THE HOUSEWIFE ASSASSIN'S VACATION TO DIE FOR

JOSIE BROWN

A BOOK BY

SIGNAL PRESS

ONE OF MANY GREAT SIGNAL PRESS BOOKS

San Francisco, CA

Library of Congress Cataloging-in-Publication Data is available upon request

Cover Design by Andrew Brown, ClickTwiceDesign.com

Digital Formatting by Austin Brown, CheapEbookFormatting.com

Trade Paperback ISBN: 978-1-942052-14-2

Hardcover ISBN: 978-1-942052-28-9

V022319

"This was an addictive read–gritty but funny at the same time. I ended up reading it in just one evening and couldn't go to sleep until I knew what the outcome would be! It was action-packed and humorous from the start, and that continued throughout, I was pleased to discover that this is the first of a series and look forward to getting my hands on Book Two so I can see where life takes Donna and her family next!"
    —*Me, My Books, and I*

"The two halves of Donna's life make sense. As you follow her story, there's no point where you think of her as "Assassin Donna" vs. "Mummy Donna', her attitude to life is even throughout. I really like how well this is done. And as for Jack. I'll have one of those, please?"
    —*The Northern Witch's Book Blog*

The Housewife Assassin's Handbook (Book 1)

The Housewife Assassin's Guide to Gracious Killing (Book 2)

The Housewife Assassin's Killer Christmas Tips (Book 3)

The Housewife Assassin's Relationship Survival Guide (Book 4)

The Housewife Assassin's Vacation to Die For (Book 5)

The Housewife Assassin's Recipes for Disaster (Book 6)

The Housewife Assassin's Hollywood Scream Play (Book 7)

The Housewife Assassin's Killer App (Book 8)

The Housewife Assassin's Hostage Hosting Tips (Book 9)

The Housewife Assassin's Garden of Deadly Delights (Book 10)

The Housewife Assassin's Tips for Weddings, Weapons, and Warfare (Book 11)

The Housewife Assassin's Husband Hunting Hints (Book 12)

The Housewife Assassin's Ghost Protocol (Book 13)

The Housewife Assassin's Terrorist TV Guide (Book 14)

The Housewife Assassin's Deadly Dossier (Book 15: The Series Prequel)

The Housewife Assassin's Greatest Hits (Book 16)

The Housewife Assassin's Fourth Estate Sale (Book 17)

The Housewife Assassin's Horrorscope (Book 18)

———————————————————

1

Fasten your seat belts. It's going
to be a bumpy ride.

———————————————————

Ladies and gentleman, my name is Donna Stone, and I'm your flight attendant today. On behalf of Captain Jack Craig and myself, I'd like to welcome you aboard—

The flight from hell.

At this time, I'd like to demonstrate the safety features of this aircraft—

Oh, who am I kidding? There are no safety features! Not for you, anyway.

For example, under normal circumstances, you should fasten your seat belt upon take-off, landing, and turbulence. To do so, you'll insert the metal fitting into the buckle, and tighten by pulling on the loose end of the strap. To release, just lift the upper portion of the buckle. In your case, however, I'd advise you to keep your belt on at all times, especially when we reach our maximum cruising altitude of fifty-one-thousand feet—

At which point I will push the ejection button that propels you out of one of the emergency exits on our aircraft, which you'll find both forward and aft.

Because of the inevitable drop in cabin pressure, the safety mask will have fallen from the ceiling. If pulling the elastic band around your head prior to extending the rubber hose gives you some comfort to imagine falling safely and soundly into a pillowy cloud, I say go for it.

Better yet: say a prayer.

Oh, and don't bother taking a bracing position—that is, leaning forward with your hands on top of your head, and your elbows against your thighs—

Because, in this situation, there are no happy landings!

"WELCOME ABOARD!" I SMILE SWEETLY AS I GREET ACME AIR'S one and only passenger, Edgar Bowden, a.k.a., Teddy Grodin, a.k.a. the guy who's on the lam for leaking classified intel to the press regarding PRISM—the National Security Administration's unwarranted surveillance program, which monitors phone calls, texts and emails moving between the United States, Europe and Middle Eastern countries.

In other words, in a post-911 world, Teddy took it upon himself to remind the rest of us that Big Brother is watching, listening, and reading up on us.

Like, duh. After that other government-contractor-turned-notorious-whistleblower, Edward Snowden, you'd think this was old news by now.

Okay so yeah, it's possible that some techno-nerds in the basement cubicle of a CIA surveillance contractor know about your Tinder.com hookup last night.

Awkward.

It may have been a crisis of conscience that inspired Teddy to open up to the press, but unlike Snowden it was the impulse to bulk up his bank account that now has him jet-setting between Ho Chi Minh City and his final destination, Moscow, via this tricked-out Gulfstream G650 luxury jet.

His ride has been provided by some wealthy corporate admirer from Iceland.

At least, that's what Teddy thinks.

By the time we land, Teddy will have given me what my employer—the black ops contractor Acme Industries—needs to know: where he's stashed the intel, and what unfriendly nations already have their grubby paws on it.

Teddy's bulk makes it difficult for him to climb the air stairs. My role as his sky geisha means rewarding his efforts with adoring glances and come-hither smiles. By the way in which Teddy's eyes sweep over my coffee, tea or me flight attendant attire—a body-hugging blouse with a plunging neckline, tucked into hot pink short-shorts—it's obvious that he wouldn't mind conducting his own unauthorized surveillance on me, once we're several miles high in the sky. Nothing says, "Come fly with me" like thigh-high boots with a stacked heel. (Or, as they used to jest at United, "Fly the friendly thighs." But I digress.)

The drool glistening on Teddy's lips is proof that he's ready to climb onboard. But his way of playing it cool is to pat my ass, then shush me with a wave of his hand so that he can listen to his newly-acquired WME talent agent on his cell phone. "Summit wants Chris fucking *Pine* to play me in the movie? No! Hell, no! Ari, I told you, either it's Gosling, or Scorsese can take a walk...Okay, *maybe* Leo DiCaprio." Teddy gives me a leer as he clicks off his cell phone. "Sorry, babe. That's life in the fast lane when you're a hero, right?"

He figures I don't read *Deadline Hollywood.* Scuttlebutt

has it that Jonah Hill has been talked about for the lead, but now that I'm standing up close and in person, Jason Segel is definitely a better choice.

So, this nerdy nobody, this tall, bulky man-boy, is now considered a human rights rock star? Give me a break. But since this mission calls for me to play along, I blink my fake lashes innocently and ask, "Really? Are you someone famous?"

"You could say that." He reaches into his valise to pull out newspapers and magazines from countries all over the globe with his homely mug on the covers. "I've just blown the whistle on our government's biggest cover-up. Did you know Uncle Sam has been conducting unwarranted surveillance on our phones and emails?"

Yep. But only since 911—unless you count the J Edgar Hoover years, of course.

Truth of the matter is that Teddy's very public revelation is old news. PRISM is just its latest—and apparently its not-so-greatest—reincarnation. Heck, back in 2006, *USA Today* reported that the NSA had already built a database with intel accessed knowingly from communications carriers like AT&T, Verizon and Bell South.

Too bad the article wasn't in the *Life* section of the paper. The public wouldn't have been so taken with Teddy's bull-shit if they kept up with our government's policies with the same zeal as they use to follow the Kardashians, the Royals or Honey Booboo.

"Then I guess that makes you the most famous person I've ever serviced—I mean, served." I giggle coquettishly at my very obvious faux pas.

The smirk comes off his face when I add, "But I doubt you're the richest."

"I'll take that bet." He makes a big show of looking at his watch. "Or I will by this time tomorrow. By then, I may be one of the richest men in the world."

I giggle. "Why? Is some old lady going to die and leave you her fortune?"

"Let's just say I've got something a lot of people want."

I look down at his crotch. "Care to be more specific?"

He actually blushes at my forwardness. "That's why we're leaving China now, and headed to Russia. President Xi was *very* interested in buying what I've got to sell. Putin is, too. Ha! Maybe I'll trade it for the Super Bowl ring he lifted off of the New England's Patriot's owner." He drops his eyes in the chasm of my cleavage. "When we land, come with me to my hotel. Trust me, I'll make it worth your while."

Just then, Jack Craig—my mission leader—comes out of the cockpit. In his sharply creased pilot's uniform with his brimmed cap at a jaunty angle, he certainly looks like the real thing.

For my sake, anyway, here's hoping that's the case, once we're airborne.

Jack salutes our one-and-only passenger. "Once we get above this low ceiling, we should have a smooth flight all the way into Domodedovo Airport, where a limo will be waiting to take you into Moscow's city center."

Teddy shrugs. Since the leak, he's used to everyone kowtowing in awe, especially those who serve him. We're merely cockroaches under his heel. Even more so, should his plan succeed.

I'll do everything in my power to ensure that Teddy fails.

As we take off, my safety spiel is more flirtatious than serious. I spread my legs before snapping the buckle on the seat belt hard, like a dominatrix shackling her favorite bottom. I purse my lips and allow them to linger on the blow hole of the flotation device. I can hear Jack chuckling into my earbud. He's watching via the cabin's hidden video cams.

When I open my arms wide to point out the safety exits, my breasts defy gravity, jutting high, front and center, thanks to Victoria's Secret Incredible push-up bra.

No surprise, Teddy's eyes never leave my chest.

Until we hit turbulence.

At that point, his eyes widen with fear.

"Well, what do you know," Jack mutters in my ear. "This dude is afraid to fly. This will be a piece of cake."

That's easy for him to say. He's not the one out here in the main cabin, tarted up like a nerd's Mile High Club wet dream.

FOR THE PAST TEN HOURS I'VE KEPT TEDDY SO BUSY WITH SLAP-and-tickle teasing and my "you're *sooooo* awesome" gushing that he hasn't noticed we're flying east, as opposed to west.

But he does notice when Jack jinks the plane—which (surprise, surprise) happens every time Teddy gets too frisky with me.

Now that we're only an hour from SEA-TAC—where a battalion of NSA agents are waiting for us—it's time to get what we need from Teddy: answers.

Jack jerks the plane to the right, a maneuver that has me toppling into Teddy's lap—but I scurry away just as he barfs all over himself.

Thank goodness my boots are vinyl. I take one of the plane's large cloth napkins and wipe off Teddy's bile so that they don't stink. Wish I could say the same about Teddy, but that would take a fireman's hose, and unfortunately that's the one thing this plane doesn't have onboard.

"I've got to take a pill," Teddy says, as he reaches for the valise in the chair beside him.

"Let me get you a glass of water." My tone is reassuring. "That is, unless you'd like something a little stronger."

"Water is…fine." His pause is the result of another turbulent dip.

As I make my way to the kitchen galley, Jack is saying something to me, but there is too much interference coming through my earbud to pick it up.

I've got to work fast, which means dosing Teddy's water with a little SP-117, Russian Intelligence's answer to the Roofie. It has the added effect that the victim readily answers any and all questions put to him. When he comes to, he won't remember a thing.

I've just put an eyedropper full of the stuff in Teddy's glass of water when I hear a floorboard squeak behind me.

Teddy is reflected in the black glass door of the microwave.

Our eyes meet for a nanosecond.

Oh, hell. He knows.

The realization that I am the only thing standing between him and a super obnoxious life of wealth is suddenly stronger than his fear of flying. He grabs a knife from a silver platter laden with brie, crackers and grapes and slashes out at me.

I break his jab with a raised arm, and counter with a front kick that catches him in the gut.

He reels backward, slamming into a cabinet so hard that it overturns. We're now dancing on shattered glass and broken china.

When Teddy lunges at me again with the knife, I dodge his first stab, but the second one cuts the top of my boot as my sidekick barely misses him.

Okay, now I'm pissed off. Hello? These boots are *vintage*.

I grab a beveled beer stein and slam it on to the counter so that what's left is just the base and a jagged shard. Yep, that'll do.

We circle the main cabin, assessing each other. On his side of the balance sheet is his height, weight, strength—not to mention his desire to live to see a couple of big paydays.

I've got speed. Most importantly, I have fear—

That I'll be leaving my three children without a mother.

This thought alone drives my next move. I take my glass shard dagger and stab at his heart.

Teddy dodges, but he's not quick enough. I cut his bicep. He cries out in pain, or maybe it's at the sight of seeing his own blood.

Angered, he rushes for me, knife in hand. He reaches me before I can grab anything to throw at him, and tosses me up against the wall. Holding the knife to my jugular, he whispers into my left ear, "You're dead, bitch."

"Kick him away now, Donna—and hold on tight," Jack whispers into my right ear.

I do exactly that—

Just as the plane goes into a sudden descent.

I'm holding tight to a drawer handle. Not Teddy. His head smacks the ceiling.

When he hits the floor, he's woozy, but he's also fully aware that the plane is gliding to Earth at an angle and speed that is conducive to the term "rest in peace."

I'm a bit perplexed myself, to say the least. Jack has left the cockpit, and he's not smiling. After cuffing Teddy, he crouches before him and slaps his face to get his full attention. "We volunteered for this suicide mission—"

Who's the "we" he's referring to?

"—because we realize the dire necessity of stopping the Chinese and Russian governments from getting their hands on our surveillance intel." He pauses for emphasis.

If he's looking for a reaction, he's getting it—from Teddy *and* me. Both of us are hyperventilating.

"We are now one-hundred-and-fifteen miles from any coast, so sorry, no hope of a rescue boat. Just so you know, I've slowed the plane's speed to one-hundred-forty-three miles per hour. That gives us only six minutes to impact. At this angle, the plane won't break up upon ditching. However, the water pressure will be too much for anyone to escape either through a door or a window. Instead, water will seep in through the wheel base, and eventually we will all suffocate in a slow death."

"What?" I shout, "Are you crazy?"

Teddy is praying. At least, I think so, but I don't speak gibberish, so for all I know he could be cursing at Jack.

Hell, I know I am.

"We're now down to a little more than five minutes." Jack stands up with a smile. If you start talking now, Teddy, I'll save us. If not, prepare to die."

The wet spot on the front of Teddy's pants is a telltale sign that he's seriously contemplating Jack's offer.

In case he doesn't, I'll do my damnedest to beat the lousy odds Jack has given us. Now let's see, maybe the angle of the plane at landing will allow me to leap out through the aft door, which should still be above the water line. But first things first. I'll need a flotation device—

"Donna, babe, I love you, and I made a promise to you that I'd never lie to you."

"Yeah, yeah, thanks Jack, very comforting for me to know, in these final moments. But perhaps you could have started by informing me *that this was a suicide mission!*" I'm looking frantically through all the bins for a parachute, a life raft--anything.

Nothing.

Don't panic... Mustn't panic... "Seriously, though Jack, I really think our time is better spent getting out of this hurtling aluminum can."

"That's just it. From the looks of things, there isn't going to be a better 'time,' so please, let me get this off my chest." He's just standing there like a man who has made peace with himself—as opposed to me, who's leaping through the cabin like a crazy woman.

"What? Just say it!" At this point, I guess my only option is to tie seat cushions to my chest and around my waist. Horrible fashion statement, but hey, the sharks won't care.

Sharks?

Oh... hell...

"Three minutes and fifty seconds, Teddy," Jack says gently, as if speaking to a baby. Then he turns back to me. "Remember the Father-Daughter dance at Mary's school last year?"

"Yes, Jack, of course! Please, get on with it. Hellzapoppin', if you haven't noticed."

"I'm sure you'll appreciate my honesty, since it's about the neighbor you despise most, Penelope Bing. If you'll remember, I danced with her that night. What you don't know is that when the band was playing a tango, I dipped her, and she gave me a lip lock that trapped me like rat in a bat's claw. Of course I pried her off as quickly as humanly possible. But still, I felt guilty that I let her get that close."

"Given the circumstances, you're forgiven." Even if Jack

won't, maybe I can pull up the plane's yoke so that it's back on an even keel. Heck, I've played my son Jeff's flight simulator video game—what's the one? Oh yeah, *F22 Air Dominance Fighter*. I'm sure the plane's joy stick is about the same.

I'm banging hard on the cockpit door, but it just won't give. At the angle in which we're dropping, I'm sure gravitational pull has something to do with it. There's got to be an ice pick in the kitchen galley drawer. Maybe I can pry it open.

"And when we were embedded in Jonah Breck's mansion—you remember, we were trying to stop the hit on Russian President Asimov," Jack blathers on.

"Yep, saved him from three—count 'em three—assassins. A career highlight, for sure." Yippee, I found the ice pick!

But then the plane sways in turbulence, and I drop it. I watch helplessly as it skitters under the dishwasher. In no time, I'm crawling on my hands and knees. I've got to retrieve it.

"Well, one night during the mission, *Babette*—Breck's wife—came on to me." Jack shakes his head forlornly. "It was right after Breck found you in his office, and was all over you. Apparently she saw the videocam feed of him attacking you."

"Ah yes, good times." I wish he'd quit yapping and give me a little help. His arms are longer than mine. He could reach that ice pick in a jiffy—

Wait…got it! With all my might I fight gravity in order to get it to the cockpit door.

"I guess Babette was jealous, and was looking for a little tit for tat. More like tit for tit, from her pick-up moves, pardon the bad pun." Jack chuckles. "Well, one thing led to another. And since our mission was to do everything we could to stay as close to the Brecks as possible—"

"You're telling me you made love—to Babette?" I'm so shocked that I break the ice pick in the door.

Dismayed at my lack of progress, Teddy whimpers and thrashes. He looks as if he wants to throw himself out one of the airplane's exit doors. To that extent, he's almost ripped the chair from the floor.

I may push him, just to put him out of his misery.

I'll push Jack, too, because he *deserves* to be miserable.

Jack snorts. "No, of course I didn't take her up on it! All she needed was someone to listen to her. You know, a shoulder to cry on. I only kissed her on the forehead. Very brotherly. Still, I felt a little guilty that I never mentioned it to you."

By now the plane's engine is sputtering. We're dipping down. Not quite a nose dive, but the angle is something I'd expect on a rollercoaster, not flying the friendly skies.

"Jack, you're forgiven, okay? Capishe?" Life is too short for this stuff.

And getting shorter every second.

Oh my God! The last cabinet in the galley holds just what we need—a parachute.

But there's only one.

Too bad. If Jack wants a ride, he'll have to hold on for dear life.

Considering the grief he's giving me, it'll be a debate as to whether I'll let him.

"In fact, it's why I feel at peace telling you about the biggest shame in my life—something I never told you, regarding the last time I saw Valentina."

In unison, my jaw and the parachute drop to the ground.

Ah. Here it is.

Jack's ex, Valentina, no longer walks the earth—thanks to my ex, Carl—but her ghost still hovers between us.

Terrorism makes strange bedfellows.

Jack takes a deep breath. "You see, she and I—"

"Please," Teddy screams. "I'll talk! I swear!" Tears are streaming down his face.

I can't say that I blame him. I'd cry, too, but now I want to hear what Jack has to say.

Teddy points out the window.

Both Jack and I turn to see that the horizon has come into view, albeit at a cockeyed angle. We are just a few thousand feet above the water, and dropping fast.

Teddy is hanging onto Jack's ankles. Between sobs, he screams, "I've got the intel in a thumb drive. It's waiting for me in a post office box in Quito, Ecuador."

Jack nods. "Keep talking. Any takers for the intel?"

"Both China and Russia have agreed to deposit funds into separate Swiss bank accounts, at midnight tonight. The minute they do, the intel goes live in different secure clouds on private servers, where they can access it."

As if he's willed the plane to straighten up and fly right, suddenly the nose of the Gulfstream lifts very gently until it looks as if we're gliding a hundred feet off the water's surface, before it rises up again into the sky.

I glance out the window. "What the hell, Jack? You mean to tell me we weren't going to die?"

Jack cocks his head to one side and grins. "Of course not. This little beauty has a state-of-the-art collision avoidance system. It practically flies itself."

"Then why didn't you tell me that all of this—this *terror* —was the game plan?" I ask as Jack jerks Teddy up by his collar and goosesteps him over to one of the chairs facing the dinette table.

Jack looks up, confused. "I did, when you walked to the

galley, to get Teddy water to take his anxiety pill. You mean, you didn't hear me?"

"No...Oh my God, I guess my earbud cut out, right as you were relaying the message."

Jack laughs. "And all this time I thought you were just acting as if you were scared—which is exactly what I wanted. Doll, I'm not teasing you—it was truly an Academy-Award worthy performance."

It's too much to hope for, but I have to ask. "In other words, all that stuff you said about Penelope and Babette wasn't true?"

"Oh, it was true, Babe. But I'm sure you'll agree I responded like the loyal and loving boyfriend I am."

A grudging nod is all he gets. Okay, now the moment of truth. "What was that you were going to say again—I mean, about Valentina?"

"Huh?" Jack frowns. "Oh…Just that she asked me to run away with her—"

"She…what?" My heart drops into my stomach. "Why didn't you tell me this, before now?"

He takes my face in his hands. *"Because it never happened.* The only reason I'd say so was to get Big Sack of Shit here"—he elbows Teddy in the gut "—to think that he had every reason to piss his pants." He looks at Teddy's crotch. "Yep. It worked."

I look away so that he can't see my tears. "You went too far, Jack."

He runs his hands through his hair. "Jeez, Donna, cut me some slack! Our relationship is built on our mutual trust, remember? It's you, always and forever."

To prove his point he pulls me close, so that I'm breast to chest with him.

So that, when I look into the depth of his eyes, the reflection I see is one of—

Me.

Yes, this is how it should be, always and forever.

Well that, and his lips on mine.

Like….now…

Joy.

Out of the corner of my eye, I see Teddy inching his way toward the galley. My sidekick puts him in his proper place.

On the ground, face down.

Jack laughs and shakes his head as he yanks Teddy back on his feet and tosses him onto one of the cabin's couches. Then he reaches into his pocket and pulls out a taser gun.

"For the next ten minutes or so, we'll still be far enough away from US airspace. If old Teddy here tries anything funny, zap him with this. We can't have bullets flying all over the place. The last thing we need is an air pressure breach. I'll be watching on the monitor." He walks to the cockpit door and unlocks it, closing it behind him.

I perch on the chair opposite our captive, and point to the television screen on an opposite wall. "Wave at the camera, Teddy. It caught your confession on video. We'll be sharing it with the CIA and the Department of Justice, to help them in their case against you."

"What you heard was given under duress! It won't stand up in a court of law."

"We're not officers of the court, so yes, we can certainly be called as witnesses regarding any statements you made to us—which include your comments to me prior to our near-fatal fall."

Teddy is paler now than he was during our nose dive over the Pacific. "But—but the Ecuadorians have promised me a secured mountaintop to live on!"

"Oh, you mean that villa you purchased a few months

ago, on Iliniza Sur?" With a click of the remote, prime real estate on one of Ecuador's seaside cliffs appears on the TV screen. "Even if you'd gotten away, sometime within the year you would have had visitors. Seal Team Six is always jonesing for another Abbottabad." I shrug. "But you didn't, so your next home is the Allenwood Federal Correctional Complex. Or as we like to call it, Dead Traitor Walking." Seeing him blanch, I add, "Don't worry. No one's been put to death for treason since the Rosenbergs. That was more than sixty years ago. For some reason the courts like handing out life sentences to traitors, as if they're gumballs or something."

His eyelids close, weighted by the reality of his situation. "They'll kill me anyway."

"Who? The Chinese or the Russians?"

"No! Some private group. It calls itself the Quorum. It was their plan to sell the unwarranted surveillance intel to foreign nations. I just thought I'd cut out the middle man and collect the hefty payday myself. But when the Quorum threatened to expose me to the NSA, I fed the reporters just enough so that the public would view me as a hero, and for Russia and China to realize the intel is legit."

"Who's your Quorum contact?" I hold my breath for his answer. It's been six months since I shoved my soon-to-be ex-husband, Carl, over a four-story banister and into the Gulf of Mexico. No one has seen or heard from him since. I'm used to his role in my life—that of a deadbeat dad and husband who went AWOL—but he has the most annoying habit of showing back up at the most stressful times.

I pray that now is *not* one of them.

"All contact was done via a blind Skype account," Teddy continues. "The guy who called wore a mask, and he never gave his name."

"Could you recognize his voice, if you heard it again?" Considering his recent Gitmo trial, we've got enough video footage on Carl to give me nightmares for the rest of my life.

Teddy thinks for a moment. "I doubt it. He was using some sort of voice-altering software."

Too bad. "If that's the case, then you better hope they put you in solitary, because one way or the other the Quorum will get to you. My advice: don't drop the soap in the shower, and do make your cellmate your bitch so that you can command him to be your food tester."

Teddy's jaw goes slack. He knows as well as I do that if anyone is going to be the bitch, it's going to be him.

For the first time since he boarded the plane, he seems small, deflated. He closes his eyes as if the sight of me is too much to bear.

So much for his plan to have me introducing him to the Mile High Club.

"You never did get me that water," he mumbles. "I think I need it now."

I nod, and start for the galley. His wrists are cuffed, so he's not going anywhere.

I am half-way there when I hear *bang* and *whoosh*. The whole plane is rattling, as if it will come apart any moment now.

"Aw, hell, he put on the phony parachute and hopped to the exit door, then used the cuffs as leverage to yank it open," Jack yells in my ear.

The chute wouldn't have opened?

And Jack is just telling me this *now*?

"I've May Day'ed Air Traffic Control," he continues. "SEA-TAC is prepping now for our emergency landing, so hold tight. Donna…Donna! Answer me! Are you okay?"

"Kinda *busy* right now!" Everything—including me—is being sucked toward the center cabin.

My arms flail as I reach for something—anything—that will keep me from following all the stuff flying out the door.

Just in time, I grab hold of a cabinet locker.

If I could, I'd crawl inside.

My life is a series of close calls.

I need a vacation.

2

Assassination Vacation

There comes a time in every housewife's (or for that matter, in every female assassin's) life when she needs to take a breather.

In other words, she needs a vacation.

The key to the ideal sabbatical is, quite simply, leaving your work behind, and with it the stress that has you frazzled in the first place.

Yeah, yeah, I know: easier said than done—especially if your job entails accurately throwing sharp knives, or crack shooting of semi-automatic weaponry, or the covert dropping of poison pills—you know, whatever it takes to bring around the untimely demise of Thugs Behaving Badly.

Yours is truly an exhausting schedule! But it can be remedied via the following actions:

Action Number 1: Get away. Just. Do. It. Seriously, drop everything. (Unless you're drowning a bad guy in a bathtub, and he hasn't yet lost consciousness. In that case, carry on!) Hit the road. Being impulsive is part of the fun!

Action Number 2: Take along someone fun. A gal pal. The

new man in your life. Your spiritual guru. Just don't be tempted to drag along your latest hit, because this little getaway isn't supposed to be Weekend at Bernie's.

Action Number 3: Don't worry, be happy! If your room looks nothing like the one in the brochure, go to a different hotel. If the airline loses your luggage, buy a thong (bikini), a sarong, and thongs (flip-flops), since that's what you'll be wearing 24/7 anyway.

Even if some mark recognizes you as the femme fatale who almost did him in, relax and enjoy the sunset.

Then go finish the job.

"MUST I GO AWAY TO CAMP THIS YEAR?" IT'S THE FIFTIETH TIME in the last five days in which my twelve-year-old daughter, Mary has asked me this same question. "I can't stand the thought of it—doing the same old things, with the same old people!"

Those "same old people" are her best friends, Babs and Midge. And those "same old things" are sleeping in tents with her besties, hiking through the woods before stopping to build forts; jumping into the lake from a tire swing; and roasting marshmallows next to a blazing campfire while telling ghost stories on a star-bright night.

I look up from folding freshly laundered sheets and towels. My scowl should warn her that I'm not up for this argument yet again. "Why? Because every year for the last three years, you've begged me to let you go to Camp Inch. Because your friends, Midge and Babs, will be there, too. Because I've already paid for it, and there are no refunds, and I'm not made of money. And because if you stay home, you're likely to...I guess I'm afraid you'll do something that you'll regret."

Like letting her middle school-soon-to-be-high school crush, Trevor Smith, roam onto third base.

Then I'd have to kill him.

Mary crosses her arms and mutters, "I see. So what you're telling me is that you don't trust me."

I sputter, but then I force myself to calm down. "Of course I trust you!"

What I don't add (only because I know she's waiting for it) is, it's Trevor I don't *trust.*

I have to watch what I say because my youngest daughter, six-year-old Trisha, has snuck into Mary's closet in order to play with her older sister's abandoned Barbie collection. Mary knows Trisha covets it, but she's not yet willing to pass them forward. At twelve, Mary is too old for Barbies, but too young for boys.

And that's what this is really all about.

I want her to stay innocent as long as possible.

I pull her down on to the bed beside me and hold onto her hands—not because she needs a lifeline, but because I do. "Mary, honey, next year you'll be too old to attend Camp Inch. Seriously, do you want to miss out on one last chance to make some wonderful memories with your best friends? We're talking about a mere two weeks, which will be over in a blink of an eye! Let this be the summer of no regrets."

No regrets.

I vow to make that my goal, too. How I long for a quiet summer, filled with days of nothing but peace and quiet. To hear about the fun experiences my children had while away from me, and to share other just as wonderful experiences with them.

To make a few intimate memories with Jack.

Mary's face flickers through a myriad of emotions: anger; stubbornness; hurt; acknowledgment—

And finally acceptance.

"Maybe you're right," she mutters. "Okay…but just so you know, Trevor isn't like…well, he isn't like that."

Ha. Famous last words.

"I wish I could go to sleep away camp," Trisha declares mournfully.

Mary jerks her head in her little sister's direction as if to say, *See? Told you! It's something for babies.*

Still, I'm not letting her off the hook—especially now that she's acquiesced to go. I smile sweetly at Trisha. "Soon, honey—when you're a little older. But right now, if you were gone for a full week, I'd be too lonely without you."

"No you wouldn't. You'd still have Daddy."

For all intents and purposes, Jack is their father—not just because he's the only one they've ever known, or because he goes under the alias of "Carl Stone," my ex-husband's name.

He coaches their league teams and he helps them with their homework.

He's home with them when I'm sent on solo kill missions.

Should I never come home, he will be their comfort. And I know in my heart that their most precious memories of me will live on *because* of him.

Should he pass before me, I will do the same for him.

You see, we are *his* family too.

I cannot do it for their real father—the real Carl, who abandoned them, and me, for life as a terrorist.

Make that a pirate. He uses terrorism to extort ransom from the countries or companies affected. His unconscionable acts have nothing to do with patriotism or a heart-felt mission or even revenge.

It's all about money.

And anyone who stands in his way—including me—is fair game.

Thank God my children don't know him.

Yes, they have met him. He's made sure of that. But he has been smart enough to stay incognito, to let sleeping ghosts lie.

He was that ghost.

And by default, Jack is the man they know as their father.

A whistle draws me to Mary's window. Below on the backyard lawn, Jack waves up to me, then points to the double hammock tethered between two legacy oak trees.

I get it. Yes, I'll meet him there.

Then I blow him a smooch.

Before walking out the door, I kiss my eldest on her fore-head. "You'll have a blast. Trust me, you won't regret it."

She shrugs.

I'll take that as a victory. One of many this summer, I hope.

JACK AND I ARE CUDDLING IN THE HAMMOCK. HIGH ABOVE OUR heads, a canopy of leaves sways in a gentle breeze.

Our collective weight has pulled us toward the center. We're just a few inches off the ground. For a few precious moments we can pretend we are hidden away from the world in this canvas cocoon.

From her open bedroom window, we can hear Trisha talking to her dolls. The smack of the basketball on pave-ment is my way of knowing that my ten-year-old, Jeff, is still in the midst of a heated game with his friends, Cheever Bing and Morton Smith. Our dogs, Lassie and Rin Tin Tin, prance and leap frantically around the boys, ignoring Cheever's curses to get out of the way.

"What time is it?" Jack murmurs between kisses on my neck. Slowly but steadily his hand has been inching up from my waist toward my breasts.

"Why do you ask?" I'm being a tease. I know he's counting down the minutes until three o'clock, when all three boys take off with Cheever's mother and father, Penelope and Peter, on their annual camping trip. An hour later, Mary leaves for Camp Inch with Babs, Midge and Babs' mom.

The plan is to feed Trisha early, then put her to bed around, say, eight o'clock, so that Jack and I can enjoy a romantic dinner for two. He's got a couple of choice steaks marinating in the fridge, which he will slap onto the grill. I've made my celebrated roasted Yukon Gold potatoes, and a mixed green salad. We'll share a great cabernet.

For dessert, I've planned a sensory experience: a few candles and some lavender scented lotion, which I will heat before caressing Jack with it.

But his massage comes with a price. He must wear nothing at all—except for the silk sash from my robe, which I will tie around his deep-set green eyes as a blindfold.

I imagine that a naughty, knowing smile will rise on his lips, not from derision but anticipation.

Very gently, I will lay him face down, perhaps on the thick Persian rug in front of our bed. In true geisha form I'll bend to my knees, and massage the calluses on his feet before rubbing out any knots in his thick calves. From there my fingers will circle his strong thighs slowly, giving him a taste of what he can expect when my hands reach his buttocks.

Once there, I will take a firm rounded haunch in each hand—kneading them gently, then firmly, creating crop circles of heated lotion before trickling it directly on his spine—

Until he shivers—

Or until he can't resist the urge to turn over in order to grab my hand and pull me down on top of him—

Where I'll ease myself onto him, because we will already be wet and willing.

I'll time my moans to his groans, my lifts to his thrusts, and his shuddering explosion to my blissful orgasm.

Then it will be my turn for a massage.

Will he lay me face down then taunt me with fingers that trail up the back of my legs like the seam of a silk stocking, stopping only when he reaches the rounded hills of my ass?

Will his hand glide over them oh so lightly, only to pause at their peaks for too many seconds, building my agony for what will come next?

Perhaps it will be a hard slap, to punish me for tormenting him just moments before.

Maybe a gentle probe with a single finger, to gauge my dampness and desire.

Or possibly a loving kiss, to honor the joy we share.

Whatever his action, I will submit to it.

I will welcome it.

I will revel in it.

So there you have it, why we appreciate every precious moment we have that is just the two of us, even if it's just cuddling together in a hammock.

And now you understand why I so reluctantly wriggle out of his bear hug.

"What makes you think I'm done with you?" Jack won't let go of my waist.

"I have to check to see if Jeff is ready to go." Despite my son's insistence that he pack his own duffle, I wouldn't doubt in the least that he forgot to toss in the 100-plus SPF sunscreen I left on his dresser. Did he leave his mouth retainer behind? He hates it so much, that I wouldn't be surprised if he did so, on purpose.

Jack groans. "You're smothering him, missy."

"Think so? I presume, then, you'll be the one who drives up to Yosemite if Jeff conveniently forgets to pack his assigned summer reading, *Lord of the Flies*? Or worse yet, what if he forgets to pack extra pairs of underwear? You know he can't wear Cheever's because he's twice as wide as Jeff. And Morton never packs any, so interrupting your exploration of my nether regions is, alas, a necessity."

He laughs. "Worst case scenario, he'll sneak into another lodge and steal a pair from some other skinny ten-year-old." When he sees I'm standing my ground, he adds, "Okay, sure, play helicopter mom. But don't be surprised how often your name comes up in any future analyses he has with some shrink."

"Ha ha, very funny." Maybe it's time to break the news to him that *we are not alone*. "The Hendersons, right behind us, have a one-hundred-thirty millimeter reflector telescope, and their sixteen-year-old son has it pointed in our direction. Top floor, southwest corner window."

"Oh, yeah?" Jack doesn't look up. He always trusts my reconnaissance. Instead he raises his hand in a one-finger salute. "It doesn't give him the one thing he needs: ex-ray vision."

To make his point, his lips meander slowly from my forehead, to my lips, down my neck, to my breasts again, until they roam down my belly, pausing only to kiss my navel.

The signs are all there: Jack is ready for some serious action.

There is nothing I can do but surrender.

I've just given in when I hear Trisha say, quite close by and quite loudly, "Mommy, look! Mrs. Breck is here, with Janie!...Hello? Mommy! Daddy! What *are* you doing in there?"

At the same time Jack lifts his head to smile and wave at our unexpected company, I scramble over the far side of hammock—

Only to flop onto the ground.

Does Babette Breck notice? Of course not. She's only got eyes for Jack.

She's still in widow's weeds so I'll forgive her. I've got to hand it to Marc Jacobs: black crepe never looked so stunning.

My guess is that she'll be out of them soon enough—and not just because her wardrobe is snug and low-cut. Granted it's been almost a year since she lost her husband, Jonah, to an assassin who he double-crossed: Carl. But considering Jonah was a philanderer who was also into rape, porn and the trafficking of sex slaves, I doubt she misses him much.

If so, she consoles herself by spending some of the billions he left her.

And you thought *your* neighbors were quirky.

"Sorry to interrupt." Her voice purrs and grates at the same time, like butter on a red hot pan, moving from melted to sizzling to rancid. "Janie and I were wondering if you could spare Trisha for a week, starting tonight. You see, we've been invited to my new beau's beach house."

Her invitation comes out like a triumphant boast. Hmmm. Maybe this one isn't after her money.

"What an interesting proposition." I try to keep my voice non-committal—hard to do, considering that Trisha is already dancing a jig at the thought of seven-day play date with her bestie. Frankly, I have mixed feelings about Babette's offer. As much as the two girls enjoy each other's company, it concerns me that, for the most part, Babette is an absentee mother. Janie's life is a revolving door of nannies, thanks to her mother's whims and jealousies.

"I'm sure the privacy would be a welcomed change of pace." Babette's declaration is delivered with sarcasm.

Okay, yeah, hanky-panky in a hammock isn't exactly an ideal scenario. Still, it gives her no reason to pass judgment on how and when I make love—unless she's offering to loan us her au pair *du jour* for an hour or two.

Then, for sure, we'll pinky promise to move the action indoors.

"I told Janie she could take a friend, so that both of us will have someone to share our fun. You know, building sandcastles, taking long walks on the beach, some horseback riding—and as much hand-churned ice cream as their little bellies can take." Her words come out in a tsunami of desperation. She must figure this guy is a keeper after all. And he certainly sounds wealthy enough to keep her in the custom to which she's become accustomed.

That is, spoiled.

"I'm sure that Donna, like me, appreciates your offer." Jack is never one to look a gift horse in the mouth. "If Trisha checks in with her mother at least once a day, Donna would give her consent."

"Call home? Well, of course." Babette shrugs, but by the way her eyes widen I'll bet the thought never occurred to her. "Does she have her own iPhone?...No? That's okay. I'll let her use Janie's cell to text a message whenever she wants. It's a great way to practice her spelling."

Trisha leaps into my arms. "Thank you thank you thank you, Mommy! Don't worry! I promise to write you every day!"

I nod reluctantly. "Or twice even. Or three times. Just... just whenever you miss me." *Because I'll be missing you, too, my baby.*

Babette pulls Trisha out of my arms. "Good, then it's settled! The limo will be in your driveway in an hour." Without even a wave, Babette turns and walks away. Mission accomplished.

As if reading my mind, Jack says, "I hope this guy knows what he's getting into."

The next thing I know, Jack has pulled me back into the hammock with him. He's almost right where we left off— somewhere below my navel—when the sound of pixie dust wafts out from my iPhone.

I glance down at the screen: the Hilldale Public Library.

Not a good sign. The library is a dead drop for my missions.

The text message reads:

AROUND THE WORLD IN 80 DAYS is being held for you and your family. Please check at Will Call ASAP.

Translation: You and Jack are to gear up for another mission, right now. Somewhere out of town. Come into the office for a face-to-face briefing.

In response to my groan, Jack asks, "Let me guess, another op."

I nod. "So much for taking the week off."

As he pulls me out of the hammock, he says, "Pack for Trisha. On the way to the office we'll drop her at Babette's monster mansion, then flip around and drop the boys at the Bings' place, and Mary with Babs' mom. Whatever this mission is, at least we'll have the kids out of our hair."

But that's just the point: I'd rather stay with the children.

It's great to know that Jack feels the same way.

3

Packing Light

Dragging heavy bags along on your journey can be a hassle. Solution: a small solitary carry-on, which can be filled with all sorts of goodies that does double duty, both for the well-heeled jet-setter and the assassin! For example:

Never leave home without a toothbrush, toothpaste, and floss —not just for dental hygiene, but because these items make great weapons! With the toothbrush, you can stab; with the toothpaste, you can gag your opponent; and with the floss, you can choke them. (Waxed floss is best because it's stronger.)

Add to that a small viscose towel, which makes a great super-absorbent washcloth (not to mention an excellent gag, too). Facial cleansers, shampoos, and conditioners can also be used to blind or choke your attacker. Bring along a perfume, which will make even the most sadistic badass squeal like a piggy when it is sprayed into his eyes.

At least three scarves and two pairs of sunglasses should also be packed, along with a great sun hat (all of which can double as ideal disguises). As for clothes, at least one pair of jeans, one pair of tailored pants and one little black dress are de rigueur, as are a pair of sneakers, some easy walking pumps, and one killer pair of four-inch heels.

And I do mean killer. If the need to eliminate a baddy presents itself, ram his jugular with your stiletto heel. It has the optimum effect—he's as dead as a door nail, and the blood wipes off easily before you sashay out the door to your next soiree!

Word of caution: Leave your machete at home. If you haven't figured it out already, you'll never clear the security gate with it packed in your carry-on.

FROM THE OUTSIDE, ACME LOOKS LIKE A SLEEPY SATELLITE office of some no-name company in any of a million anonymous mirrored-glass and concrete office parks along the 405.

But inside, it hustles and bustles with the scurry and drone of a hundred desk-bound brick agents, who supervise almost six hundred field agents—like Jack and me—through missions that can last a day, a year, or a lifetime.

Especially if that life is cut short while you're on assignment.

Our boss, Ryan Clancy, beckons us from the conference room farthest from the front door.

As we walk down the aisle toward it, we quite literally bump into Emma Hunnicutt, who is also headed in that direction. She is a rising star in the COM/INT division, which handles the communications intelligence on most of my missions. Usually she dresses in jeans, a black tee-shirt, and a black leather jacket. Today though, her usual Goth style has been toned down considerably. She wears a short, colorful skirt and a lacy tee—less Lisbeth Salander, more Forever 21.

Jack notices it, too, because he does a double-take. "Where's the party?"

Emma blushes. "I...I'm just trying a new look—but not because of anyone...Okay, maybe."

Well, what do you know? Maybe Emma's relationship with Arnie Locklear, our gadget guy, is finally heating up. His crush on her is no secret. And despite her hardcore demeanor, I truly believe she's got a soft spot for him, too.

Jack looks around the office. "No, seriously, what is it with all the women in this place? It looks like an *Esquire* reader's fantasy of the Sterling Cooper office, twenty-first century."

I follow his gaze. He's right. Every woman in the office has a bounce in her step. Of course, it helps that they're all wearing very high heels, which look great on all these shapely legs, which rise into very short skirts—

Which enhance the effect of their plunging necklines, artistically made-up faces, and softly tousled hair. "Are we expecting a visit from POTUS or something?" I mutter to Emma.

Three women, walking past, giggle when they hear my remark. I turn just in time to catch their pitying looks. I guess they think I'm wrong to have worn my yoga pants and flip-flops into the office. And granted, putting my hair in a fun bun and skipping full war paint isn't the best look, but give me a break! Today was supposed to be my day off—

Oh. My. God.

Yes, I see him, standing next to Ryan:

Dominic Fleming.

I'd know that profile anywhere. Although we've never met, the spook loops' Pinterest feeds are filled with candid photos of this blue-eyed, square-jawed, Roman-nosed golden-haired Adonis. Most of the shots show him in a tux at some foreign embassy soiree, martini glass in hand. Or else he's poolside, wearing nothing to hinder the awed stares of his broad-chested, board-flat ab'd deeply tanned well-oiled physique other than a Speedo—

Which shows only one bulge—in the right place, and too large to miss.

Always in the background of these photos is a bevy of Miss Universe-worthy women—gowned, glammed and ready, willing and able to be ravished by this year's winner of Spooklandia's annual Undercover Lover award, better known as "the Undies."

(I'm beginning to think that desk ops have too much time on their hands.)

Whereas in the previous years the award has always been a toss-up between Jack and Dominic, this year he was the hands-down winner. I guess Jack being taken off the market—by *moi*—had something to do with that.

He had to show up here, now? Of all the days for me to come in, looking like—

A mom.

No, not even a mom. More like a frump. A doofus. A bag lady—

A *hag*.

I grab hold of Emma's arm. "What the hell? Why didn't someone tell me?"

Emma shrugged helplessly. "You know very well that our encryptions aren't supposed to give away the deets of your mission."

"Couldn't you have thrown me a tiny hint? I dunno, perhaps something like 'Do yourself a favor and put on a push-up bra.' Or maybe something in Pig Latin, like 'Ominic-Day Emming-Flay ere-hay'?"

I spring my hair from its not-so-fun-anymore bun, and

tousle it. Without a mirror, I can't tell if it now looks come-hither or Hag-Holding-Poison-Apple, but I'll just have to take my chances.

Jack taps me on the shoulder. "What's the big whoop?"

How do I break the news to the man who came in second place for the Undies that the victor is only a few feet away?

As if reading my mind, Jack scans the room suspiciously. When he sees the object of his female co-workers' affections, his eyes narrow ever so slightly, and his smile hardens. "Well, well, well, look what the cat dragged in."

"You know Dominic?"

Jack's lips curl into a smirk. "Yeah, you can say we're old pals."

Oh, duh. Stupid question. But of course he does.

Jack and Dominic, a former MI6 agent, signed on with Acme in the same year. They were partnered on many assignments, some of which are quite legendary. My own training manual was chock full of their derring-do: the kidnapping of a Mexican warlord; saving a US ambassador from a terrorist plot—not to mention the time they tracked down and terminated a Russian triple agent who had defected with the schematic of our F-35 fighter jets.

But Ryan chose Jack, not Dominic, to head up the plum assignment of taking down the Quorum.

What would have happened if it had been the other way around?

This thought stops me cold. At the time I'd been angry at Ryan for presuming I'd give some stranger permission to pose as Carl in order to reel in the Quorum, which was in search of something they thought Carl had left in my house: a microdot embedded with a code that would give it access to the DaaS cloud holding Acme's digital directory, which lists every agent and every mission, as well as all our leads, assets, agents, and contacts in nations and agencies around the world.

I'd searched high and low for it, to no avail. After a while, I, and the rest of Acme, came to the conclusion that Carl took it with him. Still, we never detected a breach, which would have shown itself with exterminations of our key assets.

Only recently, we discovered why: before Carl disappeared, he attached it to his photo in the antique locket that I wear around my neck.

I discovered this right before he took a sixty-foot plunge into Mexico's Sea of Cortez, courtesy of Jack and *moi*.

Maybe it's a good thing that Carl no longer walks among the living for the sole reason that he made my life a living hell.He kept a close eye on two Acme assets: Jack and me. Needless to say, he hated that Jack lives in his house.

And that Jack sleeps in his bed.

Most of all he hated the fact that Jack took on the role of father to his children.

Is Jack cut out to play my husband?

Before the mission to take down the Quorum, Jack's reputation as a womanizer was just as notorious as Dominic's. But he won over my children. And in doing so, he won me over, too.

So, why does he feel threatened, now that Dominic Fleming is here in Hilldale?

No. let me rephrase that. He doesn't feel threatened. He feels *challenged*. I've seen that look on his face before, in our most trying times.

It says *game on*.

"Darling, they're waiting for us." Jack sounds nonchalant, but he's anything but that as he places his hand in the small of my back and guides me firmly toward the conference room.

As if he has anything to worry about. I love him with all my heart.

Still, it doesn't hurt to flirt a little, now does it?

"OLD CHAP! YOU HAVEN'T CHANGED AN IOTA"—DOMINIC Fleming grabs Jack's hand in a firm grip—"except perhaps for that slight pouch around your waist. Perhaps fake married life is agreeing with you a bit too much."

He ignores Jack's glare, choosing instead to lock and load those baby blues on the object of Jack's very real affection—

Me.

Yes, I'm blushing.

But before Jack blows a gasket, I step in between them and hold out my hand. "I don't think we've met. I'm Donna Stone."

"Ah! Finally I'm face to face with Acme's infamous manslayer, Donna Stone!" The next thing I know, Dominic has lifted my hand to his lips. I can feel his gentle kiss on the back of my hand.

I'm not old enough for hot flashes, but right now a warm tingle surges through me.

Very nice.

"In fact, I've been following your career almost since Day One, Ms. Stone. I find you…*fascinating.*" As he says this he draws out the last word, his voice strokes me—well, certainly my ego—with this velvet purr. "Your motive for joining Acme was pure of heart. Your spycraft is always spot on. Shall I say it? But of course! Everything about you is sheer genius, especially when your back"—His admiring gaze at my ass has me quite literally backing up, until I've smacked into the conference room's batten-and-board paneling—"is against the wall."

He looms so closely over me that I can admire the shadow plaid in his bespoke Savile Row suit. The musky scent of his cologne—Floris Number 89, I'm guessing (or at least it's been rumored)—is quite dizzying.

If I should faint, mouth-to-mouth resuscitation is always an option for my revival. Just putting it out there, front and center.

"Forgive me. I'm sure my adoration makes me sound like a foolish school boy." His gaze sweeps over me before seeking out my eyes, where I'm sure he can read my every thought.

And yes, I have a few. *Gimme some lovin'. Stroke me hard, fast, and often.*

But I say nothing because opening my mouth now would expose me as a blithering fool. Instead I melt into the closest chair—

Only to land on my ass.

I wasn't expecting Dominic to pull it out for me.

"Oh…a gentleman! How refreshing." I glare at those who have the audacity to snicker: Emma, Arnie, even our field handler, Abu Nagashahi.

And of course, Jack.

At least *he* has the decency to give me a hand so that I can get back on my feet.

Still, I make it a point to punish his impudence by grinding my heel into his toe. As Jack swallows a groan, I pat his taut belly. "Guess I'll have to quit making desserts until you get back into shape."

He shoves me down into the chair. "I think Ryan wants to begin."

In tandem, Dominic and Jack make a move for the chair beside me. Dominic gets there first.

"Sure, okay, age before beauty," Jack murmurs.

Dominic shrugs. "Don't you mean pearls before swine?"

"You're quoting Dorothy Parker?" Jack snorts. "Oddly enough, that doesn't surprise me."

"Nor should it, dear boy. After all, she was one of the last century's foremost wits." He scrutinizes Jack as if he were some odd specimen under glass in a natural history museum. "I dare say, your tenure in suburbia has made you quite a sexist! No doubt your female colleagues find it somewhat off-putting, what with having to endure your lascivious remarks"—Dominic's sympathetic look in my direction catches me off guard—"not to mention a compromising position or two."

I pink up as I think of all the times Jack has kept me out of the loop, or made me the unwitting dupe of his shenanigans.

Not to mention some of the compromising positions we've enjoyed.

"*What?*" Jack sputters. "Donna will be the first to tell you that *I'm* the perfect gentleman." Only now does Jack look over at me.

Seeing me red-faced, he does a double-take. His look says it all: *traitor.*

Dismayed, Ryan shakes his head. "Now, now—*gentlemen!* I hope we're able to play nice for the following week—seeing how you'll be spending it together, in Paradise."

Well, that remark certainly has turned all heads.

Ryan gives his iPad a quick tap. A verdant island, ringed with white beaches and surrounded by an azure sea, appears on the large monitor that is mounted on the wall behind him.

"Donna and Jack, you might recognize this island as Misfit Quay—Jonah Breck's former getaway." The monitor's screen has changed to show recent development on the island. "Since his demise, the trust that manages his estate has partnered with a hospitality corporation, Fantasy Properties. In fact, Misfit has been renamed Fantasy Island, and portions of the island have been developed into three very distinct resorts."

The monitor now shows a photo from a brochure. In it, a tow-headed boy and girl are building sandcastles on a beach with a man and woman in medieval dress. A thirty-some-thing couple who are just as blonde as the children toast each other while relaxing on nearby lounge chairs.

"One of the resorts is called Kamp KidStuff," Ryan explains. "Its slogan is, 'The Best of Times Have Both We Time and Me Time' because it promises parents a lot of time to enjoy each other, while their children are occupied with activities led by counselors who double as famous storybook characters."

He had me at *me time.*

The screen dissolves to another picture. In it, boardwalks raised over sugar white sand lead out to tiki huts that are suspended on stilts. On the beachside, more huts seem to be floating in the palm trees. Because it's sunset, all the people in the photo—mostly couples, although some are foursomes —can only be seen in silhouette as they lounge on beach chaises, or sip cocktails on the tikis' decks.

"This resort is called Eden Key, and it's for singles only. In fact—" Ryan pauses under the pretense of wiping his eye glasses—"both *Cosmopolitan* and *Esquire* rate it Number One in the categories of 'Casual Hook-Ups,' 'Rum-Fueled Romances,' 'Sex on the Beach' and 'Worthy of an Irish Layover.'

"Pardon?" Dominic murmurs. "Or, as the midget tart said to the bishop, 'That went over my head.'"

"It means you wouldn't mind missing your flight home, because the previous evening's drunken debauchery was worth it," Emma pipes up.

To Arnie's consternation, Emma seems to go limp with lust as Dominic graces her with a smile.

"And the third resort—a fish, game, and gambling lodge–goes by the name of the Hunt Club. Reconnaissance will be more difficult there because access is by membership only—and its members must prove an income in the billion-dollar range."

"Well, that leaves me out," Arnie says much too loudly and much too jovially.

Dead silence.

Arnie turns beet red. "By that I mean…never mind." The flop sweat dripping off his brow is creating a puddle on the table.

Before the poor guy drowns in it, I take it upon myself to change the subject. "Ryan, why the sudden interest in Misfit —I mean, *Fantasy* Island?"

"Last week, the public was enthralled with Teddy Grodin's disappearance"—I wince when he says this. I can hear the accusation in his voice. Yes, I know, I screwed up. I should have never left Teddy alone—"but the real threat to our national security is Dr. Lionel Mandrake, whereabouts unknown—until now."

"Who?" Emma asks.

"I'm not surprised you haven't heard of him," Ryan responds. "Under the auspices of the NSA, Mandrake was leading the team working on Operation Bugaboo—a weaponized plague bacteria. The plague is one of the world's deadliest infectious diseases. The infected cannot be cured with drugs."

Dominic shudders. "How barbaric."

Ryan smiles. "An appropriate word for it. In fact, plagues have been used as weapons since the Middle Ages. Infected dead bodies were left where the opposing army would find them, or rebels catapulted them over castle walls." Ryan waits for our uncomfortable chuckles to subside. "Both China and Russia have been developing strains of the pneumonic plague, which can be administered in an aerosol form. It could affect a whole building's ventilation system, even structures as large as stadiums." Ryan frowns. "Mandrake was nearing completion on an antibody-based vaccine. Last week, when word came down that government budget cuts at the NSA would affect his project, he disappeared without a trace, taking the project files and active bacteria and antidote samples with him. He has since surfaced on Fantasy Island."

"How do they know he's there, of all places?" Jack asks.

"During a routine colonoscopy procedure, the NSA encrypted him with a GPS chip."

"You mean he has a bug up his ass?" Arnie asks with a chuckle.

Ryan frowns. "Not quite. It was placed in his foot, without the good doctor's knowledge."

Emma frowns, "Isn't that an invasion of his privacy?"

Deep in thought, Dominic's finger taps the table. And yes, every woman in the room—Emma, Ryan's secretary Janine, and I—is mesmerized.

Not with the tapping, but with the thickness and length of his fingers.

Ryan shows his annoyance by snapping his fingers in Janine's face. "As a matter of fact, prior to signing on, every employee working on the project willingly agreed to the implant, except for Dr. Mandrake. The NSA agreed to his terms because of his superior knowledge and his previous discoveries in this area of research."

"And because they knew eventually they'd get the chance to implant the chip without him ever knowing about it," Emma mutters.

Ryan shrugs. "The project falls under the auspices of PRISM, and therefore unwarranted surveillance of those working on NSA projects is a matter of national security. In this case, it turns out embedding a GPS chip was a good thing, since it may save millions of lives. One scenario is that he'll use the island's guests as guinea pigs to test the plague vaccine's effectiveness. An even worse scenario is that he's meeting with a few interested parties—an enemy nation, say, or a terrorist organization—and selling it to the highest bidder."

"Do we know for a fact that he wasn't kidnapped, along with the samples?" Jack asks.

"That very well could be the case. But unfortunately for Dr. Mandrake, a crucial four hours of video footage covering the time of his disappearance has been obliterated, from both his office and condo security feeds. Also gone is his NSA photo file and ID info. All we've got to go on is one photo of him, snapped by a colleague at the department's annual Christmas party."

The photo appears on the screen. Everyone scrutinizes it silently, but it's too fuzzy to make out the sort of details we'll need to validate a suspect. "I know it's slim pickings," Ryan opines. "Even so, our facial recognition software has picked up a few features that can help our ID process. Jack, as for your question, the bottom line is that we don't know if the disappearance of Mandrake's file was a kidnapper's doing, or Mandrake's. But after the Snowden and Grodin debacles, the NSA is taking no chances that Mandrake might indeed be a traitor. Our orders are to shoot first and ask questions later."

Emma frowns. "At the same time, we have no idea what the good doctor looks like?"

"All we know is that he's single and in his late forties, around five-feet eleven inches, with dark hair," Ryan answers. "He's a loner, has no family to speak of, and he has pretty much kept to himself. His hobbies are hunting and math games."

"Other than the logical choices of the Hunt Club and Eden Key, it doesn't give us much at all to go on," Dominic and I say in unison. Instinctively I glance over at him. His sly smile makes me blush.

And yes, Jack notices this, which is why he's now frowning.

Ryan's expression warns us that all eyes should be focused on him. "He does have one distinguishing mark," he continues, "a tattoo of a mushroom cloud, at the base of his spine."

"I say, Ryan, are we to blithely ask the other guests to drop trou without so much as a promise of a dirty weekend?" Dominic chuckles as he asks the question, but he also seems intrigued by the thought.

Ryan's eyes narrow at the inference. "Prime suspects with cause for examination will be routed to the mission's honey pot."

Meaning *moi*.

Oh boy, seems I've got my work cut out for me. From what the manifest shows, between guests and staff, there are at least a hundred and sixty men on the island.

Time to change the subject, which I do without looking

up from the note I'm writing to myself. (*Lose eight pounds by tomorrow: Fantasy? Sexy muumuu: oxymoron?*) "I take it we've at least pinpointed his location to the island, thanks to the GPS tracker?"

"Yes, but he's apparently roaming all over the place—something which also merits suspicion. And sometimes the GPS signal disappears completely. All the more reason we have to bring him—and the plague samples—back to the NSA as soon as possible." Ryan circles the room. "Acme has secured six seats on Fantasy Island's weekly private charter jet, which leaves three times a day, from Orange County Airport. Each plane is met by the island's Director of Resorts, Mr. Boarke—" The photo on the monitor has changed. It now shows an elegant man in a white suit. His face is regal, and his hair has grayed just at the temples—"and Battoo, his assistant, who is also the island's head concierge."

The monitor switches again. This time Boarke is standing next to a man who is a third of his height. The diminutive man's suit, also white linen, is accessorized with a bowtie. "With Battoo's help, Boarke prides himself on knowing all of Fantasy Island's guests. Odds are one of them knows of Mandrake's whereabouts. But since the island's unspoken slogan is 'What happens on Fantasy stays on Fantasy,' we can't expect them to break protocol."

"Even if the island's other guests are at risk?" Dominic asks.

"Unfortunately, yes. But one of Arnie's jobs will be to monitor the air and water safety gauges that he and Abu will set up around the island. The first place to start is the water filtration system and the HVAC systems in all the resorts' facilities."

Arnie and Abu nod. "Right, boss," they say in unison.

"As for Boarke, he has an equity stake in the success of

the resorts. The last thing he'd want is for guests to leave in droves, and rumors of an island plague epidemic would do just that. It would be his financial ruin. And unfortunately, Fantasy Island is not under the jurisdiction of the United States, let alone that of any favored nation. When it comes to finding Mandrake, we're on our own." Ryan stands to face us. "Two agents will work out of each resort. Abu, you and Emma now have gainful employment in the Hunt Club, as a Gun Room concierge and a chambermaid, respectively. As such, you'll have the access needed to identify possible suspects. Emma, you'll have the added responsibility of assessing their backstories for anomalies."

Emma and Abu nod as they take this in.

Dominic, you and Arnie will be embedded at Eden Key. Arnie, like Emma, you'll be charged with profile validations , along with any other tech operations."

"Al*right*! Just two amigos playing with some fine ladies!" Expecting a high-five, Arnie raises his hand toward Dominic, who ignores it.

Hearing his enthusiasm, Emma's face clouds over. If that was the response he was looking for, he certainly got it. Frankly, I don't think it's one he should want.

Dominic's reaction is no more than a raised brow. "I say, chap, perhaps we should feign acknowledging each other's existence. That way, we double our efforts."

The diss goes over Arnie's head. He honors Dominic's suggestion with a fist pump.

"Jack and Donna will be based at Kamp KidStuff," Ryan continues. "Donna, if you want, feel free to take your children along for cover."

This mission seems less dangerous than most, but I wouldn't want to take the chance that I'd put my children in the line of fire. Thank goodness my real excuse for nixing his suggestion gives me the chance to at least sound like a team player. "As it turns out, all my children are away at various camps and activities over the course of the next couple of weeks."

"I see." Ryan frowns in disappointment. "Well, that at least allows for a different combination, should the situation call for it."

Dominic smiles. "May I make a suggestion?"

Ryan nods. "By all means."

"Why not embed Emma and Arnie as youth counselors in Camp KidStuff? That way, you can shift Jack to the Hunt Club. His current cover as an international financier will certainly grant him entrée. Donna and I can cover Eden Key —separate huts, of course." Dominic rewards me with a wolfish grin.

Am I flattered that he so obviously wants to partner with me? But of course.

"Sounds like a plan." Ryan scribbles something on a pad.

Emma and Arnie exchange glances and blushes. All posturing aside, their budding relationship is at that delicate juncture where trust and commitment intersect.

Jack and I are *sooooo* far beyond that, which is why I'm sure he's getting just as big a kick out of Dominic's flirtations as I am.

Or maybe not. Jack is no longer smiling. "Why does Dominic get to cover Eden Key with Donna? It just doesn't make sense. For one reason, we're a proven mission team. For another, wouldn't it be more believable for a publicly-acknowledged couple to take a vacation there?"

"I think the answer to that is pretty obvious," Dominic interjects. "It's a singles resort. We'll be going undercover, as single consenting adults"—he winks at me when he says this —"which is much better for the mission, is it not, Ryan?"

Jack's mouth drops open—then shuts again.

Because he knows Dominic is right.

He turns to me. "Donna, what do you think?"

"Well….*hmmm.* Well, I…" I turn from him, to Dominic, and back to Jack. "I'll do whatever is best for the mission."

Ryan nods. "Then it's settled. Donna, since ID validation falls on you, you'll also act as mission leader on this assignment. That said, group reconnaissance meetings take place in Donna's tiki as needed, or every forty-eight hours, beginning at nineteen-hundred hours on Day One. Along with plane tickets under your aliases, you'll also find an all-inclusive island pass, which allows you to move freely from one resort to another. Abu, Arnie and Emma will take the flight at ten o'clock tonight. Dominic, Donna and Jack will take a later one, which leaves at ten tomorrow morning." He waves his hand at Janine, who nods dutifully as she makes the necessary travel changes.

"Jack isn't piloting the plane, right?" Arnie asks with a snort. "If so, the last place I want to be is in an exit door seat."

Again no one laughs—certainly not Jack—although I detect a shadow of a smile on Dominic's lips.

Ryan sighs tiredly as he looks down at his notes. Class is dismissed.

Emma smacks Arnie on the head as she takes her ticket and heads out the door. If that's not a broad enough hint for him to cut the lame jokes, then I don't know what is.

Okay, maybe I do. But it's going to hurt.

Jack pats me on the shoulder. "Hey, this one should be fun. Sand, sun, sex on the beach"—When all eyes turn to us, he smiles—"drinks, I mean. And at least we won't have to fake the rum-fueled romance part."

Ryan looks up. "Jack, you've got it wrong. Donna *will* be faking it—with Dominic."

Ooops.

Jack stares at Ryan. Then at Dominic.

And finally, at me.

I'm too awestruck too say anything.

But Jack doesn't know that. His take on things is that I'm not supporting him.

He shrugs as he leaves the room.

"Petulant prat, eh? Not to worry, my sweet. Jealousy is a wonderful aphrodisiac." Dominic grins as he takes my hand in his. "Speaking of which, what say you join me for a bowl of mussels at that little boîte on the beach just around the corner—what is it called? Ah yes, the Sand Dollar! We can work on our cover over dinner and a good bottle of wine." Gently, with one of those thick fingers, he traces the lifeline on my palm. "We'll play dessert by ear."

As Dominic leans in ever closer, he blocks my view of Jack, who is walking out the door.

Hopefully, not out of my life.

I should go after Jack, shouldn't I? But wouldn't it be rude to jerk my hand away? Besides, Jack said it best: our relationship is built upon mutual trust.

I guess that's why I stand and say to Dominic, "So sorry, old boy. I've already got dinner plans—with Jack."

Dominic's eyes narrow even as he smirks. He suddenly realizes things aren't going the way he'd planned.

That's okay. I'm not the only one he'll respect in the morning. If this mission is going to succeed, he's got to show some courtesy to Jack as well.

I sashay toward the door after the man I love.

But he's already gone home. Without me.

By the time I've walked home, I'm sweaty, hungry, and tired.

On the other hand, Lassie and Rin Tin Tin are well-fed. Seems that Jack gave them our steaks, then went out to eat on his own.

I'm a big girl. I can forgive him. When he comes home, I'll make it up to him.

It's four o'clock in the morning and still no Jack.

This is turning out to be one lousy summer.

4

The Mile High Club

If you've yet to join one of the most coveted clubs in the world, maybe your next flight will provide you the perfect opportunity. The initiation is arduous, but certainly worth it! Here's what you'll need to do:

Step #1: Get drunk. That way, you're totally open to any lame come-on line thrown at you by a seatmate you wouldn't look twice at in any other situation.

Step #2: Be the first one to go to the lavatory. This gives you time to adjust the lighting to your best advantage. However, should this attempt set off any alarms, do your best to act innocent when the flight attendants pound on the door. (In doing so, it would help if you refasten your push-up bra.)

Step #3: Consider a little role-playing. The most obvious is "Pilot and Stewardess," but we all know you're much more imaginative than that! Go for something less obvious like say, "Bronco-Bustin' Cowboy and Wild Filly," or perhaps "Poodle meets Great Dane," both of which are worth extra bonus miles, because let's face it: anyone can do it standing up. On the other hand getting down on all fours in an airplane lavatory takes real skill! Very important tip: if your hand ends up in the toilet, don't flush.

Step #4: Afterward, expect the longest walk of shame in your lifetime. Yep, no doubt about it: everyone sitting between the lavatory and your row heard your partner's ecstatic moans, despite the number of those little tissue squares you stuffed into his mouth. Unfortunately, there's nothing left for you to do but hold your head high as you walk back to your seat—

So try hard to ignore the snickers, cat calls, and applause.

Does membership have its privileges? You betcha—bragging rights! Just think of all the gal pals you'll shock—not to mention all the man-ho's you'll impress.

THE MORNING FLIGHT TO THE NEWLY BRANDED FANTASY ISLAND takes place on a spanking new Airbus A-350, and boy, is it packed to the gills.

Jack, Dominic and I are sitting in First Class. We are all in the same row, but the men's seats are placed at each window, whereas my seat is placed with one other in the middle of the aisle.

I wish Jack's ticket had placed him next to me. Then again, we aren't supposed to know each other, let alone interact in public.

At least, that's an excuse I'm willing to live with.

I try to focus on the dossier explaining my cover. It says my name is Lotta Tallant. Supposedly I'm a sex therapist. I'm also a redhead who's into chess, math, and submission, all of which is supposed to be enticing to our target, should he be wandering through Eden Key looking for love in all the wrong faces.

The seats are really minicubicles, affording the first-class passengers the ultimate in privacy, what with high backs and curtained openings. When desired, the chairs open to a fully horizontal position.

I'd certainly desire it, if Jack were by my side.

I glance over at his cubicle, where the curtain is shut. His pouting is ridiculous.

The moment we're airborne, Dominic puts his efforts toward charming two of the plane's female flight attendants into opening a very rare bottle of cognac saved for the owners of Fantasy Air.

I've got no problem with the fact that Dominic is an equal opportunity flirt. Time that Jack realize it, too. I slip over to his cubicle and pull the curtain to one side. "You know, you're acting like a spoiled child."

He lifts a corner of his HUNT CLUB complimentary eye mask. "We're incognito, remember?"

"You were certainly *incognito* last night." I plop myself on his lap. "Where the hell did you go?"

"I did what any red-blooded fake husband would do, whose fake kids and fake wife are out of his hair for the evening. I hit a real lounge with a real bartender, where a bunch of really miserable guys were grousing about the fact their real wives and kids were pains in their asses," he says matter-of-factly. "And suddenly I realized how lucky I was."

I smile gratefully at him. "Well, I feel the same way."

"You do? You mean, you find it okay that we take some time off from each other, in order to assess what we really want out of this fake relationship?"

"No, of course not! I mean…" I don't know what the hell I mean, since I don't really think he knows what he means, either.

At least, I hope he doesn't. "Is that all I am to you—some 'fake wife'?"

"On this mission, you're not even that."

"If you're speaking of Dominic pulling Eden Key as his cover as opposed to you, I had nothing to do with that."

His look says, *we both know better than that.*

Okay, maybe if I'd squawked more, Ryan could have been persuaded.

So why didn't I?

Because it was fun watching Jack get a wee bit jealous.

I didn't realize how quickly *wee bit* can turn into *totally livid.*

Surely he agrees with me that it's time to kiss and make up. "Forget the mission for five minutes. What are we in real life?"

He pauses before answering me. When, finally, he can muster the words, it comes out in a soft growl: "Lovers. Best friends. Life partners." He stops. "I guess you can add 'heartbreaking flirt' to your side of the ledger sheet."

"Jack, be fair! You certainly do your fair share of flirting."

"It's in my job description, remember?" I don't know if his scowl is in response to my accusation, or in regard to how he feels about this part of his gig.

Our gig. "Yeah okay, well, welcome to my world."

"The difference between you and me, my dear Mrs. Stone, is that I'm not 'that guy' when I'm home with you, or when I'm in the office, for that matter." He jerks his head in Dominic's direction. "Whereas you're always…how did Dominic put it? Oh yes—'Donna Stone, the manslayer.' You enjoy turning men's heads, even as you gut them alive. And that will always be the case."

I can't see Jack's face through a scrim of tears. "You're

right. I have no excuse for ever making you feel as if you aren't the only man in my life."

Jack frowns. "That's just it. I'm not the only man."

I open my mouth to say something—

But the words don't come out.

Because I know he's right. He's got to compete with terrorists and other bad guys who want to maim and destroy. My job, like his, is to stop them from succeeding.

And doing so—being an assassin—is almost as big a part of my life—my identity—as being a mother.

Could I give it all up?

Yes. And I will, gladly—when the Quorum no longer exists.

Unfortunately, that won't happen until we know for certain that Carl no longer exists, either.

He is the ex from hell. Worse yet, he's the terrorist from hell.

We both know that Jack won't rest either, until Carl is permanently out of our lives. In that regard, so far, so good. Six months and counting. If we can go a year, I'll gladly do without the official death certificate to feel the time is right to retire.

Here's hoping Jack feels I'm worth waiting for.

In the meantime, we will complete the missions assigned to us, including this one, which we must do with the assistance of Dominic Fleming.

I have nothing left to say to him, so I turn to leave. Besides, I've got to clean up my face. No one should see me this upset.

That is, no one should see Lotta Tallant at her worst—least of all anyone on this flight, who may lead me to Dr. Mandrake.

As I bolt toward the first-class lavatories, I collide with one of the female flight attendants enamored by Dominic. Her hair is mussed, and her lipstick is smeared. I shouldn't stare, but it's hard not to, seeing how the back of her skirt is stuck in her pantyhose, revealing a thong and a tattoo of an airplane on her left butt cheek.

I'm just about to warn her of this wardrobe malfunction when she turns back around to face me. "Economy passengers aren't allowed in the first-class lavatories," she says, frowning.

"As it turns out, I happen to be a first-class passenger. Not that you've noticed. Where's all that elitist service touted in your glossy brochure?" I grab the handle to the lavatory. "Here's a thought! Get that pout off your face and fix your skirt before the passengers in Coach get the wrong idea about the glories of First Class. We wouldn't want them to think that one of the bennies is free membership in the Mile High Club, now would we?"

She opens her mouth to say something, but then thinks twice. Instead, she straightens her skirt as she huffs off.

If I'm not mistaken, there was a tear in her eye. Oh hell, I think I've made her cry. Well, too bad. I'm having my own pity party.

Oops! The lavatory door is unlocked, but it happens to be occupied—

By Dominic. He must be changing because his shirt is open and untucked, revealing the pecs and abs that have launched a thousand sighs.

He's wearing nothing else, except his boxer briefs.

"Don't leave," he implores me through a sly smile. "There's always room for one more."

Hmmm. I think I know why the female flight attendant had her wardrobe malfunction.

At that very second the plane hits a hiccup, and I fall forward toward him. I give a little yelp when I realize what I'm leaning against *ain't a gun in his pocket—*

He's just very happy to see me.

Don't….look…down…

Despite a burning desire to validate the one rumor (or should I say, fantasy) about Dominic Fleming that is most frequently and furiously bandied about the spook loops, I force myself to look him in the eye instead—not so easy to do, considering that he looms a head taller than me, and this darn lavatory is the size of a postage stamp.

As if reading my mind, he smiles down upon his God-given gift. "Yes, milady, it's real—and it's *spectacular.*"

The creak of the door is a welcomed interruption. I turn around to see—

Jack. He must have realized how upset I was, and followed in order to console me.

By the look on his face, he's changed his mind. "Sorry, Donna. I had no idea you were on your way to a scheduled rendezvous."

"Just practicing our covers for Eden Key, old boy." Dominic smiles knowingly. "You're welcome to join us. What do you say, Donna? Share and share alike?"

Jack goes at him so fast that it takes all my might to hold his arm before he can pummel the dimple in Dominic's chin into oblivion.

As Dominic massages the pain out of his jaw, he mutters, "Ah, so the rumors are true! Touché, Donna dearest! You've effectively neutered my strongest competition for spydom's Undercover Lover award." He opens his arms wide. "I'll leave you two lovebirds alone to kiss and make up in private. By the way, I've found that the Kama Sutra pose known as the *Divitala* the most ideal for these situations."

I hold Jack back from slamming the door on Dominic before it closes behind him.

Jack turns to me. "Seriously? This is the guy you want to partner with, on this mission?"

"No—I wanted to be with *you*!"

"Why didn't you say something when you had the chance?"

"Because I…"

Hmmm. Should I tell Jack the truth, that Dominic's flirtations were flattering, and that I liked the fact it made Jack so jealous?

I can't. I'm too ashamed. So instead I say, "Because he was the partner assigned to me. I…I guess there's nothing we can do about it now."

Beg me to do something about it. You know I will.

But begging isn't Jack's style. "You made the right choice. You'll learn a lot from Dominic. I have a feeling you'll also learn a lot *about* Dominic—including whether or not he lives up to all your fantasies."

Our chests touch as he brushes past me to get out the door. I'm aroused, and from the way he hardens, I know he is, too. Does this tempt him to forgive my stupidity?

No. The door closes silently behind him.

I lean over the basin to splash cold water on my face.

I wish I could take a cold shower.

It will be the first thing I do when I get to my room in Eden Key, which the brochure describes as "the epitome of sensuality, what with its heart shaped feather beds, mirrored ceilings, two-person Jacuzzi tubs, libido-warming fireplace, and plush bathrobes—optional attire, since nudity is welcomed with open arms, and your privacy is always guaranteed."

Not to mention my loneliness.

On this mission, it is my penance.

Suddenly I want to go home.

That is to say, to be in Jack's arms again.

5

How to Stuff a Wild Bikini

If your vacation includes warm weather and a beach, packing a swimsuit is a must. Oh, pshaw to your lame excuses for staying wrapped in some sack-like muumuu! Time to show a little flesh, if only for these three reasons:

Reason #1: Anticipating the day in which you can squeeze into your bikini will help curb your appetite. (Or it will make you cry. And if you're crying, trust me, so is everyone else, all up and down the beach.)

Reason #2: Putting on a bathing suit encourages you to get into the water, and we all know swimming is great exercise—especially when swimming away from stingrays, jellyfish, or sharks. Who knew you had a perfect breast stroke, and can complete it in Olympic-worthy time?

Reason #3: You need your daily dose of Vitamin D. Remember, thirty minutes of sun, each and every day, keeps the doctor away! (Or close at hand, depending on how you look in that suit. If it has his temperature rising, expect him to offer you Vitamin F injections, too.)

And remember, the perfect itty bitty for you is the Bond Girl bikini. You know the one: it has a thick belt worn low on your hips—where you'll carry your assassin's knife.

~

"WELCOME TO FANTASY ISLAND!" MR. BOARKE'S VOICE BOOMS out from the far reaches of the gently sloping lawn, which ends at the edge of the resort's private runway. As he approaches, his gait is more of a glide: leisurely in pace, but with purpose.

On the other hand Battoo is practically beside himself with joy at seeing us. He shouts, "The plane! The plane—" as he yanks a cord that pulls the large bell hanging from an enormous wooden tower.

Both men are dressed in their iconic white linen suits, as are the three drivers who stand beside the trams marked with the logos of the island's three resorts: Kamp KidStuff, the Hunt Club, and of course Eden Key.

Everyone coming off the plane gets a photo op with Boarke. After all, he is the island's celebrity. The flight crew stands behind them, straight as soldiers and beaming from ear to ear. They've arranged it so that the first guests off the plane are those heading for Kamp KidStuff. Boarke gives the parents hearty handshakes. His warnings, to slather on lots of sunscreen, leave parents just as giddy as their children as they rush to grab seats on their tram.

Many of those whose final destination is Eden Key are still primping and scoping out potential partners, not to mention the competition. This includes Dominic. He must think the pickings are slim because he has the nerve to give me a leer.

If he thinks I want to kiss and make up, he's got another think coming. My frown warns him to keep his distance. If I hadn't needed to hold Jack back, I would have smacked him myself.

Nah, he would have liked it too much.

I'm standing by three women. One, a frowzy fifty-something whose hair is too dark to be her real color, blows a perfect smoke ring over my head as she gives me the once-over. She jerks her head in Dominic's direction. "Hey Red, Handsome over there thinks you're adorable. What are you waiting for, a written invitation?"

I shrug. "Been there, done that."

"Good, then he's up for grabs." She waves him down, as if he's a taxi on Madison Avenue during rush hour.

He pretends he is one and ignores her completely. I guess he feels I've got her covered. Or for the first time in his life, he's scared of a woman. My guess is the latter.

She brushes off his snub with a smile. "His loss. The contortions I can get into would blow his mind. I used to be an aerial acrobat with *Cirque du Soleil*."

I cock my head in disbelief. "Get outta here."

She shrugs. "Okay, so I'm lying. But he wouldn't know it."

I'm tempted to say, *until you ended up in traction*, but I'm here to win friends and influence frenemies, so I keep my mouth shut.

"Let me guess, you're going to Eden Key too, right?" Cougar asks.

I give her a thumbs-up.

"My motto is 'If you can't beat 'em, join 'em,' so let's be each others' wing girls. My name is Merritt Andrews. This is Tuggle Carpenter, and that's Angie Dill, over there."

The two other women—a buxom brunette, and a willowy blonde—give me tepid waves. Obviously unlike Dominic their mottos aren't, *the more the merrier.*

Merritt lowers her sunglasses in order to scrutinize Mr. Boarke. Her consensus is a disappointed frown. "Not at all like his picture in the brochure. He's a bit long in the tooth." Like tractor beams, her eyes move right to left as she scans those male passengers who are still departing the plane. "Now, *that* one's a real cutie—and certainly young enough for some of the bedroom acrobatics I have in mind."

She's pointing to Jack.

Just at that moment he glances in our direction. I can't see his eyes because of his sunglasses. He is grinning, though, so that's a good sign.

But apparently he's not smiling at me because just then a woman brushes past me, on her way to his side. She is a slim blonde in a tight white suit that hugs every curve. She has a drink in hand—something in a martini glass. His thank-you earns him a flirtatious toss of her long, lush mane.

She takes his arm in hers and walks him over to Mr. Boarke, who smiles broadly and pumps his hand like a long lost pal as he walks Jack to the Hunt Club tram.

Apparently Jack has been assigned a personal escort, because the blonde sidles next to him in the tram.

Well, la-dee-dah.

"Aw heck, he's going to the gun club. I guess it was too good to be true." Merritt sighs. "That's okay. I've got it from an impeccable source that if you buy the midget a pint of scotch, he'll personally introduce you to the men with the longest schlongs. I guess he should know. Being knee-high to a grasshopper has to have some benefits—especially in the men's locker room, right?"

I'd rather find out if he knows Mandrake's whereabouts. But hey, since he's plugged in, it's certainly worth picking his brain.

Or pickling it. First stop: the Duty Free shop, for a bottle of Johnny Walker Blue.

As I follow my new besties to the Eden Key tram, my iPhone chimes with its fairy dust tone. It's a red letter day. Trisha has sent her very first text:

LOVE YOU, MOMMY. THE PLANE TOOK A LONG TIME, BUT NOW WE ARE ON A PRETTY BEACH. I STILL MISS YOU. KISS, TRISHA

I should be there with her, not here with the lonely and the anxious.

"YUMMY! LOOK AT THE CUTE GUY IN THE ATLANTA BRAVES TEE-shirt, out on the deck!" Tuggle is practically salivating over Tony Ebersol, a stockbroker who just made a killing on the latest Apple stock boom—something I learned after I lifted Tony's fingerprint, which he left on my vinyl bikini top as he copped a feel during this afternoon's co-ed beachside volleyball pick-up game.

I scanned Tony's print with my iPhone, then sent it to Emma, who ran it through the NSA's fingerprint database. Because Tony is a member of the Securities and Exchange Commission, Acme was able to confirm that (a) he is definitely an avid Braves fan, having held onto season tickets for years, even during the team's disastrous 2008 season; (b) that he is a partner in the Peachtree Street-Atlanta office of Merrill Lynch; and (c) that he also happens to be married.

Not that he'll divulge this interesting tidbit to Tuggle when she picks up his room card during tonight's Key party.

Key swaps are just one of the dozens of activities offered.

In any given hour, the resort's activities directors herd guests into games of all sorts. Eden Key's top picks are Strip Poker, Truth or Dare, Scavenger Hunt, and the Dating Game.

More strenuous activities include nude yoga, nude sunbathing, and nude hiking. Do you see a pattern here? The operative word is *nude*.

It's been a slow and grueling process. In the past forty hours I've eliminated only six of Eden Key's fifty-five male guests. That means a lot of flirtations and bar pick-ups, scanning the faces of possible suspects in the hope that Acme's facial recognition software will make a match with the fuzzy photo we have of Dr. Mandrake. The process of elimination is helped by anyone whose fingerprints are registered elsewhere. But other than that, we don't have much to go on—

Except for gossip. In this hotbed of hunks, tarts and hotties, the oddest of sexual peccadilloes is grist for the mill.

Tuggle, Merritt and Angie have also kept busy. Their close encounters of the male kind have reaped reconnaissance on at least another fifteen or so male guests, some who could easily be prime suspects except for the fact that they're missing the mushroom cloud tattoo.

The more my band of sistahs reveals, the more revealing they become. Turns out that Tuggle is recently divorced from the man who was her high school sweetheart. She is now looking to make up for lost time. On the other hand, Merritt, the raven-haired cougar, is thrice divorced and proud of it. One of her several mottoes—"the younger, the better"—is something she declares loudly and proudly.

The last of our clique, Angie, is a gorgeous ex-model who has never been married because (as she puts it) "men only look skin deep." To make it easy for them to do so, she adheres to the club's *Nude Is Good* policy as often as possible.

I'm beginning to wonder if her wardrobe consists of anything other than a belly button ring collection.

"What about the guy over there, in the golf shirt?" I try to sound nonchalant as I point out a fifty-something dark-haired golfer who has just come off the back nine with three other middle-aged men—brothers from St. Louis whose wives think they're on their annual fishing trip at their grandpa's old cabin on the Lake of the Ozarks.

"Haven't met him." Merritt shrugs. "And I've got no plans to do so. He's too old for me."

"If no one else has dibbs on him, I'd take him, any day," Tuggle pipes up.

"Trust me, you can do better than that creep," Angie assures her. "He's a biter! See?" She flips over onto her stomach, where an obvious set of teeth marks can be made out on her right butt cheek. "He picked me up before lunch. Said we could order room service in my suite. Oh, well, that's what I get for telling some dude I'm 'into rough stuff.' I thought he meant a little slap and tickle, not covering me in barbecue sauce and having me for lunch. I screamed so loud that he took off like a thief."

Merritt scrutinizes the manicure on her left hand. "You know my motto—"

Angie sighs. "Which one? You have so many."

Merritt folds all her fingers down, except for the middle one.

In her current position Angie is oblivious of the gesture. "The most obvious one, my ignorant little friend: 'The way to a man's heart is through his stomach.'"

"I wasn't interested in his heart. And the part of his anatomy that piqued my interest turned out to be a tiny bit disappointing." She holds up a finger of her own—a pinky.

"Ouch, never mind." Tuggle frowns. Suddenly she

notices something about Angie's bitten backside that brings her up close and personal to it. "Looks like the guy is missing one of his incisors!"

What the…? In unison, Merritt and I turn to stare at her.

Tuggle smiles proudly. "I'm a dental assistant. Then again, the tooth might have been broken above the bite line. I guess we'd need a second opinion to know for sure."

Not a bad idea. Would it be too obvious if I snapped an iPhoto of it with my cell so that Acme can match the indentations to Doctor Mandrake's most recent dental records? Like all of the Federal government, the NSA has the best medical coverage our taxes can buy.

For that reason alone, we should all work for the NSA.

Or get elected to Congress.

I doubt Angie would bat an eye if I asked. "I'll take that bet," I say nonchalantly. "I've got a dentist buddy. Mind if I shoot off a picture and text it to him?"

Just as I thought, Angie is eager to accommodate. She lifts her butt into a porn-worthy pose.

The St. Louis trio slam into each other when the first brother stops to gawk.

I hope Emma isn't around when Arnie opens this jpeg, or there will be hell to pay.

Angie stays on her belly, but she turns her head so that she's facing me. "You're a sex therapist, right? So, why must some guys bite in order to get it up?"

Good question. And I'm sure if I really were a real sex therapist, I'd have the answer to that. Instead I have to fake it. "Because they're sick sons of bitches," I tell her matter-of-factly.

"Ah! Makes sense." As she stretches out on the chaise, her bangles clink and tinkle, like Tibetan chimes in a windstorm.

Two of the brothers nudge each other.

The smile on Master Biter's face disappears when he sees the object of their lust.

Is he Dr. Mandrake? Only his dentist knows for sure. I'll get Arnie to scope out the good doctor's employee dental claims. Maybe we'll hit a match.

And then Jack and I can take some real time off, together.

6

Missed Connections

Travel can go right. It can also go terribly wrong.

It is particularly irksome when one misses one's plane and has landed too late to make the connection needed to get to one's final destination.

If you are that one, here's how to play catch-up:

First, throw down the VIP card. And guess what? You don't have to be a VIP to play! All you have to do is act like one. That means (a) proclaiming loudly that you've been inconvenienced in the worst possible way; (b) breaking into the front of the ticketing queue for those getting re-routed; and (c) haranguing the ticket agent for the best seat available. Don't hesitate to point out that your inconvenience should be mitigated by the provision of a free first-class ticket.

Next, insist on a golf cart to take you to the gate of your new flight. It doesn't matter that all the carts are in use. Nor does it matter that you're not infirm or just plain old. And it certainly doesn't matter that you'll be inconveniencing some who are too far from their gates or infirm, or old as Methuselah. What matters is that you make your point—whatever that is. (You'll have plenty of time to figure that out on your five-mile-an-hour cart ride.)

Finally, when you actually get onto that other plane, toss a hissy fit about your seat. This lets the flight attendants know you're not to be messed with again. It also signals your flight's air marshal that he should have his taser gun ready to stun, the moment one of the flight attendants give him the high sign.

Should you get tossed from this flight as well, be honest about it with the person picking you up at the other end:

Just say you missed your connection.

"Despite the fact that Jack's not here, shouldn't we start this shindig?" Abu looks down at his watch. "I've got to be back in less than thirty minutes in order to clean guns for a bunch of lazy rich dudes who couldn't hit the side of a barn with a bazooka."

I nod. "Time is of the essence. As of today there are one hundred and sixty-four men within the confines of Fantasy Island, and we've only positively cleared seventy-three of them. At this rate, we won't find Mandrake until it's too late. I've got no problem with starting sans Jack Craig."

In truth, I'm angry as hell that Jack has no respect for my turn as mission leader, but I certainly don't want the others to see it. Everyone else—Emma, Abu, and Arnie—showed up promptly, so why should they be punished?

Even Dominic is with us—sort of. He's preoccupied with posting selfies of himself and some of the comely lasses of Eden Key—eight and counting—onto his Facebook fan page. Obviously he's taking the term "undercover" quite literally.

Which begs my question to him: "Dominic, tell me—has

even one of your conquests divulged the tiniest hint of Mandrake's whereabouts?"

He doesn't bother to look up, merely waves his hand at me, as if shooing away a pesky gnat. "I don't know about you, *Donna*, but at the peak of my partners' physical pleasure, I'm the only man they're thinking about. I know this, because it is my name, and only mine, that they shout out while in the throes of passion."

"Pity. Defeats our purpose, wouldn't you agree? Tell you what, considering our time restraints, forego your usual *modus operandi*. Instead, set up shop in the men's steam room. The sooner that mushroom cloud tat reveals itself, the better."

"Aye, aye, my mistress and commander." He is disappointed. Nonetheless, he honors me with an RAF salute.

I turn to Abu. "I know it's early, but any potential suspects among the hunters, fishers, or gamblers?"

He shakes his head. "They're a chummy lot. For the most part they hang in cliques, based on their preferred pastimes. When not out playing, they're in the bar or the club's restaurant, telling tall tales. In my capacity as an 'arms facilitator,' most of my exposure is with the hunters. They break into two groups—those into tracking deer, which are allowed to roam in the woods just beyond the lodge." He hesitates, as if choosing his words carefully. "Then there are the 'big game' hunters."

That certainly gets my attention. "Big game? Like what?"

"Funny you should ask. I can't get a straight answer from any of the employees. Some think bison. Others say lions. Whatever the species, its habitat—enclosed securely, I presume—is far from the lodge. I've listened for big game sounds, but I never hear any. Each morning, these particular hunters—there is only a handful of them—are driven to the reserve in a special van. Sometimes these hunts take place in the evenings. I know this, because I'm called to the arsenal room as late as eight at night, and told to hand out infrared goggles along with the hunter's gun of choice."

"Can you tell by the ammo what they may be shooting at?"

Abu thinks for a moment before shaking his head. "It's certainly not the kind of clip that will take down a bull elephant. More in the big cat range."

Whatever is out there, I just hope it stays within its confines. I can only imagine the carnage that would ensue if some dangerous animal got loose, and made its way into the other resorts.

I turn to Emma, who's still dressed in her youth counselor uniform costume—Little Red Riding Hood. "Why don't you and Arnie fill us in on the comings and goings at Kamp KidStuff?"

She rolls her eyes. "There are no single men, just dads who have come with their wives. And most of the counselors are right at Arnie's and my age, so I don't think Dr. Mandrake is on our side of the island."

"Great. Then you'll have more time to field and assess the reconnaissance collected by the rest of us."

Emma sighs. "I'll do what I can, and as soon as possible. But sometimes it's hard to get away from my assigned group. I'm in charge of four high-school bound girls who are so boy crazy! All they want to do is hang around the pool and stare at the jocks. I mean, come on already! If they cared half as much about math and science as they do their tans, their nails, and their hair, they wouldn't need to worry about whether or not they impress a bunch of deadbeat testosterone-crazy dudes."

Arnie slumps down to the floor. "You think you've got it

bad? Every time I think I've got a bead on Mandrake's GPS signal, I've got to break up a fight between a bunch of antsy ten-year-old boys who don't want to do anything other than stay inside all day and play video games."

What the heck? This isn't supposed to turn into a gripe session. Time to pull the mommy card. No, make that the mission leader card.

I point to Emma. "Look, I know you've got a lot on your plate. But don't forget that your prime objective is monitoring your iPhone for our reconnaissance. As for your camp duties, let the girls flirt, for goodness' sake! What harm can it do? If one of them allows a boy to go beyond a lip lock, shove them into the pool. Granted, she'll be mortified that her hair got wet, but it'll show her that you mean business."

She gulps and nods.

"As for you, Arnie," I flip around to face him, "boys love competition. Your Acme duties come first. Confiscate all the game gear, pick two leaders, and schedule a prize for the team that builds the best fort."

He salutes me.

That's more like it. "Now, in which camp have you found Mandrake's GPS signal?"

"I swear, every hour the dude is somewhere different. This morning, it was the Hunt Club. After lunch, it was Kamp KidStuff. And an hour ago, he was close enough to this tiki that I thought you'd caught the wily bastard."

"He was *here*?"

"Cross my heart."

"That's crazy. I've been here—*alone*—for the past two hours, writing up my reconnaissance report!" Something is definitely not right.

"Ah yes, the mundane duties of a mission leader." The

voice, coming from behind me, has caught everyone's attention. "The only one that counts right now is reconnaissance."

It belongs to Jack.

He looks as if he's spent the day working on his tan. Considering his company as of late, maybe that's a good thing.

Unless it's been on Eden Key's nude beach. Son of a bitch better have a tan line.

He's in a tux, so I can't check for one. Ha. I guess he's got more formal plans for this evening. With whom, I wonder? My guess is Boarke's blonde.

I force a smile onto my face. "Pardon?"

His grin is just as frosty as mine. "You need to pull Arnie and Emma out of Kamp KidStuff. They've been assigned the most strenuous covers. At the same time, they have double duty on this mission, which includes assessing our intel. Their camp duties are slowing down the mission."

"Is that so?" My declaration was rhetorical, but Arnie and Emma seem to have taken it as the answer to their prayers because both are nodding—

Until they see my eyes narrow in their direction. Then they look at their feet.

Keep calm. That a girl. "We're following Ryan's orders, remember?" I'm tempted to stick out my tongue at him, but I'm too much of a lady. Besides, that would seem childish.

Jack loosens his tuxedo tie. "Stop me if I'm wrong, but aren't you this mission's leader?"

"Yes, of course I am." Casually I lean against the wall. He knows my body language. To put it delicately, I'm signaling, *better shut up while you're still breathing.*

"As such, you can change their orders as you see fit."

"Oh! Well...I..." Damn it, he's right.

And I'm stubborn. "But I don't 'see fit' to do so."

"Pardon?" he says as he leans against the wall across the room. He's daring me to deny this.

But I can't. It was Dominic's suggestion that they be placed at Kamp KidStuff. At the same time, our British team member has been rolling in and out of beds all day, and what does *he* have to show for it? Several hickeys, and that's about it.

Still, if the team sees Jack win this battle, I'll lose the war. "Emma and Arnie will just have to suck it up. We need reconnaissance at that resort, too."

"Here's an idea. Why don't you and Dominic swap places with them? I'm sure he can easily ingratiate himself to a few other desperate housewives."

The operative word here is *other*—as in me being the first.

Or is it *desperate*?

"True that, old boy." Dominic smiles broadly.

The narcissistic dolt has taken it as a compliment.

That's it. I've had it with both of them. I fake a lazy yawn. "I promise to give it some thought. In the meantime, why don't you enlighten us regarding your own reconnaissance efforts, Jack?"

"I thought you'd never ask." His smile disappears. "My international banking credentials have endeared me to Mr. Boarke. He wants to expand the amenities offered here at Fantasy Island, but he's having a hard time convincing his silent partners—who are represented by a Canadian venture capitalist—to go along with his plan. Let's just say that my offer to be an outside funding source has given me a few special privileges."

I can only imagine.

"To that extent," he continues, "I've requested a full tour of the island before making my recommendation to my employer. This allows us the opportunity to scope out locations that coincide with Mandrake's GPS coordinates—that is, if Arnie is freed up to track them during my tour, and feed them to me. So what do you say, Donna? Can Arnie and Emma be relieved of their Kamp KidStuff duties?"

Checkmate. Under the WWRD (What Would Ryan Do?) rule, I've got no choice but to say yes to Jack's initial suggestion that Arnie and Emma be transferred.

I shrug. "Okay, sure. Arnie, turn in your notice immediately. You too, Emma. Then book yourselves here, at Eden Key, under different aliases. Make sure to put yourself on a plane manifest, just in case the resort does a cross-check."

"No prob, boss lady!" Arnie says. He and Emma high five each other. At least it's not a chest bump.

Jack turns to me. "I'd appreciate a second pair of eyes for this reconnaissance mission. If you're free tomorrow, Donna, I can pass you off as—well, as my date."

If I'm free?

Heck yeah, I'm free. For tomorrow, and the rest of my life.

If this is Jack's way of calling a truce, I'm all for it. Nonchalantly I say, "With Emma moving here to Eden Key, I'll certainly make the time."

"Good. Then it's settled. The Boarke Buggy will be at your tiki door promptly at ten in the morning."

As everyone files out, I place my hand on Jack's arm. "Thank you for your input tonight. I want to do my best to succeed on this mission. I never want Ryan to doubt his trust in me."

"Ryan is quite aware of all you have to offer. You'd never let him down. He knows it"—Jack pauses—"and I know it, too."

"Oh!...Well, thank you for your vote of confidence."

"I'm not talking about the mission, Donna. I'm talking about us."

Ah. Even better.

As with everything in life, actions speak louder than words. To that end, the tenderness with which Jack takes me in his arms speaks volumes regarding his feelings for me.

As does the gentle way in which his lips fall onto mine.

As well as the way his mouth hungers for my own.

I hate it when we're at war. I love it when we make love. I am *such* a hippy that way.

The buttons on Jack's tuxedo shirt are hidden behind a pleat. Still, it doesn't slow down my game plan to strip him out of it—

But the lipstick on his collar sure as hell stops me cold.

When I point to it, the anticipation goes out of his face. "So…um…you know how to get rid of that, right?"

I think for a moment. "Sure no problem. A bullet hole will do the trick. Stand still for a second while I get my Glock."

He must be afraid I'll make good on this threat because he holds tight to my hands and looks me in the eye. "Nothing happened. *Nothing*."

"Sure, okay. Nothing." I shrug him off and head back to the mirror. Suddenly I feel claustrophobic in this room. It's much too small.

Or maybe the bed is much too big. Not to mention heart-shaped.

And empty.

What a damn waste.

Not that I'll let him in on that secret. Instead, I reach for my mascara wand and work on making my lashes long and lush, just like the packaging promises. I force myself to sound cheerful when I say, "I look forward finally to meeting Mr. Boarke. I'll do my best to be utterly charming."

"Unfortunately, he won't be with us. His assistant, Julie,

will be showing us around." Jack hesitates then adds, "In fact, I'm meeting her when I leave here."

"If that's the case, then don't let me keep you any longer."

He waits a moment, but I don't turn around.

There is nothing he can do but leave. The door closes silently behind him.

This mascara also claims to be waterproof. I can tell you first hand that it is not.

7

Cruisin' for a Bruisin'

Everyone should take at least one Mexican cruise in their lifetime.

In fact, one cruise is the most many of us can stomach. Perhaps the term "stomach" is wrong, considering the amount of food you'll find on a cruise buffet, not to mention the effect of ocean waves on your stomach.

This brings us to six things you should never do on a cruise:

Thing #1: Overeat. Why? Because the more food in your belly, the more likely you'll barf it over the rail in a storm. And yes, there is always a storm.

Thing #2: Don't drink too much. See Thing #1. Add to it a hangover.

Thing #3: Boast that you're "worth millions" when you're drunk. Why? Because (here's a shocker) dineros, the Mexican currency, aren't a one-to-one match with the US dollar. Then again, none of your newfound cruisin' buds know that you're talking in dineros as opposed to dollars.

Thing #4: Have sex with a stranger. Thrilling? Depends on how fast you can run when his wife catches you together.

Suggestion: Before your cruise, make sure you're slim enough to climb through a porthole. Second suggestion: Forego the cruise buffet, in case you need to be slim enough to climb through that porthole.

Thing #5: Marry a stranger at sea. Certainly not anyone you met while you were drunk. Or one who is already married. Most marriages are recognized in international waters as well as on land.

Thing #6: Fall overboard. By that I mean, get pushed. Hey, it happens—especially after impetuous weddings at sea to strangers who hear you boast about your bank account and presume you're talking dollars, as opposed to dineros.

"HIT ME AGAIN, BATTOO." I'M A GLUTTON FOR PUNISHMENT.

And for a good vodka martini.

Battoo makes them mean and dirty. He's my kind of guy.

And right now, he's the only guy in my life, since I chased off the love of my life.

All because I wanted to impress an indiscriminate man-ho.

No amount of vodka, vermouth, olive juice, and olives can wash away my stupidity, but I'm sure as heck going to give it a try.

"I should cut you off, Red. You know that." Battoo smiles as he pours my drink.

It should bother the spy side of me that Battoo has lost his Polynesian-French accent, but it doesn't. More disconcerting is how comfortable I feel with him—and not just because he's the only bartender I've ever seen who walks *on* the bar when he hands over your drink.

He's been handing out a lot of them, and not just to me,

either. Turns out Merritt is a sad drunk. She carries a sack of quarters in her Dolce bucket bag in order to feed the lounge's juke box, just so she can croon along with Carrie Underwood covers of Patsy Cline's classics.

To the shock and dismay of everyone in the bar, all it took was two drinks for Tuggle to channel her Coyote Ugly—and I'm sorry folks, but it just ain't pretty. I don't think the bar's patrons appreciate an interpretive dance which melds classical Russian ballet with the Charleston and the Funky Chicken.

Certainly not when bumps and grinds are eagerly anticipated.

"Not bad looking. But maybe it would help if she had a pole," mourns one of the bar's patrons, a cop who took one of his two weeks of vacation in the hope of finding women willing to open their hearts, minds, and legs.

"Forget that. Maybe if they'd put a burlap bag over her head," mutters his buddy, a firefighter. "But no, that wouldn't cover up the parts that jiggle when they shouldn't."

I'm just about to offer to cut off the jiggly bit nearest and dearest to him when Battoo murmurs, "Where's your other friend? You know, Tall, Blonde, and Naked?"

Good question. I shrug. "Who, Angie? Ha! Hadn't noticed. Maybe she got lucky. She gets that—*a lot*."

"Having the Biter know which room is yours isn't 'lucky.' More like creepy." He shudders as he grabs a bottle of Oval Swarovski Crystal Vodka from the bar only a nanosecond before Tuggle kicks it into the fireman's lap.

I may be drunk, but I'm not stupid. "Battoo, are you trying to tell me something?"

He nods. "Ah, but you are a perceptive one! Here's the thing: Boss Man wants to sell out. Therefore, Boss Man can't afford a scandal that has the lovely ladies fearing for their lives. So Boss Man can't let people know there's a serial killer on the loose, tying up our female guests and eating them—with his own special barbecue sauce, if you catch my drift."

Of course, I do.

If there was ever a reason to sober up, I guess saving a new pal from a cannibal is as good as any. I shove my martini glass back in his direction. "You really do know everything that happens in this joint, don't you, Battoo?"

He nods, but he doesn't smile. "When you're my size, it's easy to be overlooked. For the most part, I consider that a blessing. Times like this, I realize it's also a curse."

"Not when you can save a life." I grab a pen from my purse and scribble on the napkin under my drink then slip them back his way. "If I don't come back in twenty minutes, send in the Cavalry. Even without Boarke's permission, one way or another, this is one problem that's got to go away."

He takes my information. Then he turns his back to me.

But the folding knife he uses to slice lemons and limes is left on the counter.

I may not need it, but I pocket it anyway. Better I should have it than for Tuggle to slice open her foot while attempting a split.

WHEREAS MY TIKI HUT SITS ON A BOARDWALK OVER THE SAND and surf, Angie's vacation abode is one of the staggered duplex tree houses. If I'm to sneak up on Hannibal, I'll have to avoid crunching palm fronds underfoot.

I solve this problem by tiptoeing onto her neighbor's deck, then leaping from it onto her bedroom balcony.

I can peek in. I don't like what I see. Angie is tied down, spread-eagled, on her bed. Her breasts are drenched in a dark liquid.

I guess it's the barbecue sauce that Battoo warned me about.

At least she is still alive. I know this by the look of terror on her face.

I try the French door that opens from the living room balcony. Thank goodness it isn't locked. I enter the dark room, and feel my way toward the bedroom, but unfortunately I bump into the coffee table. Angie must have left her bangles on it, because they clink together.

I freeze.

Apparently, so does Hannibal.

But only for a moment. When the door opens from the bedroom, I duck behind a chair. Did he see me?

I certainly see him—all of him. He is buck naked as he walks slowly through the room. In a singsong voice, he murmurs, "Here, pussy, pussy, pussy. Come out, come out, wherever you are."

I'm sorry, but likening a woman—or any part of her—to a helpless animal pisses me off. When he's just a foot away from me, I stab his calf with the knife.

He hollers like a banshee as he goes down on one knee.

I get up before he does, and I slam my knee into his face. Then I jab a bent elbow into the back of his neck. When he's flat on the floor, I kick his kidneys—first the left one, then the right.

If he asks why I did this, I'll tell him it makes them tender. He should appreciate that.

I leave him on the floor, moaning, as I run into the bedroom.

Tears stream down Angie's face as I loosen the bindings

on her feet. She's choking on her gag as she tries to thank me—

No, I guess she was trying to warn me. I only realize this when Hannibal smacks me solidly on the head with a picture frame.

I fall onto the floor. Before I have a chance to get on my feet, he grabs me by the hair and slams the back of my head into the wall.

Just before everything goes black, I hear him say, "You've got more meat on your bones than I usually like. But what the hell, who diets when they're on vacation?"

Those last eight pounds always get me in trouble.

"Hey, do you like liver? You know it is nature's most potent super food." Hannibal lifts my head by the roots of my hair. "No joke. There are at least ten—if not a hundred—more nutrients in liver, than any other organ."

The last thing I need from this maniac is a lesson in nutrition.

I'm almost afraid to look over at Angie because she's moaning so loudly. I look at him instead. His lips are smeared with something red.

I want to throw up.

He laughs. "Relax. It's just an extra-spicy rib rub and it's *mmmm* good! I've decided to make you the main course, and leave skinny over there for dessert." He stares over at Angie. She's finally silent, which means she's either dead, drugged, or passed out. In any case I'm sure it's a blessing for her.

I've got my own problems. One is Hannibal's insatiable appetite.

Just in case he's concerned about his cholesterol, I think I should remind him, "You called me fat."

He shrugs. "Let's just say you're pleasingly plump."

"And you're a sicko." I try to move my hands, but I can't. He has them bound behind my back. I'm naked now, except for the silk sash around my throat and around my ankles. The way he jerks on it, he makes sure I know it may also serve as my noose. In fact, if I try to straighten my legs from a crouching position, I'll choke myself.

He slams my head down, deep into the couch cushion. My head is facing the coffee table. On it, six very sharp instruments are laid out on a towel.

Hannibal picks up the one that looks like a kebab skewer, and very slowly runs it up my spine. I try my damnedest not to shiver.

He slides the skewer to my neck, right below my ear where it meets my jaw. "Did you know there's a pressure point, right here? It reduces your appetite." He pinches my waist. "Guess not, eh?" He giggles as he presses down on the skewer.

The pain is excruciating, but I bite the inside of my mouth to keep from screaming out.

He laughs—and lets up. The skewer clicks against the carving knife as he tosses it back on the coffee table. Then he picks up a bowl filled with something thick and moist. "You know, you and your scrawny little gal pal in there are providing me with a veritable feast! It's like having an early Thanksgiving at the beach. In fact, while you were out cold, I took the time to make some stuffing. Here, tell me what you think of it."

He sits me up so that he can slather some on my breasts. After they're covered, he dabs even more to my right nipple. He stops a moment to admire it, then he licks it off. "Wonderful, you find this stimulating! Hey look, me too!" He points at his crotch.

He's lucky I'm all tied up. Otherwise I'd kick the shit out of him, starting with his tiny wanker.

He shoves some stuffing into my belly button, but stops when he gets to my Brazilian wax job, so that he can scrutinize it. "Well now, that won't do! I'll have to shave it all off before I finish stuffing you, my little turkey-lurkey. In the meantime, you can suck on this." He jabs his stuffing-laden fingers into my mouth.

The fool. I bite down so hard that I can taste the tartness of his blood.

When he's finished screaming and cursing at me, he tosses my head back down between the seat cushions. While I'm choking, he sticks something long and hard in my hand.

"Zucchini," he whispers in my ear. "It's on my diet." He slaps my ass with it, hard. "Now it's part of yours, too. Of course, when I get through with you, all your friends will be asking who did your lipo."

What, now he's looking for referrals?

"Like the firmness?" Slowly he slides the vegetable down the small of my back. I feel it moving toward my crack. "Only twenty calories. A gram and a half of *dietary fiber*." He caresses those last two words, as if they are porn.

In his hands, they are.

And in his hands, apparently my ass is delectable. He bites me, and it's my turn to scream.

I may lose those eight pounds yet.

He yanks the silk sash so hard that I gasp. I can't black out, not now.

"*Shhhh*," he whispers in my ear. "Now the fun part begins."

I feel his fingers separating my ass cheeks. His thumb slides down my crack until he finds what he is looking for—

No, it slides even lower, until it enters my vagina. With thumb and finger he widens it, then he places the zucchini on its lips. "I'll bet you've never been fucked with a summer squash."

He's got that right.

I brace myself for the worst lay of my life.

Instead, I hear the sweetest sound to any victim's ears: the whoosh of a bullet as it hits your tormentor in the back of the head.

Then the thud of his fall as he lands on top of you, pushing you deeper into a cushion, at an angle that has your bindings choking you.

Then a whisper in your ear, from your savior: "Donna? Oh God, Donna! Are you okay?"

Even a simple nod of your head will take you into darkness, so you wait until your savior has moved the dead body of your captor to one side and unties your bindings before cuddling you in his arms and swearing that he'll never let anyone hurt you, ever again.

All at once you're thankful he got to you in time. And you're embarrassed that he has to see you like this—all tied up, as it were, *ha ha*—

But seriously, this is no time for jokes, now is it?

He throws a sheet over you and carries you back to your tiki. Then he bundles you up into bed, and lies beside you—

And holds you as if he'll never let you go, as long as you both shall live.

When you wake up in the middle of the night, you whisper, *Jack I love you*, over and over again.

Maybe in the morning you'll break the news to him that zucchini is off the menu until you can stomach it again, but for now you let him sleep because the best time in the world is when he holds you in his arms.

If you don't break the spell, perhaps you'll never have to leave them.

~

MY PHONE IS BUZZING ITS CRICKET RING TONE.

I open one eye. Jack is still beside me and still deep in slumber.

I roll over and look at the Caller ID on my cell. It's Arnie. I click on it. "Speak to me."

"Sorry it's taken me so long to get back to you on the tooth mark, Donna. Ready for this? It belongs to the heir to the Bannaker Steel fortune, a guy named Connor Reems. I guess that makes him wealthy enough to pay to have his rap sheet buried in the bowels of Pittsburgh's police department's data archive. No convictions, but Reems has got a propensity for picking up single women who, for the most part, are never seen again. The few who got away have some pretty wild stories to tell, like food fetishes—even cannibalism!"

"Really? Ya think?" Hey, I can't blame Arnie. I'm the one who put too much on his plate (excuse the pun). I'm glad Jack set me straight about that.

"By the way, Donna, Battoo asked me to tell you that your friend, Angie, is safely on her way home. But the other two are ready to partay, as soon as you can break away, they're there for you."

Thanks, but no thanks. This isn't supposed to be a gal pal getaway weekend.

When I hang up, Jack mutters, "Who was that?"

"Arnie. He got around to some reconnaissance I requested." I flip around so that we're nose to nose. "I was out of it, but did I hear you say that Dominic got Angie to safety and Abu took care of whatever is left of Hannibal?"

He nods. "I take it Arnie confirmed he wasn't our suspect."

"No, unfortunately." I entwine my hand in his. "I'm beginning to feel as if we're looking for a needle in a haystack. Oh well, maybe the tour today will put Mandrake in our laps."

Jack frowns. "Oh yeah, about that…When I mentioned to Julie that you wanted to tag along, she didn't seem too keen about it. She's concerned that Mr. Boarke won't like it."

Yeah, right, I'm sure that's her real concern.

"Mr. Boarke owes me, big time," I mutter. "If I have to remind him about it, I will." One of Boarke's problems is solved. He's got a new one: *me.*

I yawn. "We barely have time to jump in the shower before we have to meet the Boarke buggy. Love that rich Corinthian leather."

Jack grins. "We'll have plenty of time if we shower together."

"Last one in has to scrub the other's back." I roll out of bed. "Oh, I just remembered! If you see a bite mark, just ignore it."

Jack checks out my backside. "No way. I want to take my time examining you for bruises, then kiss them and make them better."

I've no doubt he will. And I'll love every minute of it.

8

Oh, the Places You'll Go!

One of the joys of traveling is seeing new sights, and making new friends. Here are some tips that will help you expand your horizons in ways you never thought possible:

Tip #1: Travel alone. "Alone" doesn't mean you'll be lonely. It means going without your usual BFF, bestie, bro, or SO. Seriously, why do you need an entourage, anyway—to carry your purse, or your suitcase, or your miniature dog? (Just get a bigger dog, and he can drag your suitcase—problem solved!)

Tip #2: Reach out to strangers. You'll meet so many nice people on planes, trains, or automobiles. Hint: if (a) the selected mode of vehicle is a hippy bus, and (b) drugs are being offered, and (c) everyone on the bus worships a guy named Manson, pass on the lift. Better to keep that thumb in the air. Trust me on this one.

Tip #3: Don't be afraid to open up. Tell your new friends your name and where you're from. Give them a glimpse of the real you. However, no need for diarrhea of the mouth. Leave out such info as (a) your home address, (b) your ATM pin number, (c) your

Twitter and Facebook passwords, and (d) any sexual peccadilloes or kinky predilections you may have.

Tip #4: Keep your eyes open, and enjoy the view! From the plane. From a mountaintop. From your hotel room—especially if the couple across the street are going at it, like bonobos in heat. In fact, this alone is a perfect reason why you bring binoculars—

Which can also be carried by your new pack dog.

"I THINK IT'S JUST ADORABLE THAT YOU TWO MET ON THE PLANE to Fantasy Island!" Mr. Boarke's assistant, Julie bats her lashes so furiously that I wouldn't be surprised if she took flight.

I've been watching her do it all morning. She does it when she talks. She does it as she walks. She does it when she giggles. And she does it as she drives.

Unfortunately, she hasn't shut up *or* quit giggling since we started our road trip through Fantasy Island. Worse yet, she can barely drive and talk at the same time. I don't dare test this theory by tempting her with a piece of gum. We may find ourselves hurtling over one of the island's many shore-hugging cliffs.

I look straight ahead in the hopes she'll do the same. "Oh, *pshaw*! I bet cute meets happen all the time in this lovers' paradise."

"To be honest, yes." She blushes. "In fact, thirty-six percent of our guests have found their future spouses at Eden Key."

"How romantic." I'm tempted to ask her if there is a statistic for how many guests leave the island in a body bag.

We've been touring for the past couple of hours. Already we've taken in the highlights of Eden Key—the tricked out huts, the large heart-shaped communal pools with swim-out bars, and of course its infamous nude beach.

We've also seen the joys of Kamp KidStuff, what with its cute family cabins, each with verandas boasting large porch swings. The cabins are set far enough apart that each has its own lawn. While parents indulge in massages, tennis, golf, yoga, and romantic walks on the beach, their children play games of all sorts, supervised by fresh-faced youth advisors (minus two, now that Emma and Arnie are officially ensconced in Eden Key—in separate tree houses, of course).

While I'm busy talking nonsense with our guide, Jack is listening to a different chatter. Arnie is feeding him Dr. Mandrake's GPS coordinates through his earbud.

Suddenly Jack gives me a thumbs-down. I guess that means we're out of range again. This Mandrake guy is always on the go! I'm beginning to wonder if we'll ever catch him.

"Hey, Julie, this tour of the resorts is great, but I was hoping to go off-road, too. You know, see areas of the island that lend themselves to future development. In fact, I have some specific regions in mind." I guess Jack is worried. Why else would he make his request so directly—

Make that so blatantly. As he moves the map closer to her, his hand grazes her thigh. She gasps a bit, but shifts even closer to him—

And almost drives us off the road.

Quickly, I reach over from the back seat and jerk the wheel, steering us away from the shoulder.

Do I get a thank you from either of them, for saving their lives? Nah. They're too busy looking soulfully into each other's eyes.

"I...I'll have to get proper authorization for those areas," Julie stutters.

"I'll make it worth your while—and Mr. Boarke's of course."

I give the wheel another quick jerk—to straighten out the Jeep, if not my relationship with Jack.

The maneuver causes Jack to hit his head on the roof of the Jeep. "Shit…*Ouch!*"

"I'm sure Julie will happily kiss it and make it feel better," I hiss at him.

Julie, still embarrassed, takes the wheel. But this time she keeps her eyes on the road.

We pull into the Hunt Club right at lunch time. The club, which sits behind a tall stone wall deep within the island's thickest jungle, resembles a rustic Victorian lodge. It is made of worn stone and aged-wood beams that look as if they were salvaged from old ships. White Adirondack chairs are scattered, in pairs, over its velvety green perfectly manicured grass.

Beyond the lawn, the lush jungle lays undisturbed, except for the shrieks of parrots, no doubt in response to the rumbling footsteps of the wild beasts roaming through the ferns at the base of the tall moss-veiled palms where the birds have taken sanctuary.

Julie ushers us into the lobby, which is filled with men clustered according to their toys of choice: rod and reel, guns and ammo, or cards and chips.

"Ah, the deep sea fishermen are back!" Julie gives a happy sigh. "Their catches–mostly tuna—will be prepared to their liking at dinnertime by the lodge's legion of world-class chefs."

All around us, hunters are swapping tips on the best routes to stalk the island's wild game. "What kind of animals are they after?" I ask her.

"Mostly red stag," she answers, "Although our puma, black buck, and wild boar safaris are popular, too."

I nod, as if fascinated. "I hear the Hunt Club also has a private reserve, just for its VIP guests. Does it have a different, more exotic prey?"

My question wipes the smile off Julie's face. "I've heard rumors to that effect."

Give, queenie. "*Ooh!* Are we talking endangered species? Elephants? Lions?"

Julie glances over my head, at a security camera, I presume. When she turns to Jack, her lashes are batting a million miles an hour. "I hardly think Mr. Boarke would do anything that would displease our guests."

That's just the point. How far would he go to please those who pick up the tab?

And who exactly are the partners he wants to cut out?

More importantly, how does Dr. Mandrake fit into this equation?

"As for a tour of the club's private reserve, sorry, no. It wouldn't be fair for those who have paid top dollar for the privilege." Her frown turns upside down as she faces Jack. "But you'll be happy to know, Mr. Stone, that the part of the island you've requested to see is next on our itinerary! I've arranged Battoo to be your guide, since he's more familiar with the terrain than me." Her eyes sweep over me. "Your sundress is precious, Miss Tallant. But considering that most of your journey will take you off the beaten path and within the animal reserve, you'll have to change into camo. We don't want to scare the animals, now do we?" She takes Jack's arm in hers. "Take your time. We'll wait for you up in Mr. Stone's suite. I have to go over a figure or two with him."

Hers, being the prime integer.

Let the games begin.

Too bad she can't tag along on the rest of our tour. It would have been interesting to point a rifle in her direction, if only to see how fast she can run in those heels.

❧

"You look ridiculous in that get-up," Jack mutters.

At least he's waited until Battoo is a good fifty feet in front of us on this rocky path before chastising me for what I'm wearing.

I shrug. "Hey it's not my fault that the women's attire in that so-called 'gear shop' was slim pickings at best. Camouflage bustiers and short-shorts? I mean, come on already!"

Jack raises a brow. "Admit it. You counted the wolf whistles from the guys in the lobby."

Six, but I feign ignorance with a shrug. "Can I help it if your new gal pal, Julie, has cornered the market on Ralph Lauren safari wear?"

I'm being serious. Her outfit was downright elegant: a long-sleeved belted beige linen tunic over formfitting khakis.

He shakes his head. "Don't be so jealous. She's a nice kid."

"She's no kid. And that's no normal hunt club, either. The only other alternative was a Playboy Bunny outfit! No wonder this place is called 'Fantasy Island.' Tell me honestly, Jack, what kind of woman would wear this get-up in a hunting lodge?"

"One who's looking to bag a man with a humongous bank account." He swats away a mosquito. "And believe it or not, the lodge is crawling with that kind of woman—sometimes on all fours and tied to a leash by a studded collar around her neck, and wearing a pair of antlers on her head. We've only been on this island for thirty-six hours and already I've been invited to three orgies with the theme, 'Fuck a Fawn.'"

"If you think Dr. Mandrake will show up, you should certainly attend."

"He's not. He's out here somewhere. At least according to his GPS reading as of thirty minutes ago. But if Mandrake were there, yeah sure, I'd play along. We're here on a mission, and we both know it."

So that he doesn't see me grit my teeth, I feign interest in a beautiful bush with pale pink tulips that hang upside down from its branches. But before I can touch it, Battoo slaps my hand away. "Miss Tallant, don't! That is Devil's Breath. It turns those who touch it into zombies."

"Wow! Thanks for the warning." I've already had one run-in with the drug that comes from it: succinylcholine. My ex, Carl, used it on me then waltzed out of Guantánamo Bay, with me as his cover.

And you wonder why I wanted a divorce?

"Mr. Stone, we've gone as far as the path will take us." Battoo sounds worried.

Jack's green eyes darken as he stares deep into the jungle. "I understand that, Battoo. But any investment in Fantasy Island dictates a due diligence that goes beyond the boundaries for the already established resorts. I'm sure you and Mr. Boarke understand my need to investigate even further."

Battoo hesitates for a long moment. Finally he nods. "Yes, of course. But I caution both of you to follow me closely. We are only a twenty-minute walk from the crest of Mount Fantasia, the island's most spectacular vista point. Still, the jungle is fraught with danger."

His warning weighs heavily on the already moist air enveloping us.

An even bigger warning is the poison dart that whizzes past my head.

Jack jerks me back just as another one flies by, spearing the trunk of a dwarf palm.

I follow closely at his heels as he leaps into the bush, taking us off the footpath. We don't dare stop and turn around. The sounds of the darts slamming into tree trunks and shredding palm leaves are all the incentive we need to keep moving.

We've run a quarter of a mile when suddenly Jack stops short—

At the ledge of a cliff. The drop is at least six hundred feet into a copse of thick foliage, and who knows how far below it? To climb back up is impossible because the wind has stripped any vegetation off the cliff's sheer face.

From what I can tell, there is only one way to escape. Somehow we've got to leap to the other side of the trail— which from the looks of it, wraps around the hillside.

But where does it end?

Jack turns to face me. "It's a seven-foot leap. With a head start, you can clear it."

"What? Are you crazy?" I shake my head so that he gets the message:

No. Fucking. Way.

"It's a broad jump. You did it in high school, right? There's no difference here."

"Oh yes sir, there is a very big difference. I'm twenty years older! And back in the day if you fell, you cut your knee—you didn't *kill yourself!*"

"Listen to me, Donna, you can do this! And I'm certainly not going without you—so, ladies first!"

Ladies first, eh? *Now* he pulls the etiquette card?

Then I see it. Long, strong, and swaying over my head, from a ledge that juts out over the abyss:

A vine.

I take off in a dead run. I grab it just as it waves past me, twisting it around my wrist and holding on tight—

And I take a flying leap.

I glide far, far over the chasm—

Until I'm swaying over the path on the other side.

Drop the vine—now! Drop it…

I do, and I flop down onto the muddy path. *Yes! Yes!* I'm on the other side!

When I turn back, Jack is staring at me in awe.

He looks hurt. "What the hell, Donna? You couldn't have waited for me to grab hold of it, too?"

I shrug helplessly. "But you said 'Ladies first'!"

He waves me off, annoyed. At least my weight gave the vine the needed momentum to sway back toward him.

Thank you, God, for those eight lousy pounds that won't come off.

Jack takes a flying leap, grabbing hold of the vine as it goes overhead. Then he swings back over the abyss, toward me.

But then his face twists into a grimace. At the same time he jerks forward—

Oh my God, he's been hit by a dart.

His grip is slipping. His eyes open wide at the realization that he may not make it. But when they shift toward me again, I see love and hope and determination—

Until he falls.

I run toward him, praying that I make it in time.

I slide to the edge, belly flopping just in time to stop, and to grab him.

Yes! I've got his hand. But…barely.

The rest of him dangles over nothing but thick, moist air.

And silence. Except for the shrieks of birds.

I wish those parrots would shut the fuck up.

Jack's grip is softening. I do my best to hold tight with both hands, but he's much too heavy. Any second now, he'll slip away from me.

From the life we've built together.

From the love we share.

The look in his eyes is not fear. Nor is it resignation.

It is adoration.

It is…surprise?

Something has grabbed hold of my legs.

Whatever it is pulls me back, across the rocky ground. And because I'm still holding onto Jack, he is being dragged up and over the edge.

I don't let go until he is a safe distance from the ledge. Then I turn to see who saved us.

An ape?

No, it's a man—

A very hairy man.

A very hairy, naked man.

So there really is a Sasquatch.

Ha. Cute ass.

Jack is cold. His body stiffens. I don't want him to die this way. Please God, don't let him die.

But if he does, at least it will be in my arms.

Make that Sasquatch's. He turns around and comes back to us, if only to yank Jack up and over his shoulder, like a sack of potatoes. He practically runs down the path with him.

Leaves slap my face as I fly through the brush after him. I round each curve just in time to see him disappear around the next—

Until I don't.

I stop short. The bushes are once again thick on both sides of the path. I backtrack about twenty feet, scrutinizing every palm leaf and every fern, every nook and cranny of the hill towering over the path—

Until I find it: a tiny crack, half hidden in a thatch of vines.

I have to turn sideways and bend to the waist to enter.

It is pitch black inside.

I've lost them.

Is Jack now Sasquatch's bitch?

"Don't worry. He's just stunned." Sasquatch's voice is coming toward me from the deep recesses of the cave.

I hear sharp scratching sounds. The next thing I know, flames are flickering in a pile of brush, creating shadows that dance on the cave's walls.

Jack is lying beside the fire. I run over and kneel beside him, cradling his head in my lap. "You—you know English?"

He lets loose with a husky chuckle. "I'm from the South, darlin'. You Yankees are the ones with the accents, and don't you forget it."

He saunters back over and crouches down beside Jack, whose eyes are wide open, but he's shivering. Sasquatch turns him over on his stomach, then runs his hand over Jack's back.

I shove it away. "What the hell do you think you're doing?"

"I'm trying to save, him, pretty lady." He grasps both my wrists in one hand, while the other continues across Jack's shoulders. When he reaches the right one, he stops. "Ah, there it is." He plucks a tiny feathered dart from it, and holds it up for me to examine. "See?"

"Oh!...Thank you." I pat Jack's head. "How long will he be like this?"

He tilts his head as he assesses Jack. "Depends. It didn't go in too deeply, and at least it hit muscle. Maybe an hour."

Much too long. I look around the cave. "Will—will they follow us?" There's nothing to make a weapon—no stones, no stakes.

"Calm down, lady. They never have before. They don't have the guts to make the jump." He smirks. "Or else, they're too damn lazy."

"Who are 'they,' anyway?"

"The island's original native tribe. Boarke pays them to act as game trackers. Can't have a bunch of hunters sitting there with thumbs up their asses and bored out of their gourds, now can he?"

"If they track animals, why were they shooting at us?"

He stares hard at me then laughs. There is no joy in his cackle. "You really don't know, do you?"

But I can guess. *Somehow, we've blown our covers.*

"Are you—are you Doctor Lionel Mandrake?"

He freezes when he hears the name. "What do you know about Mandrake?"

"Please, there is no threat here—not after all you've done for me, and for Jack." Can he hear the gratitude in my voice? I hope so. "We were sent to retrieve the bacteria—"

Fear darkens his face.

No, it is resolve. He reaches against the wall and pulls up a gunnysack, then he makes for the cave entrance. Once there, he tosses a thermos at me, along with his answer. "To get back to the lodge, head right out of the cave, then down the hill. When you come to the fork, turn left. Another mile and a half, you'll find yourself on Eden Key's beach. If I were you, I'd get off this hellhole of an island. Otherwise…let me put it this way, if you don't leave now, you never will."

He's gone.

Jack moans, and moves ever so slightly.

From the determination in his eyes, I can tell that he wants to get out of here. I do, too.

Gently I pull him up into sitting position then I bend his knees. This allows me to pull him up. He tilts against the wall, but with my support he can take baby steps.

Another part of our journey begins.

IT TAKES US TWO LONG, ARDUOUS HOURS TO GET AS FAR AS THE fork Sasquatch mentioned. Jack has been walking slowly, but he seems to get stronger with each step.

Battoo is waiting for us there. He stops pacing when he sees us. Relief floods his face. He may be short, but he's also strong. He leads Jack into the back of the jeep.

We bump along until we hit asphalt, about a quarter-mile from Eden Key's main gate. At that point, Battoo stops the car. "Please know I would never have put either of you in danger."

I turn to face him. "Then tell me: who shot at us?"

"The natives of the island need us for their livelihood."

"And they make money by hunting down the island's guests?"

"No! They aren't hunting, they're—" He stops cold. "They are just supposed to tranquilize the prey, to slow it down. That is all."

I laugh at what we both know is not funny. "Jack and I

weren't on all fours, Battoo. You were there with us. You know this. Why did they shoot at us?"

He looks down at his lap. "I really don't know, Miss Tallant. Maybe someone suspects the truth—that you aren't who you say you are."

If he's right, there goes the mission.

"Can you find out if that is the case?"

Looking up again, he nods. "Yes."

"Is it Mr. Boarke?"

It's his turn to laugh. "He thinks Mr. Stone is his savior. It can't be Boarke."

Well, that's good to know. "If not him, I'll need to know who it is."

"I will do my best, Miss Tallant."

"Call me Donna. Stone."

He puts out his hand, and I shake it. I can tell the gesture means a lot to him.

Our lives depend on this supposition.

He drives us to my tiki hut, and helps me to unload Jack from the Jeep. He insists on walking us to the front door.

I'm glad. I'm bone tired and Jack must be, too, because he winces through each labored step.

Gentle waves lap against the posts that lift the tiki's boardwalk over the sand. It is high tide, but the planks are raised just enough that the water isn't a problem.

The sun is setting, and the light has shifted. The water below us, cellophane clear in bright sunlight, is now navy in hue. We can no longer see the tiny colorful schools of fish beneath us.

Suddenly bubbles rise to the surface. "Look!" Battoo points at it. "A shark!"

I'm sure it won't be the last one that crosses our path.

9

Language Barrier

A wife should always look her best for her husband. Granted, sexy dresses make it so difficult to hide a weapon! You can't exactly strap a Magnum to your sparkly belt or an AK-47 over your shoulder as if it were a pashmina.

Helpful Hint: Some Berettas are compact enough to fit into even the smallest evening clutch. For example, the Tomcat is only five inches long, and yet it packs quite a punch! And in a really tight squeeze, there's always the folding stiletto. (Down to three inches! Fits into most hollow-heeled Louboutins.)

"YOU SAY JACK WAS HOBBLED BY A ZOMBIE DART? HOW perfectly odious!" Dominic waves an open palm in front of Jack's face. "Chilling stare it's left on the poor fellow's clock, wouldn't you say? Can't have the old boy scaring off all the women and children. Here's hoping the effects wear off soon."

Jack slaps his hand away. "It *has* worn off, you oaf."

"Now, now, boys! No bickering. We have a full day ahead of us." I smile encouragingly at Team Fantasy.

(Like the name? You should see the logo! It will look very cute on a French tee, which I will order in all team members' sizes—

If we survive this wretched mission.)

I turn to Arnie. "My guess is that the feral man I met is our suspect."

Jack shakes his head. "I beg to differ."

Really? You're arguing with me in front of the kids—again? And after all I've done for you? Still, I keep my voice level when I murmur, "Based on what, might I ask?"

He ignores my glare. "Based simply on the fact that there is no evidence to validate your suspicions."

"How about this for facts? Fact number one: we went out specifically to find him, and there he was. Fact number two: Obviously he's living off the grid, which is why we haven't been able to find him, despite eliminating, by now, over eighty-three male guests. And fact number three"—I pause, because really, I have no third fact. However, this works with the kids, so I'll try it now—"because I say so."

Jack smothers a chuckle with a cough. He is smart enough to know that my revenge is a dish best served with some toxic ingredient, and when he least expects it. Nonchalantly he adds, "Excellent deductive reasoning, for sure— and easily validated with, say, a DNA sample. Were you able to pluck a hair or two?"

I smile, but shake my head. "No, sorry, I was busy at the time." *Saving your life—or don't you remember?*

"How about a few other deductions? For example, how old did he look to you?"

I stop to think. "Late thirties, maybe early forties."

Jack nods. "And Mandrake is in his late forties, so

certainly in the wheelbase—except for the fact that Sasquatch is also at least six inches taller than the good doctor, not to mention strong enough to carry *me* over his shoulder."

"I say! He really *is* a beast," Dominic murmurs.

Jack ignores him. "This brings us to the final and perhaps most important evidentiary component."

I roll my eyes. "And what would that be, Sherlock?"

"Mandrake's mushroom cloud tattoo." Jack smiles. "You said yourself he was naked. And you walked behind him—for quite a distance, in fact. If you're correct and he's Mandrake, surely you would have noticed one."

"I..." I feel my cheeks heat up at the thought of Sasquatch's....well, his cheeks. "Okay, no."

Dominic leans in, fascinated. "No, you didn't look at his arse? Or no, he didn't have the tattoo?"

I look from one of my tormentors to the other. "Okay yes, I...looked. If he had one, I would have noticed—and he didn't."

Jack frowns. I guess giving him the answer he wanted backfired. "I rest my case."

"But remember, we were out there because Mandrake's GPS coordinates led us there." I turn to Arnie. "Can you check our coordinates at around, say three-thirty, with those of Mandrake's?"

Arnie diddles with his iPad screen then projects a video onto the wall, so that we can all view it. "Here they are, side by side. As you can see, he was certainly in the vicinity." He points to our GPS readings, and that of Mandrake's, which are close to ours, but oddly enough are following a different trajectory. While ours move in tandem, and in line with the mountainside, Mandrake's comes in from a different angle.

I glance over at Jack. "But how could that be? We were on

a trail that hugged a cliff, for God's sake! For him to have followed the route shown here, he would have been floating in a cloud!"

Jack thinks hard for a moment. "Or else he was in the abyss below us." He points to the break between the lush greenery on both sides of the path. "Arnie, can you zoom in, right here?"

With the touch of his index finger and thumb, Arnie is able to magnify the screen so that we can actually visualize what was below us. "See this?" He points to a flurry of white and gray. "It's flowing water, and it's almost at sea level. You were hanging over some sort of river."

"I guess that means Mandrake was standing *below* you," Emma murmurs. "Perhaps he was in a boat?"

Abu shakes his head as he points to the screen. "You're half right. Not in a boat—unless he was carrying it to the river. You see, here, where he came from? Only moments before, he was traipsing through the underbrush, below your footpath."

Curiouser and curiouser.

"Donna, do you remember Sasquatch's reaction when you asked him if he was Mandrake?" Jack asks.

"Yes, of course. He wanted to know how I'd heard of the good doctor—but he didn't deny he was Mandrake."

"You then mentioned the missing bacteria plague," Jack reminds me.

I nod. "It spooked him. He couldn't get out of there quickly enough."

"He also gave us directions, and then warned us to get off the island as soon as possible—before we couldn't leave, for whatever reason."

Dominic frowns. "It doesn't sound as if he's the perpetrator, only that he's concerned about the havoc Mandrake could wreak on our little idyll."

"Is he scared of Mandrake, or the bacteria?" Emma asks.

Arnie squints in thought. "What does it matter?"

She shrugs. "I'm still not convinced Mandrake is Dr. Evil. If he is, wouldn't he be hanging out with the swells, as opposed to traipsing through the jungle, like this other lonely guy?"

This certainly gives us all food for thought.

Abu lets loose with a long, low whistle. "So then, who is Sasquatch, anyway?"

"Good question. But not one we'll find out tonight, anyway." Jack stands up and stretches. "Emma does have a point. More than likely we'll find Mandrake at the Hunt Club. Here's an idea, Dominic: why don't you use your pass to hang in the casino tonight? You can participate in the big baccarat tournament. The winner takes home a million dollars. It's sure to draw a crowd—including Mandrake, who loves to gamble. You and Donna should meet me in the tournament room, nine o'clock sharp." He glances at me, sheepishly. "Boarke's assistant asked me to go with her, but I told her I'd already asked 'Lotta.'"

Good boy.

"In fact, Dominic," Jack continues, "I'll introduce you to Julie. See what you can get out of her."

Dominic's response is a shrug. I'm sure he's contemplating what he can get *into* her instead.

I turn to Abu. "You're part of the wait staff for the event, am I right?"

He nods.

"Perfect. The four of us will be wearing our eyes and ears so that Emma and Arnie can monitor possible suspects. Class dismissed."

My phone hums the "Pleasure Island" song from *Pinoc-chio*—my ring chime for Janie Breck's phone. Trisha's message puts a smile on my face:

LOVE YOU MOMMY! GUESS WHAT? I MADE FRIENDS WITH A PIRATE! HE IS THE NICEST ONE I EVER MET! LOVE TRISHA.

What a girl. What an imagination. I miss her so much.

And Mary and Jeff, too. But Mary must still be mad at me. Otherwise she would have called by now.

As for Jeff, he must be having too much fun.

The easiest way for a parent to get into their children's good graces? Buy her way back in. If Dominic wins at baccarat tonight, I'll use the money to take everyone on a shopping spree.

But of course he'll win. He always does.

And if he doesn't, what's the worst that can happen?

10

Gambling Resorts

Housewives face a quandary when given the opportunity to go out for the evening. After all, who will watch the wee ones?

Babysitter vetting can be made simple, if you follow these instructions. First, a background check. Next, a list of do's and don'ts, including who is allowed into the house. And finally, a torture session, to ward off any notion that your instructions be ignored.

Granted, you'll never get the same sitter twice, but ask yourself: if the sitter breaks under pressure, would you really want that person back in your house?

THE HUNT CLUB'S CASINO IS DEEP IN THE BOWELS OF THE lodge. Dominic and I are the only ones in the elevator, and the ride down is moving slowly. I guess this is the club's way of building tension.

If you want to feel important, you better look important. Frankly, tonight I could give Miss America a run for her money. I'm wearing a body-skimming sheer silver beaded halter back gown, by Naeem Khan. Granted, it was a splurge at the Eden Key boutique, but I have to look the part of a financier's arm charm, don't I?

Besides, I've left the tag on, so that I can return it after tonight.

"You look stunning," Dominic murmurs, as he nudges the price tag back under my armpit. "I'm glad of that, because tonight I'll need you to walk up behind me and kiss me on the neck, so that the players will be thinking about your neckline and not about their cards. Do you think you can handle that?"

"Yes, I can," I assure him, "But I won't. Tonight, *you* are the decoy, or have you forgotten? Please don't. The more you win, the more attention you get."

"Speaking of which, I presume Acme is funding my stake in the game?"

Yikes. Didn't see that one coming.

"Ryan has given me some petty cash—for incidentals. You know, bullets, knives, paying off sources. That sort of thing." Okay, yeah, this princess-worthy gown wasn't on any requisition order, but I can't very well walk into a casino in yoga pants, now can I?

If all goes well, Ryan won't find out about it until I turn in my expense report.

I open the clasp on my Judith Leiber Swarovski-gemmed clutch purse. "Well, okay. I guess staking your place at the table qualifies as petty cash. It's like, what, a hundred bucks or something?"

His laughter echoes through the elevator. "Your naiveté is always so endearing! I see now why Jack sticks it out."

Go ahead, Dominic old boy, stick it out. See what I do with it.

"No, my darling Donna, you'll have to stake me *ten thousand dollars.*"

Gulp. This dress was almost that much.

My clutch slams shut. My only regret is that Dominic's tongue wasn't caught in it. "Wait…don't *you* have the money? I know for a fact that the pay scale for an international man of mystery is more than that of a housewife assassin."

"No limit *Tenez Les Cartes* Championship baccarat tournaments cost more than your suburbanite pastimes of bridge and bingo."

"No shit. And I'll bet that Rolex you're wearing was a pretty penny, too."

"Omega." He shifts the cuff of his crisp white tuxedo shirt so that I can admire it. "The sponsorship fee was too high for me to turn down. And yes, it's around nine thousand pounds. Granted, not as much as I get for tooling around in my Aston Martin DBS, but enough for a pint or two when out on the town."

"Exquisite," I coo. "It has a modified black steel-on-steel Seamaster Planet Ocean 620 millimeter, does it not? *Ooooh,* and look! It's got a transparent sapphire crystal porthole! Very cool."

He's in bliss by the fact that I know my Omegas. "It's one of a kind, you know."

"Well then, what can I say?" I open my purse and pull out the last of my Euros. "Don't lose. Otherwise we'll all be swimming home. Unless that car of yours doubles as a submarine."

"It does, in fact." He drapes himself over me. "But there's only room for two."

While the fingers of my left hand run playfully up his tux shirt, the fingers on my right unclasp his Omega.

It costs almost as much as Acme's grub stake. One way or another, I'm not walking out of here empty-handed.

The ping of the elevator announcing our arrival on the casino level distracts Dominic, and not a moment too soon. He takes one last look at himself in the shiny mirrored doors then walks out without a backward glance.

So much for ladies first, not to mention pearls before swine.

~

DAMN IT, WE'RE LOSING OUR SHIRTS.

Or in my case, my dress.

Maybe it has something to do with all the martinis Dominic has guzzled—three measures of Gordon's, one of vodka, half a measure of Kina Lillet, shaken over ice and served with a slice of lemon peel, yada yada. The dude bores the whole table with the intricacies of his order.

I want to kick his stool out from under him.

Hey, if I do, maybe he'll play better.

If it isn't the drinks, maybe he's too distracted by Julie's generous cleavage in skin-tight whore couture, all the more prevalent whenever she nuzzles the back of his neck.

On the other hand, I don't dare allow myself to sweat, otherwise I won't get away with my dress return in the morning.

To keep my mind off Dominic's poor hands, I scan the room for anyone at all resembling the measly details we have on Mandrake. Frankly, it could be at least a third of the eighty or so men in the room. They are all cut from the same cloth.

Jack and Abu also have their eyes peeled, but thus far Emma's and Arnie's responses to the faces we feed them have been negative: Everyone here is either very rich if not so famous, or a known mover and shaker.

Boarke and Battoo are also floating through the crowd. While Battoo overseas the croupiers, Boarke is ever the consummate host. He shakes hands, laughs at bad jokes, makes small talk, and compliments every woman in the room.

When Jack introduces me, his eyes sweep over me, scrutinizing every detail. "Ah, she is a heartbreaker," he murmurs through lips that hover over the back of my hand before grazing it gently.

If my mission were no issue, I'd smack him black and blue for allowing Reems to harm Angie and countless others. Instead, I simper and preen, then murmur, "I'll take that as a compliment. Besides, you know as well as I do that all men deserve what they get."

My answer has him scurrying off under the pretext that there are so many guests to greet and so little time.

Soon he will make time for me. He has to know Mandrake's whereabouts. I'm sure of it now.

One face which has already been scanned, analyzed and cleared stops me short. There is something familiar about it, but I can't seem to place it. "Arnie, what about the man sitting opposite Dominic, at the table?"

"Abu spotted him first, yesterday. Our facial recognition software has cleared him. His name is Lee Chiffray. He's a Canadian venture capitalist and entrepreneur who makes his money in software—a single guy, here with his girlfriend and her kids."

I can see why he'd interest Abu. The man is the right height and age to be Mandrake. And the fact that he sits across the table from Dominic in this high stakes game says something about his mathematical aptitude.

But he's got a mug that only a mother—or a desperate golddigger—could love: his nose is flattened, and there is a large, ragged scar on his cheek. The only handsome feature on his face is his deep blue, piercing eyes. They remind me of Dominic—

Who—heaven help us—is suddenly having a stroke of great luck. Suddenly the chips are piling up in front of him. The way things look now, Acme will be a million Euros richer.

Julie, tickled pink, squeals with delight. I don't blame her. I'm tempted to do a cartwheel myself, but if I tear this dress, I own it. Hell, I'm trying hard not to breathe in it, and I've been walking like a mummy. So much for any attempt to look sexy.

How many gowns would a million Euros buy—minus Acme's initial stake, of course? And I wonder: would Jack want a submarine Aston Martin? His birthday is coming up. Maybe it's worth checking into.

Oh hell, what's wrong with Dominic? His face has turned white. He leaps up from the table, spilling what's left of his martini on the baccarat table. He lunges toward the elevator doors, clutching his collar as if he can't breathe.

I run after him, and reach the elevator just as the doors are closing. "Dominic, what's wrong?"

"Going into…anaphylactic shock…must have been something in…in my martini. I'm guessing Digitalis."

"Oh my God! What should I do?"

"Get me to my car. There's a MediPack in the glove compartment."

"Your *car*? It's here on the island?"

"Part of the deal, ducky. It's written into my contract. Brought it over on the plane." A feeble shake of his head registers his disdain at my apparent naiveté.

Once again the elevator moves so slow that I'm afraid he'll die on me before we get out. It doesn't help that the doors open midway to the ground floor and a couple of hunters, still in camo, hop in.

They don't realize I'm propping Dominic up and slapping his face to keep him from dying. They just think he's got himself a redheaded tart who loves to play rough.

If only they knew.

WILDLY, I WAVE THE ASTON MARTIN'S KEY FOB IN FRONT OF the car's near-field electronic lock. Finally, the doors opens.

I shove Dominic into the passenger seat, then reach across to open the glove compartment. Yes, the MediPack is there. I grab it and rip it open—

Spilling its contents all over the floor—mostly colored vials, crowned with tiny surgical needles. I scoop up what I can and put it in Dominic's lap.

"We've got…less than two minutes." His words come out in fits, starts, and gasps. "Rev the engine so that you can… can…charge the portable defibrillator…which has to be attached to my chest by the leads."

I leap into the driver seat, attach the defibrillator to the battery outlet, and rev the engine until the lifesaving device comes to life.

My hands shake as I rip open his tux shirt and attach the wires to a waxed and tanned chest that has elicited its fair share of *ooohs* and *aaaahs.*

"The combipen—the needle connected to the blue vial— holds Lidocaine. You've got to jab it into my jugular vein, in my neck. But right before you do, you'll have to hit the red button on my defibrillator."

"Got it. Red vial, blue button."

He nods.

I get ready to stab him—

But then I see that he's shaking his head, agitated. "No, no! *Other way around*! Blue vial, red button!"

The needle stops a hair's breadth away from his vein. I drop it, and scramble frantically to find the blue combipen. *Where the hell is it?*

On the passenger seat floor.

As I crawl over him again to get it, Dominic pats my backside and whispers, "A few pounds less and you'd have a perfect ass."

I take great pleasure in stabbing him in the jugular.

As he passes out for a second, I debate if I should hit the red button on the defibrillator that will bring him back to life.

Okay yeah, I hit it. But only because we've still got a seat in the tournament, and we can still win it.

Suddenly Dominic's eyes pop open. He sits up, spewing me with bile.

This dress needed something, but I had a bauble in mind, not my flop sweat and Dominic's fixings for a designer martini. I use his pocket kerchief to wipe off as much of it as a can.

At least he's bright-eyed and bushy-tailed again, as frisky as a pup on Christmas morning. He rewards me with a broad smile. "Tell me, was it as good for you as it was for me?"

"Heart-stopping, to say the least." I take his arm and lead him back into the Hunt Club. "Shall we?"

Something tells me his luck won't run out this time.

❧

Wrong. I am *so* wrong.

Dominic is losing again—and badly, to the only player still left in the game: Lee Chiffray.

Finally, Dominic takes my high sign: This hand is to be his last.

If it's a loser, he'll have to throw in the towel—preferably over me, now that this dress is ruined.

He turns over his cards—

Four kings. *Yes! Yes!*

I'm about to break out in my happy dance when Chiffray flips over his hand, revealing—

Four aces.

What are the odds of that?

I need a drink.

⌒

I've just taken the last empty barstool when my cell phone rings. The Caller ID reads WICKED WITCH.

It's Penelope. Oh no, what did Jeff do now?

Quickly I hit the TALK button. "Penelope, is everything okay?"

She's sobbing. "No…they're….horrible!"

Oh my God, has something happened to Jeff? "Who? My son—is he okay?"

"My God, Donna, don't be so dramatic!" She practically snickers. "The Yosemite park rangers, that's who! Listen, there's been a slight change of plans, which I'm sure you won't mind at all, since it works to your benefit."

"Oh?" My spidey senses are tingling. Whenever Penelope claims that something will work to my benefit, invariably it means I'm about to get screwed.

"Turns out the Yosemite Park service 'conveniently' lost our reservation."

For once, it's nice to hear the sarcasm in Penelope's voice aimed at someone else.

"They claim it was some kind of technical glitch in the reservation software," she sniffs. "Frankly, I think they did it on purpose, what with all the brouhaha last year. You remember, don't you? Something about Cheever coercing the other boys to carve a peephole into the woman's shower room—as if they were little pervs, or something! Can you imagine?"

I can, actually, although I wouldn't dream of saying that to Penelope. In her mind, Cheever is still four years old, and mommy is the sun to his moon.

"In the meantime, we've been sleeping in some odious recreational vehicle for the past few days in the hope that a cabin opens up, but the park is booked solid," she continues.

"So, you'll take the boys home, I presume?"

"That was the original game plan—until we heard that *you* went off to some tropical paradise—Fantasy Island, right? In fact your hubby—how you ended up with such a sweet, generous man is a miracle, I swear!—came up with the brilliant idea that we join you there! He even suggested that the two of you would take the boys for a few days, in Kamp KidStuff, so that Peter and I could spend a few romantic nights in Eden Key."

"How thoughtful of him." I crane my neck until I find Jack. When I catch his eye, I crook my finger at him.

He smiles and walks through the casino toward me. *Unwitting fool.* If he were smart, he'd run in the opposite direction—and fast. I'd have a helluva time catching him in these heels, but I'll do my damnedest.

"We'll be there, bright and early tomorrow—and not a

moment too soon. The boys are getting antsy—not to mention gassy. Such active little bodies! But the boys' seats are in coach, while Peter and I will be up in First Class—away from the firing range, as it were. See you in the morning!" Penelope hangs up without further ado.

I guess the Stones are checking into Kamp KidStuff for a few days after all.

Or maybe Jack is, by himself. Something tells me the Hunt Club is where all the action is.

Dominic must think so, too, now that Julie is proving to be such an amenable consolation prize. Good enough. As far as I'm concerned, his next heart attack is her problem.

I snap my fingers at the waiter. "Vodka martini, please."

The bartender nods. "One of our guests has started a new trend. We call it 'the Dominic.' It has three measures of Gordon's, one of vodka, half a measure of Kina Lillet, over ice and with a twist of lemon."

Aw hell, why not. I quit slamming my head on the bar just long enough to give him a nod.

"Would you like that shaken, or stirred?"

I yank him closer by his bowtie. "Do I look like I give a damn?"

He takes the hint, and hands me a bottle of Skyy 90 instead.

Good boy. Let the guzzling begin. But I've got no cash for a tip. I'd leave him the Omega, but it is property of the National Bank of Acme.

Jack leans against the bar beside me. "Who was that on the phone?"

I lick the vodka trickling from the corner of my mouth. Too late. It's already made a wet spot on the front of my dress. Will the sales clerk notice? It's not like it reeks with some fruity infusion, or something. Okay, maybe some throw-up, thanks to my success in resuscitating Dominic. In fact, another couple of spills, and I can pass off this gown as a Jackson Pollock original. "It was our very dear neighbor, Penelope. She's excited about taking you up on your invitation to dump the boys on our doorstep in the middle of our mission."

He grimaces. "Oh yeah, about that—"

"What are you trying to do, Jack? Blow this mission?"

"No, not at all. She just sounded so stressed out. And when she mentioned that she and Peter were having trouble, I thought, hey, why not be a good neighbor?"

"You should have asked me first. I'm the lead operative here, remember?" I take another swig of vodka. "That's what this is all about isn't it? The fact that Ryan put me in charge as opposed to you—or for that matter, Dominic the Douche."

"So, you think he's a douche?" He's trying to sound nonchalant, but he can't stop his lips from lifting into a smile.

"Oh, I see now. You're so jealous that you arranged for me to babysit the boys!"

"You're wrong, Donna…Okay, yes, to be perfectly honest with you, I was a wee bit jealous. I guess I shouldn't be surprised that another man finds you as beautiful and interesting and fun to have around as I do."

That earns him a lip lock—

And an apology from me. When I resurface from the bliss of his kiss, I sigh. "I hope you can forgive me for buying into Dominic's shenanigans. I was a fool, I admit it. I'm also a woman in her mid-thirties, with three kids. So sue me for being flattered that the world's most charismatic spy asked to partner with me on a mission."

"You'll just have to settle for the world's second most charismatic spy wanting you by his side for the rest of his life." He squeezes my hand gently. "Donna, seriously, when I said yes to Penelope, it was under the assumption that being around at least one of the kids would put you in a better frame of mind."

"Not if Mandrake plans on poisoning us all—or have you forgotten why we're here in the first place? If the bacteria plague gets loose and Jeff gets ill because of it...or worse..." I can't speak though because I'm choking on my tears. "Jack, I'm not as callous as Carl. He had no conscience about endangering anyone, let alone our children. But I can't stand the thought of putting them in danger again."

He frowns. "I'll call Penelope and tell her it was a rotten idea."

"No, never mind. Your heart was in the right place. And besides, Abu and Arnie have been diligent in monitoring the safety gauges." I grab the vodka bottle in one hand, and his hand in the other. "Look, since it's the last night we have to make wild unabashed whoopee, I'm taking you some place special." I hold up the keys to the Aston Martin.

His eyes light up. "I'm in!"

We practically run out to the garage.

There it is—the car.

And there he is: Dominic—fogging up the windows in the throes of passion.

Damn it, I thought I'd locked the car door! Now, he's beaten us to the punch.

We rock the car. Then we run off.

Time's a'wastin'. It won't be long before the boys are back in town.

11

Are We There Yet?

Seeing your vacation through the wide and innocent eyes of your children can be enlightening and memorable. Needless to say, don't be surprised if you get the following questions. Here are some answers that will satisfy their curiosity:

- *Question: "How do we know where we're going?"*
- *Answer by being candid: "Because despite your father's propensity to ignore her, the GPS lady is telling us how to get there."*

- *Question: "I have to pee. Can we stop?"*
- *Answer with a hygiene warning that may save your little one's life: "Yes, but don't touch the toilet seat. Do what everyone else did before you and make the best of it—which means peeing on the floor."*

- *Question: "Can I sleep in the bed with you and daddy?"*
- *Answer in a manner that won't traumatize your child,*

and result in years of therapy: "Trust me, you don't want to. Daddy hogs the covers and farts in bed and if I let him—and I won't!—he'd be on top of me...Oh, never mind! Sure, hop in."

- *Question: "Are we there yet?"*
- *Answer by being precise—but firm: "No. And at the speed in which your father is going, we may never get there. In fact, we will probably still be in this car when it's time to celebrate your sixteenth birthday, which is great because then you'll be old enough to drive us. It will be a hell ride, but anything is better than this."*

Granted, your child will spend the rest of the trip sobbing at the thought of all those wasted years in the back seat of your car, but it's better than hearing him ask the same question over and over, now isn't it?

"HEY, CAN WE GO TO THE NUDE BEACH?" JEFF'S FRIEND, Morton Smith, must think this specific page in Fantasy Island's thirty-eight page four-color brochure opens into a centerfold because he turns it sideways.

"Why bother? We can just watch a porn channel," Jeff declares, without moving his eyes from the television set. "This joint has got three of them. What does 'BSDM' stand for?"

Jack rips the brochure out of Morton's hand. Then he grabs the TV remote from Jeff, and turns off the set. "Get off your cans. Go out there and be boys–you know, build a fort, or a sandcastle. Throw ice on the girls hanging by the pool."

I dig my nail into Jack's palm as my way of

saying, *thanks but no thanks*. "Cheever dear, I think what Mr. Stone is trying to say is that you should go out and enjoy the many activities Kamp KidStuff has to offer. It's why you're here, isn't it? Did you know you can parasail, and go fishing? Why, there's even a pirate party! They tell stories about real pirates, like Blackbeard and Jean Lafitte, while roasting marshmallows by the campfire. And there are treasure hunts—"

Cheever falls off the couch, laughing. "What do you take us for, babies?"

I grab Jack's arm before he picks the kid up by the scruff of his neck and tosses him out the door. We've had the boys for only six hours, and already they're driving us up a wall.

Jack glares at Cheever. "No, in truth I've got you pegged as a future serial killer. Let's see, you've only been here a few hours and already you've buried one of the other kids up to his neck in sand, and scared one of the poor counselors into thinking you were drowning so that she'd give you mouth-to-mouth resuscitation."

"Until she saw he was getting a boner," Morton snickers.

"The other boys hate them, and the counselors run in the other direction when they see them," I mutter to Jack. "At this point, I don't think we could pay someone to babysit them."

Cheever shrugs. "Toss me a Benjamin and I'll stay out of your hair."

Jack snaps his fingers. "Hey wait. That's not such a bad idea."

I shake my head. "Are you crazy? Pay them to watch themselves?"

"Why not? In the real world, an employer would compensate them, am I right?"

"Yes. But I don't owe any of these slugs a living, except

for this one here"—I jerk my head toward Jeff—"and only through college."

"That's just the point. We'll make it a job, and tie their pay to proven productivity."

"I don't know about that," Cheever whines. "I come from a long line of Socialists. We believe in a strong welfare state—"

Jeff slaps his hand over his friend's mouth. "I've got my eye on an iPad Mini, so shut up and let's hear what they have to say. Go on, Dad."

"It's very simple. Every day you'll be out of the bungalow by nine, and back here by six. Three times a day, one of you is to document your activities to Mrs. Stone, on video, via your iPhones. At the end of the day, you'll each get paid with a twenty dollar bill."

"What a rip! For nine hours, that's not even minimum wage," Cheever mutters.

"Listen up, you little union agitator—this isn't exactly the coal mines of Kentucky. You're getting three square meals a day—none of which is tofu, like your mother would feed you—*and* you're living in paradise." Jack opens his arms wide to make his point. "Also, there's a bonus plan to sweeten the pot. Five extra bucks a day if you get a counselor on video singing your praises for making nice-nice with the other boys on the island."

Morton frowns. "Some of those dudes are real dweebs. And their leader is a moron. The only reason we buried him in the first place was because he pissed off Jeff when he called Mrs. Stone a fox."

A fox? Me? Jeff and I turn almost the same shade of pink.

Morton turns to me. "Don't worry, Mrs. Stone. Jeff set him straight. He told the boy you were probably older than his mother. When the kid heard that, he barfed. It was a hoot!"

Ah, how chivalrous of my little man. Note to self: Remind Son that any compliment toward his mother is a *good* thing—not worthy of belittling, beatings, beheadings or for that matter, *the truth.*

Jack looks at the clock on the wall. "It's two o'clock now. You can put in half a day's work, if you want. That's ten bucks each, and any bonuses you can scrounge up."

Morton looks at Jeff, who glances over at Cheever, who nods.

Oh, boy. If Cheever is the boss of this mob, we'll have our hands full, despite Jack's offer. That's okay, it's not as if I have a lot of petty cash lying around to pay them.

The boys troop out the door just as the cell phone rings. It's Abu. I put him on speaker. "Hey, what are the chances you and Jack can make it over here?"

I brace myself for the worst. "Trouble?"

"Not at all. In fact, we may have stumbled onto Mandrake's lair."

Jack laughs. "Quite an interesting word for his hideout."

"Only because it appears to be in an interesting place, and I don't mean the plush gambling salons of the Hunt Club. If we're right, we may be able to wrap up this thing tonight."

"Nothing would make me happier. We'll be right over." As I ring off, I turn to Jack. "What should we do about the boys?"

"Call Emma. She can watch the little monsters while she monitors our mission. They'll be putty in her hands. Jeff still has a crush on her, you know."

"He could do worse." I pick up the garment bag holding my Cinderella gown from last night.

"What are you doing with that?" Jack asks.

"Returning it. Between the tricks I know with crushed aspirin, meat tenderizer, lemon juice, salt, baking soda, hydrogen peroxide and liquid dish soap, it looks as good as new."

I shut one eye and hold it up to the light. Well, almost. If the sales girl is blind, I may just get away with it.

SINCE OUR BUNGALOW AT KAMP KIDSTUFF IS UNDER THE NAME of Donna Stone, Jack had no reason to give up his suite at the Hunt Club. The whole mission team is already there, except for Emma, who's listening in via speaker while she hangs at the bungalow until our little hellions come home, hopefully with all appendages still attached.

But just in case one doesn't, I've left her a MediPack.

Arnie has a map of the island projected onto the wall, for all of us to see. "Emma and I have tried to detect a pattern to Mandrake's travels over the past couple of days. What we've noticed is this: he stays on the outskirts of the resorts, but rarely does he go inside their boundaries."

"There was one exception," Jack interjects. "His signal was picked up near Donna's tiki hut, that one night."

Arnie nods. "Yes, that anomaly stumped us, too—at first. But even then, it had one thing in common with all the other verified coordinates: he is never far from a body of water. Even when he was next to the tiki hut, he was hugging the beach, along the shallow part of the surf."

Jack shakes his head, confused. "Does that mean he's traveling by boat?"

Abu runs his finger over the map. "Could be. Although, from Arnie and Emma's research, it looks like he comes on shore periodically, but certainly he never wanders too far from the coastline or one of the island's many tributaries."

"So, what does this tell us?" I ask.

Dominic taps the wall beside the map. "My guess is that he's not a guest. But he's not being held captive either."

I'm confused. "So, he's squatting—like Sasquatch?"

"Even so, they're obviously not working together," Jack counters. "Otherwise Sasquatch wouldn't have been spooked at the mention of his name."

"Arnie, tell them the great news." Emma's voice echoes from the speaker.

"Whereas in the past he seems to have been moving continually, for the past few hours he's been hanging in one specific quadrant." He stabs the map.

"Could he be dead?" asks Abu.

Arnie shakes his head. "Every now and then he moves slightly. More than likely, he's injured."

"Where is it?"

Abu scrutinizes the map. "From what I can tell, it's very close to the VIP reserve."

Jack shrugs. "Well, since we don't know why he's still and how long he'll stay that way, I suggest we go there as soon as possible. Abu, both you and Julie mentioned that sometimes there are night safaris. Do you know if any are taking place tonight?"

Abu shakes his head. "Not that I'm aware of."

"Good," I say. "Less chance of us running into someone who may not appreciate our presence. I say we work in pairs. We'll equip ourselves with video lenses, earbuds, and night-vision goggles. Until we know Mandrake's business here and we secure the bacteria, shoot to stun, not to kill. And since we'll be in uncharted territory, prepare for anything and everything."

"Lions and tigers and bears? Oh my," Dominic murmurs.

He may be joking but after our run-in with the Fantasy Island pygmies, the thought of being chased by something with fangs sends a shiver up my spine.

Not that I can show my team how I feel. "Okay grab your gear. Let's meet off-grounds, in exactly an hour."

"Well done, boss lady. Very Hillary, but with just the right dollop of an Anna Wintour chill." For a fleeting moment, Dominic's smile fades. He takes a lock of my now brown again tresses in his hand and sighs. "Already I miss that clueless hussy, Lotta Tallant."

I have to laugh at that. "Thank you…I think. Look around you, Dominic. Everywhere you turn there are a lot of Lotta Tallants—especially on this island."

He nods. "True that. But too much of anything becomes a bit of a bore. Pra'ps its time I settled down, like you two old sods."

He actually sounds wistful. I think of what it would mean for Hilldale to have him in its midst. The women would go gaga. The men would be insanely jealous.

It would be Nirvana for him—

For all of a week.

But no, it would never work. International Men of Mystery don't live in Orange County, California. They don't put down deposits on McMansions on quiet Cul-de-sacs. They don't trade in their Aston Martins for Lexus sedans or BMW SUVs, then double down with the requisite John Deer mower and a coveted Napoleon Mirage gas grill.

They have to save the world, and while they're at it, a pretty girl or two.

They don't have wives and children. They don't attend meetings at school with teachers who tell them what they already know about their kids, let alone wince when the teacher has the guts to say that their son is too lazy for his own good, or that their daughter is too boy crazy.

Or that they've got a little assassin in the making.

Yep, the kid is a chip off the old block.

Besides, if the Dominics of the world opt for everyday lives, who will stop the really bad guys?

Not that I can say this to him.

In truth, I don't have to say anything. He already knows it.

The Jacks in this world are few and far between—those men driven to get into the game, who excel at it, who are used to its junkie high.

And yet, should they come across Ms. Right in their world travels, they would readily trade the thrill of the chase for the love of a good woman.

I know, because he proves it to me every day, and in so many ways.

Dominic would be very lucky to find his own soul mate. But I won't hold my breath. Hell, I have to do that enough in my line of work, what with all the people who try to choke or drown me.

Instead I smile and say, "Sure thing. Go for it. And I'll be the first to welcome you into the neighborhood, with my world renowned cherry pie."

"If it's as good as you say, you'll have to give me the recipe," he murmurs as he saunters out the door.

Well, la-dee-dah. I didn't see *that* one coming.

I hurry out after him.

MANDRAKE'S GPS COORDINATES TAKE US AROUND TO THE south side of the island, moving west. We're on an undeveloped beach, very close to where Battoo picked us up the other day, when Sasquatch saved us.

Not much of the beach is sand because the mountain's gentle rise seems to start almost at the water's edge. The mountainside is blanketed in a thick carpet of trees, vines, and pungent flowers. Running water can be heard if not seen, in both directions. It's dark enough that we're wearing our night-vision goggles.

"Mandrake's GPS signal is coming in weakly," Arnie mutters in our earbuds. "He's somewhere between the hill and the beach."

"If past experience is any indication, the hillside may be dotted with caves. I wouldn't be surprised if the surf has carved one or two of them within the inlets along the bay. He could be in any one of them," I say. "And since his MO is to stay near water, why don't we break up into teams?"

Jack nods in agreement. "Abu and I will follow the spring, up the hill. Donna, you and Dominic can follow the shoreline."

I'm glad he finally realizes this pairing gives him nothing to worry about.

Dominic grabs me by the hand and practically drags me after him. "Let's go, ducky. The sooner we find the bloody wanker, the sooner we get off this Godforsaken island. Back in London at Boodle's, there's a martini with my name on it."

"You don't say? And all this time I had you pegged as a Groucho man."

"Ouch! You do know how to hurt a bloke, with or without a gun…Oh my dear, watch out for that vine there. It seems to be moving. Ah, I see why now. It's really a green tree pit viper…Donna? Slow up! My God, woman, I do believe your 400 meter sprint is worthy of an Olympic gold medal!"

~

DOMINIC AND I HAVE BEEN TRAIPSING ALONG THE SHORE FOR AT least an hour now when suddenly Arnie gives a low whistle in my ear. "Donna, Mandrake's GPS signal indicates that he's just a few feet from you."

"In which direction?" I mutter.

"Ahead, and to the right," he answers.

Dominic points to a mound of branches and brush beneath a stone outcropping, right at the water's edge. The mound is tall enough to form a wall. The leaves and vines above it create a natural canopy.

I put a finger to my lips, and indicate that we should approach slowly. Dominic signals back to allow him to go first, and to cover him. I nod.

He steps closer slowly, then motions me to do the same. The sand is soft and wet around us, so, we aren't making any sound as we inch closer to this natural fortress. If we're lucky, Mandrake will be in there, possibly sleeping or injured, and his capture will be a piece of cake.

Oh hell. Hell oh hell. No, Mandrake isn't there.

Just a crocodile. She is protecting several dozen eggs.

Make that two crocodiles. Her hubby is there, too, on the far side of the nest.

Realizing this, Dominic takes one step back—

And cracks a branch.

Daddy Croc looks up. Its eyes narrow. Mommy Croc shows her fear with a high-pitch scream. Not Daddy Croc. Its large, pointed snout opens, revealing sharp jagged teeth.

It hisses and bellows and lunges towards us, lifting so far off its front legs that it looks as if it's walking toward us.

We're out of there, in a flash.

It follows, and it's just as fast. No, it's faster. With each stride, it gains more ground.

Instinctively I run the way we came. Dominic is on my heels—

Until I trip over a log. As I fall down, he stumbles over me, flipping onto his back in the wet sand.

The air has been knocked out of him. He is left gasping.

The croc weighs his options. I'm punier, and obviously weaker than Dominic. But he's immobilized.

Realizing this, the croc crawls toward Dominic.

The log that tripped me up is about four feet long, and around a foot in diameter. It's also heavy, like petrified wood, but I pick it up anyway, and run after the crocodile.

He's no more than six feet from Dominic when I slap it down onto his tail.

Yep, that got his attention. At this very moment I feel like a dog chasing a car. What am I going to do, now that I've caught it?

His thunderous howl echoes up the mountainside, frightening the wild parrots out of their perches. They fill the air, frantically circling over us. Their shrill screeches mimic the crocodile's surprise.

The croc whips around, mouth open wide. Those sharp teeth are bared in a ghoulish grin, as if it's about to let me in on some gut-busting joke.

I have no intention of being the butt of it.

When his jaws swing open wide and around for me, I cram the log between them with both hands.

Try as he might, the crocodile can't close his mouth.

I don't want to wait around to see how long the croc

takes to snap the log into bits, or to choke it down. I help Dominic stagger to his feet, and we run back down the path. To play it safe, Dominic detours onto the higher road, in the hope that it takes us out of croc country.

I pray he's right.

In my earbud I hear Jack's voice. "Donna, I need you to see something—now."

"What? No 'Hey honey, sorry I couldn't be there with you, in your hour of need?'" My words come out in fits and spurts because I'm huffing as we run uphill now.

"We'll commiserate when you get here. Arnie, send her my coordinates."

This doesn't sound good.

But seriously, can it be any worse than what we're running away from?

12

Death Takes a Holiday

Admit it: you work too damn hard.

Someday, you'll regret it.

Yes, you will curse all those workaholic weekends, when you should have been going to your son's ball games, or your daughter's piano recitals.

You'll kick yourself for having allowed your vacation time to accrue over several years, only to lose it because you didn't use it.

You'll rue the day you worked through the occasional three-day holiday. Just who were you trying to impress—your boss? Well, guess what? He didn't notice. He was having too much fun on vacation.

Then there were all those times your spouse said, "Hey, take it easy, slow down," and you'd answer, "There's plenty of time to do that when I'm dead."

Really? Is that what you think?

I'll let you in on a few secrets. Hell may be hot, but it ain't no tropical vacation.

As for Purgatory, think of it as getting stuck at Newark

airport in a snowstorm: no food, no toilet paper, and lots of people whining about their plans being cancelled.

Even if Heaven is paradise, will you still think so if the one you love most never makes it there?

Life is a one-way ticket, so enjoy those wonderful vacation days while you can. And the cost of making special memories? Priceless.

JACK AND ABU ARE SNAPPING PHOTOS OF BODIES IN A MASS gravesite.

There are at least sixteen of them. But between insects, parasites and scavengers, there isn't much left of the corpses, so it's hard to tell. They must have been dug up by wild animals, which is why Jack and Abu were able to find them.

The skulls and bones are all sizes, so apparently the victims weren't uniquely adult males.

I pick up one of the smaller skulls. "Could this have belonged to a child, or one of the pygmy tribesmen who attacked us?"

"Based on this charm bracelet, I'd say no." Very gently with a stick, Jack prods aside a fallen leaf, exposing the skeleton's radius bone, which is still attached to a half-eaten hand.

Around the wrist is a link chain bearing charms that spell out AWESOMESAUCE.

"Could this body have belonged to one of Jonah Breck's sex slaves?" Emma asks over our earbuds.

I hear Morton shouting in the background. Emma covers her headset, but her muffled threat to him—that he better shut the heck up or else she'll give him a Vulcan mind probe and leave him outside in his underwear—is followed by dead silence.

That's my girl. It's her last shift as a camp counselor. Even if it wasn't Morton I couldn't really blame her for letting loose with the threat.

"Good question, Em," I respond. "My guess is no. There's still too much skin, hair and clothing on at least this particular body."

"This is a mass grave, but all of these bodies are in various states of decomposition," Jack points out. "Apparently this is some sort of dumping ground."

Everyone goes silent. All around us are sounds of the jungle—rustling leaves, bird whistles, and faraway howls.

I bend beside another body. The head is no longer attached, but there is still skin on its bones. I shiver, but at least I can hold down the bile trying to climb up my throat. "Everyone, grab bone and skin samples from each of the bodies, and then let's get out of here. Tomorrow we'll ship them off to Ryan so that Acme can do a DNA test and some carbon-dating...Oh my God!" I cover my eyes with my hands.

Jack puts his arms around me. "Donna, what is it?"

I point to the backside of the body. It has a tattoo of a tiny airplane.

"She was the flight attendant on our plane!" I grab Dominic and shove him toward the remains. "Do you recognize that?"

Dominic stares down at it then nods slowly. "Unfortunately, yes, from...well, from our quickie, as one would say. In hindsight I'm not at all surprised she ended up this way."

I can't believe my ears. "What the hell do you mean by that?"

"If her questions to some of the other men she met on

Fantasy Air were half as pointed as the ones she asked me, the wrong sort of fellow might not appreciate it." He shakes his head sadly. "I warned her that might be the case."

When I bumped into her, she was certainly upset and frustrated. At least now I know the real reason why.

I don't like her being exposed like this, with her skirt hiked up around her waist. But when I reach down to cover her up, Jack stops me. "For all we know, she—and some of the others here, too—were victims of Mandrake's bacteria plague."

Good point.

Abu, ever at the ready for any occasion, hands out surgical gloves, along with a bunch of small portable plastic bags. The others follow my lead as I put on a surgical mask.

Jack picks up a jawbone with teeth. Dominic bags a skull with patches of scalp and hair.

For me, it's a manicured finger from the hand of AWESOMESAUCE.

Whomever it belongs to it was once somebody's baby. Are they sick with worry, wondering what may have happened to her?

Suddenly I long to hold Mary. To talk to Trisha. To hear Jeff chatter on aimlessly about sports, or Iron Man, or how much he hates all the girls in his class.

I could tell him that hate is a pretty cruel word—that it should be reserved for those people who kill and maim, and for those who have too much anger buried inside themselves. Now that he's almost eleven, I think he'd understand that words can hurt others, or instill shame, or motivate retaliation.

Whoever did this to these people deserves my hate, and my retribution.

But right now I need to feel love, and to be loved.

I keep thinking of how much I want to call the girls. It'll be the first thing I do when I get back.

Make that the second. First, I'll cuddle Jeff, even though it may embarrass him in front of his friends. Every hug may be the last.

WHEN WE GET HOME, THE BOYS ARE ALREADY ASLEEP.

"They went to bed early. I guess they were worn out," Emma explains.

Arnie is there, too. He takes his toxicity tester and runs it over all of us: Jack, Dominic, Abu and me. Then he does the same to the bags of bones.

"Looks like everything is in the clear."

"Ryan will certainly be happy to hear that."

"Good, then it's tea time!" Dominic beams and glances around. Where do you keep your martini shaker?"

Before Jack can answer him crudely, I interject, "Sorry, old chap! You'll have to hit the bar at Eden Key. I've got three boys here, who know how to stay in trouble while sober. No need to keep liquid incentive lying around."

"Ah, righto! Boys will be boys, eh? And men will be men. Being one of the naughtier ones, I'm off to the Hunt Club, where the women are easy and the bartender now has my martini down pat."

"Speaking of business, Dominic, your next task is to get as close to Lee Chiffray as possible. The fact that the representative of Boarke's largest investor is on the island the same time as Mandrake may not just be a coincidence. Make it your primary objective."

He graces us with a grand smile. "I won't surface until I've got the goods."

"Or Chlamydia," Jack mutters.

While Abu and Dominic take off, Emma and Arnie open the bone bags and begin the process of sorting and cataloging the samples by text and photo. The bones will be put in a Fantasy Island souvenir box addressed to a safe house owned by Acme, but marked HOLD AT AIRPORT, where Ryan will retrieve it so that the Acme labs can do a full analysis.

While Arnie packs the samples, he looks over at me. "Dominic and you were right next to Mandrake. Why didn't you grab him when you had the chance?"

I shake my head in disbelief. "Excuse me? The only things in our path were two crocodiles—one of which chased us halfway through the jungle."

Arnie stares down at his iPad. "No way!"

I stare him down. "Way."

He frowns and fingers open a new screen on his tablet. "Look, I wasn't seeing things. Here's a replay of your GPS coordinates and Mandrake's, after you split from Abu and Jack."

My dot is pink, whereas Dominic's is purple. Mandrake's is flashing gold. The video tracks us moving west before coming to a standstill.

Suddenly our dots backtrack on the path. The gold dot follows, but then slows along with ours, which I presume is the place where Dominic fell.

"Look!" Jack points to the screen. "Your dot and Mandrake's are almost together."

"But how can that be?" I ask.

"Maybe living with prehistoric reptiles is his idea of fun," Emma mutters.

Jack shrugs. "Yeah, he's a regular Crocodile Dundee."

Emma's eyes narrow in confusion. "Who?"

"Never mind. It's a pre-Gen Y reference." He hits the replay button, and we all watch again.

And again.

Finally Jack says, "Could he have been running after you, to help?"

I shake my head. "If so, he never showed himself."

"Maybe he was there, but you just weren't looking for him," Arnie chimes in.

"In any event, he stayed with the croc, as opposed to following you and Dominic back to the bone yard," Jack points out.

"Won't it be sick if he needs the crocs to test the plague bacteria?" Emma wonders out loud. "And maybe the fact that their eggs are about to hatch has something to do with it, too."

"Yeah, 'sick' is the right word for it." Fear and fatigue weigh on my eyelids. I don't know what Mandrake is up to, but I do know one thing: it's dangerous for everyone here on Fantasy Island.

Once again I'm hit with the urge to hug a child.

I open the door to the boys' bedroom. It's such a warm night that I'm surprised to see they have the blankets up over their heads. I'm walking toward Jeff's bed to make sure he's not too hot when my cell phone chirps.

Damn it.

So as not to wake them, I scurry out of the room and shut the door behind me.

The Caller ID reads CAMP INCH. Mary must finally be missing me as much as I miss her, and decided to call. "Hello? Mary?"

"No, Mrs. Stone, this is not your daughter. It's Rebecca Granger, the lead counselor of Camp Inch. We've been calling your house all day—"

"Oh my God! Is Mary alright?"

"The only thing hurt may be her pride. You see, she and her cabin mates, Midge and Babs, are no longer welcomed at Camp Inch."

I go into my bedroom and close the door behind me before sitting down on the bed. "Ms. Granger, what happened?"

"Last night Mary and her friends were caught with boys in their cabin, playing Spin-the-Bottle. As you know, the camp has very strict rules about that sort of thing."

"I have strict rules for my daughter, too. Apparently she chose to disobey both of us." As relieved as I am that Mary is okay, I'm certainly disappointed in her, especially after the talk we had. I guess it's time for another.

"The parents of the other girls have already retrieved them. I presume we can expect you some time tomorrow?"

"I...I can't! I'm out of town."

"Oh, I see." Ms. Granger's tone reeks of accusation—that I'm the worst mother in the world.

No, I'm just the mom of a boy-crazy 'tween girl who just so happens to be several thousand miles away and needs me now, more than ever.

"I'll send her Aunt Phyllis to pick her up. She can be there by eight in the morning."

Ms. Granger sighs condescendingly. "Our rules specifically state that a suspended camper can only be released into the custody of her parents. Since you're out of town, I'll make an exception, but just this once."

She hangs up before I have a chance to point out to her that there will be no "next time," since this was to have been Mary's last year, anyway. I guess this blows it for Trisha, too, when she's old enough to go.

Jack peeks through our bedroom door. Seeing that I'm off

the cell, he enters the bedroom and flops down beside me. "Who was that?"

"Camp Inch. Mary got kicked out. I've got to call Aunt Phyllis to pick her up. I don't think Mary will be too happy with that arrangement."

"Certainly not when she finds out Jeff is down here with us." Jack smiles. "Hey, why not have Phyllis bring her to Fantasy Island? Phyllis can hang here, too, with the kids. That way, Emma is freed up to do her work from Eden Key."

"Are you crazy? I don't want Mary here for the same reason I'd like to see Jeff and his pals and the rest of us get off this wretched rock! There may be a mad scientist on the loose, the place is crawling with pygmies who shoot poison darts—and let's not forget that we don't know what kind of wild animals are roaming around for those gun nuts in the Hunt Club! Oh, and did I mention that Dominic and I almost got eaten by a crocodile?"

"You, I can understand," he says, as he licks the tip of my nose. "You're sweet as sugar. But Dominic"—he shrugs —"he's an acquired taste."

"Apparently so. By many, and often." I wrap his arms around me.

"Remember, Donna, we're monitoring the water, food, and air for toxicity. And we've come very close to capturing Mandrake, if tonight is any indication."

"That's just it: as close as we've been, how do we keep missing him?"

Jack shrugs. "For the life of me, I can't figure that one out."

Regarding Mary, what choice do I have? None really. "Okay, maybe you're right about Mary and Aunt Phyllis. I'll make their reservations for tomorrow morning's flight. They'll be here just before dinner. After I get them settled here at

Kamp KidStuff, I'll meet you and the rest of the team over at the Hunt Club. Dominic is right about one thing—it's where all the action seems to be." I stretch and yawn. "I'm sure Emma will be happy to leave Kamp KidStuff for Eden Key, once and for all. And I need to have a heart-to-heart with Mary."

His smile falters. "Just be kind."

I smack him on the nose. "You know me well enough. Why, would you imply otherwise?"

He rubs out the sting of my slap. "My point exactly."

Ah, I get it. "So that's what you think of me? That I'm too hard on her?"

"I think Mary would like a little more space, yes. I also think we've had a very long day. And tomorrow is shaping up to be the same. The double tub in there would be a great way to wash off any crock stank, not to mention the work of collecting a few bones from the recently departed."

No arguments there.

By the time I've made my aunt's and eldest daughter's necessary travel arrangements, Jack has already started our bath. I watch as he twists the tub's faucet knobs in order to get the temperature just right. Then he strips down.

When he sees me staring into space, he takes it upon himself to do the same to me. He raises my left leg onto the side of the tub so that he can unlace my sneaker and pull it off along with my sock. Next to go are my shirt, my belt, my pants, my bra, and panties.

His lips inch, kiss by kiss, up the back of my thigh, and beyond the curve of my ass to the small of my back; then up my spine, to my shoulders.

When I think of how close I came to missing his kisses for a lifetime, I want to cry. Instead I graze the top of his head with my lips and whisper, "Never let me go."

He nods.

Then we sink together into the water. At least for the next hour I can forget that this paradise is also hell.

JACK SITS UP IN BED. "HE'S DEAD."

"What?" I roll over, but I'm so sleepy that I can only open one eye. "Who?"

He turns to me. "Mandrake. He was eaten by that crocodile."

"In other words, you don't believe Emma's theory—that he's testing his plague on the critter?"

"It makes more sense that Mandrake was eaten, GPS and all. Full-grown crocs move fast. In order to finish their kill, they've been known to toss their prey around in order to break off their limbs. That monster could have eaten a grown man with no problem."

"Ha! Not to mention a grown woman." The memory of those jaws makes me shudder.

Jack snuggles down and pulls me close to him. "If Mandrake arrived on the island even the week before us, he'd still be moving through the damn animal's digestive system. For that matter, the GPS could last forever in the crocodile's gut—or until it was excreted out of the crock's body." He pauses in thought. "I've heard that crocs can go four months without eating again. So, if it wasn't hungry, why did it attack you?"

"To protect the mama croc and her eggs, of course. You'd do the same thing. A more important question is what was Mandrake doing out there in the first place?"

"Running away," Jack says through a long exhausted

yawn. "But from whom? And when he escaped, did he take the bacteria samples with him?"

"Good questions. And if not, who has the samples now?"

Jack's gentle snoring tells me he's down for the count.

Too bad, because now I'm wide awake.

I spoon Jack tightly. Just knowing that killer crocodile is out there may keep me awake all night.

I wake up to the hum of my cell phone, which insists *I Only Have Eyes for You*, the ringtone that always announces Jack's texts. This one reads:

Early rendezvous with Julie. All in a day's work. BTW, I broke the news to her that "Lotta Tallant" is in fact my wife and that you're here also for business: doing research for your next book on modern mating rituals. Knowing this, maybe she'll get off my back.

I don't know if he means that literally, but my guess is yes. Ha! As if a mere wife will stop the hussy from digging her claws into him.

Jack's message continues:

Since you've moved to Kamp KidStuff with the boys, I suggest we meet in my room at Hunt Club for call with HQ after Mary's flight comes in. FYI: Bring a killer dress. Boarke is treating us to dinner. Xo

Speaking of the boys, the bungalow is as silent as a tomb. I guess the little hellions are out too, thank goodness for that.

I look at the cuckoo clock on the wall. *Oh my God, it's already ten-fifteen!*

My flight tracker app shows that Mary's plane is running late. It won't land until four.

In the meantime, I've got work to do. I send a text to Arnie:

Need Mandrake's GPS signal archive from the moment he landed until his signal moved into the VIP reserve for the very first time. Also need guest+ Boarke arrival photos ASAP.

By the time I'm out of the shower, Arnie has texted back:

Both attached here. LOL Jack almost got caught lifting photo thumb drive from Julie's computer. Guess that ain't so funny, but still… —A

I smile as I read about Jack's close call. I can't wait to find out how he got out of that one.

Then again, maybe I don't want to know.

My eyes are crossing by the time I'm ready to head over to the Fantasy Island airport. I've scrutinized every male guest in every photo with a photographer's loop, and I know every pore in Boarke's face and every tooth in his mouth. His smile never changes. If I didn't know better I'd think it was molded out of hard plastic.

In every photo, the flight crew is lined up behind Boarke. Whenever a photo includes the female flight attendant whose body we found in the jungle, my heart races a little faster. Do her co-workers wonder what happened to her? Do they ask each other why she didn't make the flight home? Their faces are now so familiar to me, I'd recognize them anywhere.

I consider making the time to ask one of them today while I'm on the tarmac, but then I think better of it. I'm there to pick up Mary, and it's more important that I give her my full attention, at least until it's time for me to leave for the Hunt Club.

I'll be relieved to see her, but I'm sure she won't be happy with what I have to say. There are many ways to grow up fast. Breaking rules to impress her friends isn't one of them.

13

Family Reunion

The best getaways of all are those spent deep within the pillowy bosom of a loving family.

However, just as some bosoms are rock hard, not all families are loving. If your relatives are more like the Munsters than the Waltons, here's how to survive your next reunion:

First, have no expectations. For example, try to live with the realization that your brother-in-law the doctor will still charge you two hundred dollars for a six-minute earwax removal visit, despite the fact that a loan from you put him through med school.

Next, rejoice in the good luck of your family members! The scary and ironic news that your Cousin Cletus has been granted an early release from prison due to a technicality is a perfect example.

And finally, don't hold old grudges. Just let bygones be bygones, okay? Unless they have to do with your ex-husband having once slept with a sister, cousin, mother, or favorite pet.

THE SHORTCUT TO THE FANTASY ISLAND AIRPORT TAKES ME right past Eden Key. I'm passing the pool when I receive a video selfie from Jeff. Good boy, he knows how to keep his mother happy.

In the video, he, Cheever and Morton are standing on boogie boards, giving the camera the thumb-pinkie surfer salute.

A Kamp KidStuff counselor, dressed as Aqua Man, comes up behind the boys and puts his arms around them. In a voice that sounds a bit too boisterous, he says, "These little guys are the *real* super heroes!"

Cheever nudges Morton, who winces but then joins him in shouting out, "Best vacation ever, Mrs. Stone!"

"Cut," Cheever mutters through gritted teeth. Immediately Jeff's camera shifts downward, toward his bare feet.

The counselor can't be seen, but the tone of his voice is frigid. "Okay, you little SOBs, I want my—"

Suddenly the video cuts off.

Hmmm. Okay, something's not right here.

I'm replaying the video when I hear "Hey, Lotta! Over here!" shouted in a foghorn holler. I look up to find Merritt Andrews and Tuggle Carpenter waving at me.

Ouch. Just my luck to run into the Sisterhood of the Traveling Thong.

They are sitting poolside, just a few lounge chairs over from three other women who are being straddled by the pool's lifeguards while lotion is applied to their naked backs.

One of the women is moaning so orgasmically that when her mimbo hops off, I won't be surprised if she asks for a cigarette. The broad back of her masseur glimmers with droplets of water. He may have just gotten out of the pool, but the bulge in his Speedo FastSkin brief—not to mention the drool on Tuggle's lips—attest to the fact that he'll never have to worry about shrinkage.

Merritt lowers her sunglasses to reveal an arched brow. Obviously she's enjoying her ringside seat to the best hand job in the resort. "Yo, Lotta, our turn is next! Want to join us?"

"Would if I could, Merritt, but I can't. I've got to meet the plane."

The moaner suddenly bucks up and churns her head to see who's talking, almost tossing the man off her back.

He retaliates with a slap on her butt. "Down, li'l filly," he murmurs.

I wouldn't be surprised if she whinnied. Who does he think he is, the Slut Whisperer?

Apparently so, because every muscle in her body freezes—

Except for her mouth, which hisses, "Oh, what a bore! Is that you, Donna?"

Penelope Bing.

Ah, yes, now I remember that bony ass.

She sighs. "What are you doing here? Shouldn't you be with the boys?"

"Boys?" Merritt perks up when she hears that. "Why, you little Puma! Have you been holding out on us?"

"Um—no, Merritt!" *Think of something, quick.* I whisper to her, "Penelope is talking about a few guys I met recently— over thirty. She's a bit of a man chaser, if you catch my drift."

"You're telling me," Merritt mutters. "I've got the tiki hut next to hers. It's busier than Grand Central Station."

Wow! Coming from Merritt, that's saying a lot. Maybe Jack was right to give Peter and Penelope a break from Cheever.

All the more reason not to let her intimidate me—especially in front of my new besties, who know me under an alias. "Nice to see you too, Penelope. Oh, and look, the man straddling you is not your husband, Peter!"

Her two newfound gal pals whip their heads around to face each other. The look they exchange is not lost on either Penelope or me.

Penelope waves her life-guard-slash-masseur away with a Benjamin, which she folds into his Speedo. He rewards her with a sly nod before mounting Merritt.

Ride'em, cowboy. High ho, Silver! Away.

Merritt is so busy with her new boy toy that she doesn't hear Penelope mutter, "Ix-nay on the arriage-may! Peter and I are…well, we're taking a 'break,' if you catch my drift."

"Yeah, I get it. Whatever happens in Eden Key, stays in Eden Key."

The redness in her face has nothing to do with her tan. "I…I'd prefer if you didn't mention this, you know, when we get home."

"Sure, Penelope, whatever you say—*friend.*"

"Sure…*Lotta.*" She rolls her eyes. Still, she gets the hint: *I own you, bee-yatch.*

I'm not the kind of person who likes to rub salt in a wound —unless it's a bullet hole. To play nice, I pull out my cell phone. "Here's what Jeff and Cheever were up to, this afternoon."

I play the video, up until the part in which it's obviously bogus. It puts a smile on her face, and a tear in her eye.

"Do you miss him?" I ask.

She nods.

"I'm sure the Fantasy Island reservationists wouldn't mind if you traded in your tiki for a Kamp KidStuff bungalow."

She stares at me. "What? Are you crazy?"

I can still hear her laughing as I walk through the airport gate.

～

I'M NOT THE ONLY ONE MEETING THE PLANE. AS IS THE USUAL custom, Mr. Boarke and Battoo are here as well.

By the look on Boarke's face, I see he is trying to place me. Since slipping over to Kamp KidStuff, I'm back in mommy mode. My hair, now brown, is pulled back into a ponytail, and I'm wearing one of Jack's tee-shirts over lululemon yoga pants. In other words, I'm no longer the sultry redhead in a designer gown that he remembers as his financial angel's arm charm.

He has to turn away when he's accosted by Lee Chiffray, the big winner of the baccarat tournament. Whatever is on Lee's mind must not make for pleasant conversation, because both men are scowling. With the financial problems Boarke is having, I wonder if he shorted Chiffray on his winnings. That would be stupid. News like that would kill his gambling business.

I walk over to Battoo, who is leaning against the bell tower and scanning the skies for the Fantasy Airplane. "The plane is going to be late, Ms. Stone."

I shrug. Great. As it is, I'll barely have time to meet with my team before we have dinner with Boarke.

Noting my disappointment, he smiles and changes the subject. "Is your Kamp KidStuff bungalow to your liking?"

I laugh. "I don't miss my heart-shaped bed, if that's what you're asking."

He joins me with a chuckle. "I'm sure there are a lot of things you don't miss, including your lonely hearts club."

"Hey, at least they *have* hearts. I hate to think of all the ones who disappeared from this place without theirs."

His smile fades. "The other women here have you to thank for that."

I am modest enough to shrug. "Thanks, Battoo. I know you wish no harm to anyone. Now I need your help on something. In the undeveloped part of the jungle to the west, we found a mass gravesite. Do you know whose bodies might be buried there?"

Despite his tan, I can see the blood go out of his face. "Perhaps infighting between the natives—"

"No," I say firmly. "There is evidence that at least some of the victims may have been guests."

"Perhaps the cannibal's prey?"

I shrug. "Perhaps. Then again, perhaps not. You see, the victims are both male and female."

"Well I..." He closes his eyes. "I can't say."

"You can't, or you won't?"

He glances in the direction of Mr. Boarke and murmurs, "Other than translating Mr. Boarke's directives to the natives, I am not allowed into the VIP reserve."

"I didn't realize that part of the island is part of the reserve."

He nods. Then he stops. Just over my shoulder, something has caught his attention. "Sorry, I must go. As you can see it's show time."

He grabs the bell rope to alert the others while shouting, "The plane, the plane!"

Gotta give the people what they came for, right?

I make my way over to the tarmac. Mr. Boarke is on his way there, too.

Not Mr. Chiffray. He's headed back to his driver and car. But he catches my eye, smiles, and tips his Panama hat. I wonder if the daughters of his girlfriend are around Mary's age, and if so, would they like to hang out with her?

Maybe I should wait before I ask him. Mary is walking down the air stairs now, between a gaggle of giggling college girls ready to go wild in Eden Key and two families with toddlers. With that scowl on her face, you'd think she's being sent to the electric chair instead of a fashionable resort.

Aunt Phyllis wears oversize glasses, and her head is covered in a large straw hat. Her muumuu catches a down draft and puffs out, like a balloon. Spotting me, she waves frantically. "Donna! Over here," she bellows, to Mary's mortification. If my daughter thought she could slink off into anonymity, she's mistaken.

Time to face the music.

Mary scans the crowd. Seeing me, she gives a hesitant wave. I raise my hand in return as I trot over.

Whereas Phyllis hops up and down as she hugs me, Mary hangs limp when I put my arms around her—not a good sign.

"What a ride! What a place!" Phyllis waves the brochure in my face. "This joint has everything—*and* gambling!"

Oops. How could I have forgotten about my aunt's obsession with Vegas' slot machines? Or as she once told me, "Nothing that hard feels as good in my hand."

Time to sign her up at OurTime.com.

Or else get her a decent dildo.

If I break the news to her that I need her for babysitting duty, I'll have two sad lassies on my hands—and a possible mutiny.

Okay, deep breaths. Smile. Exude kindness. "Ladies, I'm so happy you can join us here! Mary, I know you were looking for a change of pace from camp this year. With your father here on business, this may fit the ticket."

Mary's eyes shift from anger to wariness. "You mean you're not upset with what happened at Camp Inch?"

I force my smile to stay on my face. "I wouldn't exactly say I'm pleased with your expulsion—especially since we'd talked about the importance of your last year there, and all the memories you'd be making."

Phyllis snorts, "Oh, I'm sure she's got a couple."

Mary blushes. But before she gets defensive, I take her arm in mine. "Phyllis, Jeff can't wait to see you. In fact, why don't you hop on the Kamp KidStuff tram with the luggage? Mary and I will walk over. It'll give us a chance to catch up! Right honey?"

Mary nods. I presume the four-hour flight with Aunt Phyllis was three hours too long.

"Gotcha. Maybe I can catch a poolside game of Texas Hold'em." Phyllis grins at me. Before I can tell her Kamp KidStuff is a gambling-free zone, she's half-way to the tram.

Ah well, she'll find out soon enough. Right now, it's time to break the news to Mary that Fantasy Island is a trouble-free zone as well.

We walk by Mr. Boarke, whose greetings to the Hunt Club's newcomers are filled with superlatives: his joy at seeing them, his awe for the women accompanying them, and his assurance that this will be the vacation of a lifetime.

Certainly if that plague gets out, it will also be their last vacation in their lifetime.

As we head down the lane toward Kamp KidStuff, I notice that Mr. Chiffray's car is still here. The window is down, which may be why he's still wearing his sunglasses. It may be my imagination, but his head seems to turn slightly as Mary and I walk by.

Yes, he's watching us. I know this because he waves at

me again before commanding the driver to roll up his window and drive on.

~

WE'VE WALKED IN SILENCE ALMOST TO THE GATES OF KAMP KidStuff. Finally I come out with it: "So, what happened, Mary?"

Mary stops short. She looks down at her feet. I'm sure she's wishing a few clicks of her heels will send her to Kansas, or any of a dozen places other than here, with me.

Well, too bad.

"Mary, I've only heard Ms. Granger's side of it, and that is certainly not fair to you."

Still she says nothing.

I sigh. "And it's not fair to me, either. I put a lot of faith in you. I'm sure you're aware of that."

She frowns. "If you must know, I did it on a dare. We saw the boys across the lake, around sunset. Babs bet me I'd screw up a Morse code message to them, to meet us after midnight in our cabin."

I give her a brownie point for a fluency in Morse code, since it is a survival skill that I myself have found handy. However, I take the point away because she used it for something frivolous and stupid, like signaling boys who obviously had an ulterior motive other than singing songs around a campfire.

In other words, we're back to zero. "Well, since they showed up, I guess you got it right. Did you use a flashlight?"

"No. Midge had a lighter on her—"

"A lighter? What was she doing with that?"

Are the girls smoking cigs? Or pot? Hashish? *Crack*?

What kind of camp is that Granger woman running, anyway?

Mary bites her lower lips. "It was, you know, to start campfires."

"You really expect me to believe that? I know for a fact that everyone in your camp tribe earned a badge last year for learning to start fires with a flint!"

"Midge cheated, okay?" Mary winces in frustration. "I wasn't supposed to tell!"

"Oh…okay." I can't tell her but I'm happy that I won't have to tap into her college fund for drug rehab. "I guess it doesn't matter since none of you are welcomed there, anyway. Did you feel having the boys come over was worth the expulsion?"

Mary shrugs. "What do you think?"

"I think you know what I think. I'm asking you how you feel about it."

"Okay, no, it wasn't worth it. But I wouldn't have known it if we hadn't tried. Until then, I'd only been kissed by…well, Trevor. You know that, because you caught us."

I nod. It was one of the reasons I wanted her to have a summer away from Trevor. Be careful for what you wish for, right?

"The boys from the other camp were harmless! It wasn't as if any of us knows what to do."

"That's a relief to hear. But what if it had gone the other way? What if the boys had—you know, forced themselves on you?"

"Dad showed me a few moves that can help me defend myself. Do you remember? I was trying to"—she glances away, embarrassed—"to impress Trevor."

I do remember. Trevor developed a crush on me after I stopped a robbery in a toy store parking lot. Mary resented it, but with Jack's help she got over her insecurity by learning some impressive tactical moves of her own.

"Of course I'm proud that you know how to defend yourself. But Mary, love, I never want you to find yourself in a situation that you can't handle, which can easily happen when you trust the wrong person."

As I say this, I think of Mary's real father—the real Carl Stone. For many years, I presumed he was dead, and that he had died nobly in the service of his country. When he contacted me to let me know he was alive, I wanted to believe his story: that he was a hero who had faked his death in order to protect us and his black ops mission.

Instead, I discovered that he's a terrorist.

Not only that, but he'd be fine with killing me if it saves his mission.

I lived. His terrorist mission failed. But boy, it was a hard way to find out about love and commitment. Let me put it this way: any trust issues I have now are because of him.

Which brings me to Mary. "While we're here, you're to follow the same rules as Jeff and his friends: make a few friends. Make sure they aren't prone to getting into trouble. And check in with me at least three times between breakfast and dinner. Lights out at ten for everyone—no ifs, ands, or buts. Do we understand each other?"

"You have nothing to worry about. In fact, I plan on staying inside for the whole time."

"Sorry, no, that doesn't work for me. Mary, look around you! You're in paradise! Make the best of it. The boys are enjoying themselves. I'm sure you will, too."

She snorts. "Mom, come on already! This place is called 'Kamp KidStuff.' The name alone qualifies anyone staying here as a dweeb. I'm not surprised Jeff and the Terrible Two fit right in."

I wince when I hear her call Jeff's friends by my nick-name for them. Still, I can't have her moping around while I'm trying to figure out what happened to the plague bacteria. "I'm sure the resort has several girls close to your age. They can't all be 'dweebs.'"

I point toward Kamp KidStuff's pool, where four girls lay on chaises. Unfortunately, they're a few years older than Mary. In other words, they're still jailbait, but this doesn't seem to bother the five teenage boys flocking around them. Why should it when three of the girls are front side down, with their bikini tops unlaced?

It certainly bothers me—especially when Mary says, with a sly smile, "Maybe you're right Mom. I've got to learn to be more sociable."

No. Oh, no.

Do I have to keep her under lock and key until she goes off to college? We both know that's not possible.

Better idea: build a torture chamber in the basement, for any boy who goes too far with her. *Hmmm.* I wonder if I can convince Jack that it will add to the value of our home.

In any regard, until construction is completed I'll have to trust her.

As if reading my mind, Mary pats my arm. "Don't worry, Mom. I wouldn't do anything with anyone who doesn't really love me. I promise."

I reach out to grab her arm, to make her look at me, if only for a moment. "Mary, falling in love is a wonderful experience—especially with the right person and at the right time of life—which by the way *is not twelve*. Soon you'll be dating. And some of the boys you meet may not be looking for 'the right person,' or be experiencing the same sensations you may be feeling. It's okay to tell them no."

"But that's just it, Mom. What if I want to say yes, even when I know they're not 'the one?'"

"You may think you do, but you don't, really. How could you? You're only twelve!"

Mary's eyes narrow. "But just last week you told Dad that you think I'm 'very mature' for my age."

By that, I meant to say she was bounding into womanhood much too quickly—both physically and socially.

Not that I'd say that to her. Instead, I spin it this way. "True, I was impressed with how you've handled yourself in the past, when faced with complicated moral dilemmas. But after Camp Inch, I'm not so sure I feel the same way. I mean, come on Mary! You said yes to a dare, knowing full well that the consequence for getting caught was expulsion from the camp. That doesn't sound too mature to me."

She's not paying attention to me. One of the boys at the pool gives her a knowing smirk. She smiles back.

By the time she's ready to answer me, her eyes have hardened. "Okay, yeah, I made a mistake. It won't happen again."

What was the mistake, getting caught? Is that what she vows won't happen again?

She knows me well enough to feel my doubt. With a shrug, she mutters, "I guess you'll just have to trust me."

No, I don't. I have to watch her like a hawk.

I'll have Arnie link me to her cell phone's GPS tracker. He can also put a video bug on her favorite faux diamond stud earring.

"And I'm sure you'll do everything you can to earn my trust—especially after this past week." I put my arm in hers. "But first things first, dear. Why don't you unpack?"

I point to our bungalow. It's pretty in pink. Best yet, it has a bird's eye view of the pool. In other words, I can see everything that goes on. "Oh, and by the way, I hope you don't mind sharing a room with Aunt Phyllis."

Seeing her grimace, I add, "Yes, sweetheart, I know, Aunt Phyllis snores. No worries! Just prod her, and she'll stop right away. Think of it this way, such tight quarters gives us all time to bond, and that's really what family getaways are all about."

Of course she's unhappy. She wants to experience life on her own terms—even if it means sneaking out of her room at night to do so.

We both know this. But I don't have to accept it. And I won't. Her life journey will be pocked with speed bumps, and she's going to have to take it slow. My job is to see to it.

She storms into the bungalow ahead of me.

Really, I don't need this grief. The way it stands now, I don't even have time to dress here. Instead, I'll throw a few things into a garment bag before heading out to the Hunt Club.

It takes me all of five minutes to narrow it down to two dresses. The white one is too short, too low-cut, and too see-through. The other fits skin-tight, and red hot.

I take the latter, and a pair of four-inch stilettos to match.

I knock on Mary's door. When she doesn't answer, I say in my firmest mom voice, "Dad and I will be back by ten. We'll talk more then, okay?"

Still no answer.

I'm about to knock again when my phone riffs its pixie dust chime. Trisha texts me:

MISS U MOMMY! GUESS WHAT! THE PIRATE TRADES ME LITTLE TREASURES FOR MY SNACKS. HE'S SO FUNNY! CAN I BRING HIM HOME WITH ME?

Sounds like she's having a good time. Glad she's made a friend—

A pirate? Gotta love the kid for having such a wonderfully active imagination. I wish I could say the same about Mary.

14

Where the Boys Are

The true test of any housewife is how she treats her guests! From the moment they walk through her front door, they should feel welcomed. They should be wined and dined and feted until they are sated. They should be in awe of the guest list, comfortable in the lush surroundings you've created for them, and riveted by your scintillating conversation.

Important Tip: Avoid arsenic in any dishes. Seems that a dead guest has a way of putting a damper on a party. Go figure.

BY THE TIME I GET TO THE HUNT CLUB, MY TEAM IS ALREADY there. Abu, is in his Hunt Club khakis, Emma and Arnie wear the Hawaiian shirts and shorts that peg them as Kamp KidStuff Kounselors, while Jack and Dominic are dressed in their tuxes.

I kick off my flip-flips. I'll dress after our conference call with Ryan..

I dial him now, and put him on speaker.

Immediately, we get down to business. After a nod from me, Jack and Emma start by giving their competing theories regarding Mandrake.

Ryan listens without saying a word. Finally he murmurs, "I lean toward Mandrake being croc food. It's the most rational explanation for the misleading GPS signals."

"If Mandrake is dead, is the mission over?" I ask.

"Unfortunately, bringing him in was just part of the job. Frankly, the plague bacteria samples are even more important." Ryan coughs—which is his tell that he's got something on his mind that I may not want to hear. "Donna, if Mandrake took the stuff with him into the wild, we'll need to retrieve it."

"Just how will we do that?" Jack asks.

"We've been tracking the GPS since the first day he disappeared. You'll have to retrace his footsteps, in case he released it accidentally or intentionally before his death."

"But how do we know if the GPS coordinates are his?" Abu wonders out loud. "If the crocodile ate Mandrake, whose steps will we really be following?"

Ryan thinks for a moment then sighs. "Unfortunately, we don't know when he had his run-in with that croc. Since we don't know the answer to that, I'd suggest you start with the first day's coordinates."

"Ryan, if Mandrake is dead, isn't it possible the bacteria plague died with him?" I ask.

"I wish that were the case, Donna. But human contact with it is inevitable—particularly as development on the island goes forward. Some animal might become infected, and in turn pass it along to the tourists who are coming in from all over the world. If one—or several—also become infected, it could cause a pandemic. And if it is ever discovered that the plague was created at NSA headquarters, the international community will hold the United States responsible. Some countries may even consider it an act of war."

"Then I guess we'll draw straws as to who's going to go back to the croc's nest." I laugh so that I don't cry at the thought of our mission's failure, and the inevitable consequences. "Ryan, do you think the bone yard we discovered has anything to do with Mandrake's disappearance?"

"In that regard, the bone samples have a lot to tell us. In any case, time is of the essence. Jack, do you see Boarke as friend or foe?"

"He's so anxious to get new funding that he'd be my bitch, if I wanted."

"Dog's bollocks!" Dominic exclaims. "Now, there's a vision for you!"

If looks could kill, Jack's stare would have stopped Dominic's heart faster than a speeding bullet.

"Good," Ryan continues. "Because something tells me he knows more than he lets on. At dinner tonight, why don't you and Donna play 'Good Cop, Bad Cop'? Donna, be the nice guy, if you catch my drift."

Sadly, I do.

And so does Jack, by the way he's wincing.

"I'm here for anything you need, so don't hesitate to ask," Ryan reminds us. "Donna, I hope you realize I have all the confidence in your success." He clicks off.

I wished I believed him. He's just making the best of a bad situation.

The others know it, too. I can tell by the looks on their faces.

Time for a pep talk. Nothing inspires your team like a solid plan. Here's hoping I sound as if I actually have one. "We all heard the man. New rules: Arnie and Emma, pull up every male guest who arrived on the day Mandrake's signal showed up here. By now, most of them may already be cleared via Acme's facial recognition software. Cross-reference those yet to be ID'ed with any intel you the can dig up on them. As to anyone who hasn't already been eliminated, track their every move from that day forward, via Fantasy Island's security feed archives. Anyone who has been on a VIP hunt when Mandrake's trail goes into the VIP reserve should be our first priority."

Even before the command is out of my mouth, Arnie and Emma are on it. Their hands swipe furiously on their iPad screens.

"Abu, is there a VIP hunt scheduled for tonight?"

He thinks for a moment. "No. The next one is in three nights. Why do you ask?"

"If we are to retrace Mandrake's path through the VIP reserve, we don't want to be running into any hunters."

"Or pygmies, for that matter," Jack mutters.

My nod seconds that thought. "Any remaining suspects may know why and how he disappeared. They may even be implicit in his death. If any of them fit the bill, we'll search their rooms for the plague bacteria." I turn to Dominic. "Ask the croupiers if they recall a player with Mandrake's extraordinary gaming skills. Or perhaps one of the bartenders or wait staff remembers him. Certainly some of the eye candy that seems to be on permanent vacation here must have caught his eye. Someone has got to remember a man fitting Mandrake's description!"

Dominic honors me with his already patented and no-doubt-soon-to-be sponsored smile—Colgate, perhaps. "Right, boss lady."

I'm beginning to like the sound of that. "By the way, are you making any headway with your 'interrogation' of Julie?"

"Oddly, no. In fact, I'm beginning to think she was the one who put the Digitalis in my drink during the baccarat tournament." He frowns. "In any event, she's made it clear that I'm not exactly her type." His gaze moves from me, to Jack, and then back to me.

Ah. Gotcha. All in a day's work.

The look on my face has everyone scurrying out.

Except for Jack. While my heart crashes and burns in a barren field of doubt, Jack steps nimbly through the debris of my pain. "We should hurry. In twenty minutes we're to meet Boarke in his private dining room. You've barely got time to get dressed."

I open my garment bag and lay my gown on the bed. As I step out of my sundress, I keep my eyes on the mirror over the vanity. "We'll make it with plenty of time to spare if you stick around and zip me up—unless you have better places to be. You know, it's all in a day's work."

As he catches the reference, he also catches my eye in the mirror. "You asked for something. I got it for you. Mission accomplished, right?"

Wrong.

He unzips the dress from the bag and walks over with it. When we're face to face, he drops down on one knee. "Step into this," he commands.

On this particular mission, I'm calling the shots. We both know that. But in our relationship, we're equals, which means I have a choice.

He looks up at me, waiting for my decision.

I raise one foot and place it into the dress, then the other.

Very slowly he raises my gown over my calves. The silk feels smooth against my thighs, and caresses the curves of my ass. The boning in the bodice hugs my abdomen as he raises it upward. Because the dress is sleeveless, he lifts my breasts gently, so that the décolleté makes the most of what I have to offer, which is perhaps too generous.

Obviously he thinks otherwise or he wouldn't be admiring them.

He moves behind me. One hand stays firmly on the small of my back while the other takes hold of the zipper. With a gentle tug, it begins its slow journey up my spine. Through the mirror I watch as his eyes move along with it.

Then he steps back to admire his handiwork. Unconsciously, he gives a slight nod.

Mission accomplished.

No, sorry. As far as I'm concerned, I will never be business as usual.

I brush past him without a smile or a glance, let alone a thank-you kiss. "We're hurrying, remember? We don't want to be late."

He turns toward the mirror to straighten his bowtie.

Or to hide the frustration I've already seen in his eyes.

When this mission is over, I'll request a commendation for him. In this line of work, being a perfectionist has to count for something.

I'M NOT AT ALL SURPRISED THAT JULIE MAKES OUR DINNER WITH Boarke a foursome. And I'm certainly not surprised that Jack is just as attentive to her as to me.

Make that more so. If and when he takes time to glance my way, he calls me "my little wife," as in, "my little wife has seemed quite content in my absence," and "my little wife is keeping so busy that she barely misses me."

Each time he calls me that, Julie snickers, as if the joke is on me.

Oh yeah? Well, his little wife happens to carry a very big gun. When we go powder our noses, she better hope it doesn't go off by mistake in one of her nostrils.

Even if we hadn't spatted, Jack would have found it hard not to stare at her cleavage, which is barely contained in her leopard skin halter dress. A brass key dangles in the deep chasm between her breasts.

On the other hand, the way Jack ignores Boarke has our host practically jumping out of his skin.

Do my ecstatic compliments about his resorts make up for it? Just barely. During the sublimely roasted tomato soup, I rhapsodized about the roominess of the bungalows. And during the artichoke appetizer, I complimented him on the size of his beachhead.

From his leer, I realize he took it the wrong way.

Story of my life.

It's now dessert time, and I've almost run out of platitudes. Okay, this one's a blatant lie, but it can't hurt. "Mr. Boarke, your Kamp KidStuff counselors are so sweet. They've been very attentive to our son, Jeff, and his friends."

"We do our best to give our guests everything their hearts desire." Boarke pats my arm appreciatively. But when I try to slip out from under his grasp, he holds onto it as if it's the last lifeboat on the Titanic.

The man is desperate.

As if on cue Julie turns to Jack and says, "You've barely touched your pie. Perhaps we have something else that might entice you. Follow me to the dessert alcove."

He nods obligingly. Why? Is there a mattress in there, perhaps made of angel food cake?

"I'm happy to hear that you're enjoying yourself, Mrs. Stone." Boarke leans in closer. "The success of Fantasy Island depends on it."

"How very gracious of you to say so, Mr. Boarke."

His smile disappears. "I mean it. As you know, Mr. Stone's visit means a great deal to me." Slowly, his fingers trace the palm of my hand. "Any encouragement you can give him to fund *our* little paradise will be aptly rewarded."

The way he elongates the word *our* sends a chill up my spine.

"In fact," he continues, "I'm not above sharing my good fortune with the right benefactress."

"Are you trying to bribe me, Mr. Boarke?"

"A more important question, Mrs. Stone, is, 'am I succeeding'?"

My chuckle seems to set his jaw on edge. "Anything you want, Mrs. Stone. I'm being serious."

Wow. He's handing Fantasy Island to me, on a silver platter. Why is he so anxious to get out from under Lee Chiffray's thumb?

I've got to admit, though, his offer is tempting. Okay, what do I want, really? Indiscriminate liaisons with any and all delectable man candy? Won't do it for me. The way I feel about men right now, Boarke's pretty cabana boys would count their blessings if I didn't castrate them. Should I ask that the gaming tables be tilted in Aunt Phyllis's direction? Nah, I'm not sure she'd share her winnings with me, even if it could get me out of hock with Acme for Dominic's tournament loss.

At the very least, Boarke wouldn't charge me for the dress that Dominic puked all over.

Sadly, none of these trifles will get me any closer to the bacteria plague. Ergo, none of us gets out of this hell hole.

Whoa, I've just had the most brilliant idea.

"I know just the thing to win my husband's enthusiasm,

Mr. Boarke. But it will cost you a five percent commission on his loan."

He frowns. "I…I can live with those terms."

"Good." I grace him with a smile. "Oh yes, and one other thing! Tomorrow is his birthday. Please arrange for one of your renowned VIP hunts. It would delight him to no end."

Getting into the private reserve without worrying about getting shot? Priceless.

He frowns. "I had no idea that Mr. Stone appreciates hunting, let alone the type of quarry stocked in our VIP reserve."

"Trust me, he's totally at ease with big guns —*and* unusual prey." I lean back into my chair. "To tell you the truth, he was a bit disappointed that it wasn't offered to him before now. In fact, Miss Julie has done her best to discourage it, don't ask me why." I shrug. "How exciting! I already know it will be the highlight of our trip because of what Mr. Chiffray said about it."

Boarke's eyes narrow. "Oh? And what was that?"

As I suspect, he hates the thought that Jack may know his investor.

"How did Mr. Chiffray put it? Oh yes! He called it, 'the thrill of a lifetime.'"

Not really. I read this hackneyed line in the Fantasy Island brochure. It's time this resort got a new ad agency.

Boarke's smile hardens. "Yes, as you can imagine, such a hunt is very exciting!" He traces my hand with his finger. "Perhaps you'd like to pick out your husband's prey for him?"

His offer certainly gets my attention. I quit focusing on all the ways I could torture Boarke and reward him with an inquisitive smile. "Really? It's allowed?"

"We insist! It makes it all the more interesting, should

you come face-to-face in the wild. Of course, the hunter always has the upper hand."

"By that, you mean the gun."

"Yes, in part."

"And the night goggles."

"Certainly both are an advantage—but not the only ones." He rises and moves behind me. I feel his eyes studying me. "A face-to-face allows the hunter to size up his prey. Even in his sleep the night before, he dreams up ways in which to beat a quarry that knows all too well why it has been caged in the first place. Finally, when it is tracked and cornered, one's eyes fill with resignation, the other with resolve." He proffers his hand to lift me out of my chair. Can you guess whose is which?"

"It's not hard at all. I've seen your trophy room." I take his hand.

His laughter leaves me hollow. "Such a quick wit you are, Mrs. Stone! Now, to our private stockyard."

He guides me out of the dining room, to a small side elevator that needs a brass key, which he pulls from his hanky pocket. It could be a twin of the one Julie wears around her neck. "I'm glad you will be accompanying your husband, Mrs. Stone. Men live to share their victories with those most dear to them. I look forward to your inspirations on my behalf, as well."

I'd like to think Boarke is talking about his loan, but I wouldn't bet on it.

~

THE ELEVATOR DROPS US DEEP BELOW THE HUNT CLUB'S CASINO, into a long hallway that seems to go on forever. Every twenty feet or so is a guard, dressed in mufti, with a gun and a whip on his hip.

At the far end of the hall is an elegant iron door. The lock is recessed, but it opens with a hydraulic hiss when Boarke's brass key is inserted.

Does it smell like a livestock yard? No.

Fear has a unique stench of its own—not at all surprising when you're housing about a hundred people in thick Plexiglass cages.

There are both men and women here. From what I can tell, some are old enough to have grandchildren, whereas others are as young as Mary.

They are of all nationalities, colors, and races. The only thing they have in common is their prison garb: thin white cotton vests and loose pants.

A badge on each vest sports a Hunt Club logo, as if these people are its employees, not its prey. In the middle of the logo is a number but no name, as if reinforcing their place on the island's food chain.

An Asian man cowers in the corner of his pristine cage, babbling prayers to a God who doesn't seem to hear him through industrial strength plastic. Another man, with a shock of white blond hair and deep blue eyes, bangs and shouts angrily when he sees us, but the walls are too thick for us to hear his curses. I blink away my own tears when we come across a girl—Middle Eastern, perhaps?—who sobs uncontrollably as she dances around in circles.

Some of the prisoners are spread-eagled and shackled by all fours, on the farthest wall of their cells. Their eyes have darkened with the realization that the rest of their wretched lives will be spent in these pristine cages until the anointed moment of their release—

In which they will be hunted down and killed like wild animals.

Wretched is a relative term. The prisoners are clean and groomed. They show no bruises, and it is obvious they are well fed.

In other words, they are the perfect prey.

I keep my voice as level as possible as I ask, "Where did you get them?"

"As you might guess, they are from all over the world. We are the 'last resort'—do you like my little pun, Mrs. Stone? Miss Julie thought of it, so I must give her the credit —of countries seeking the most extraordinary rendition imaginable." Boarke shrugs. "We are truly killing two birds with one stone—so sorry that the puns are running rampant today! But yes, our VIP hunt seems to fill two unique niches. A country wishes to remove political undesirables from its shores. At the same time, world class hunters seek the ultimate prey. Humans are just that, are they not? Maybe not as strong as an elephant or as fast as a jaguar, but certainly as cunning as the hunter."

I stare at the people in front of me. "And how do you keep the righteous tourist from finding out The Hunt Club's politically incorrect secret?"

He puts a finger to his lips, as if to hush me. "For one thing, it's why no reporters are allowed on the island. And for another, all VIP reserve guests must put up a large deposit, via a Swiss bank account." He laughs at my surprise. "It is held in trust for their heirs, and released upon their deaths. Yes, it's true, we buy their silence—with their own money, no less! On the upside, the interest is generous. Best of all, it's tax-free." He shakes his head proudly. "Such financial incentives easily assuage any untoward remorse, I can assure you."

I smile. "You've thought of everything, haven't you, Mr. Boarke?"

"I really shouldn't take all the credit. Again, it was Miss Julie's idea—not to mention her marketing skills are second to none! The Hunt Club has an annual occupancy of one hundred percent. In fact, we're booked solid for the next three years. Best of all, advertising costs are nil, as it is all word of mouth." He nudges me down the hall. "How about you? Is your preference something easy"—He points to the Middle Eastern girl—"or something that will give you a run for your—I mean, for *my* money? Oh, and please don't worry about a deposit. Should you or your husband be struck with qualms of guilt, your equity stake in Fantasy Island will be leaked to the press."

"No worries there. I presume Miss Julie has assured you he has no conscience at all, particularly when a sure bet is involved."

He purses his lips, but just for a moment. "It would be gentlemanly to presume that her discretion in the matter is the better part of valor, but then I know her too well. She too enjoys 'collecting scalps,' as they say. I assure you, if Miss Julie had been making headway with Mr. Stone, we wouldn't be standing here, Mrs. Stone."

I hope to hide my relief regarding Jack's fidelity by changing the subject. "Considering the success of the Hunt Club, I'm surprised you need any additional financing at all."

Boarke grimaces. "Our largest note comes due very soon, and our investors are anxious to move their money into less unorthodox ventures. At the same time, we'd like to expand the VIP reserve program." He holds his arms wide, toward the seemingly ongoing rows of prisoner bays. "Unlike the rest of the animal kingdom, the human is not yet an endangered species. We've had to turn away some potential client countries. It works to our advantage that we're the only game—another pun, do excuse me!—in town, and we'd like to keep it that way. Other resort management companies have been snooping around, eager to learn our success. But I'd be shocked if their stockholders would fully appreciate this concept." He moves in and whispers, "A more obliging partner would be welcomed with open arms."

I avoid his hint by easing away. I start down the aisle slowly, glancing into the cages on both sides of me. Boarke doesn't realize it but he's also put me in a box. Obviously, Jack and I can't—we *won't*—shoot a prisoner. Frankly, I'd like to see how fast Boarke could run through the jungle with me tracking him.

Or Miss Julie. Especially in the Louboutins she was sporting tonight. The faux leopard fabric would provide a bit of camo, but not much.

Better yet, just let the prisoners have a go at them—

At least one prisoner.

Sasquatch.

He is two cells in front of me, on the right. They've got him shackled to a wall. His eyes are closed against the bright lights coming up from the floors on all sides of the cage. With his long hair, he looks almost medieval.

He opens one eye. At first my face doesn't register with him. When it does, he strains against the iron wristbands that hold him back from charging at us.

"That one," I say, just loud enough for Boarke to hear me.

Boarke's eyes grow large. "He...he may not be the best choice. Only recently he was put in the stockyard—"

"It's him, or I tell my husband I'm bored with this joint, and that it's time to call it a day. Not the best customer satisfaction review, wouldn't you say?"

Boarke's stutter dies in his throat. "No, of course not. Yes, alright, your fantasy is my desire. But so that it doesn't turn into a nightmare, I insist on sending you along with a trusted guide."

He must mean Battoo.

"Works for me," I murmur. "May I…would you mind if I touched him?"

Boarke doesn't speak at once. When he does, his tone is slick, even as his words are crisp. "But of course. His shackles will hold."

"What a shame," I purr. "I can just imagine the fun if they didn't." Sasquatch, loosened from his bindings, could snap Boarke like a twig.

And I'd enjoy watching him do it.

Boarke's key fits into the keyhole to the side of the cage. Soundlessly a door, built into the front wall, slides to one side.

I stand directly in front of Sasquatch. His grin curls into a snarl, but he stays silent and doesn't move as I lay my hand on his belly. My left index finger meanders up his firm abs, then over to a nipple. It is already taut before I flick it with my tongue.

He shudders at my touch.

"Does he meet your approval?" Boarke's tone is derisive. Yes, he is jealous.

"He is perfect, thank you. What's the saying? Oh yes, 'one good turn deserves another.' You're a lifesaver. And you'll be duly rewarded."

I keep my voice jovial, but my eyes on Sasquatch. Only he can see the look in my eyes: *I will get you out of here.*

Sasquatch gets it. He winks then looks away.

The door hisses again as it closes behind me.

15

Island Fever

Bored in Paradise? It happens.

Endless days of sun, surf and sand aren't stimulating enough for a brain that seeks to be challenged. Or a mind that must be entertained. Or a heart that longs for provocation. Here's how you know when it's time to start packing up:

Telltale Sign Number 1: Whereas once the thought of a jaunt to Paris had you cursing "Merde," now you think, "Mais oui," and spend hours devising the quickest and cheapest routes from your isle du jour to Ille de Louis;

Telltale Sign Number 2: Whereas once you poo-pooed any interaction with those tourists who refused to learn the local lingo or eat at local boîtes, you now cling to the ankles of homeward-bound travelers, begging and pleading them to "Take me with you, oh please pretty please." A sure sign the local charm is not so charming anymore.

Telltale Sign Number 3: Whereas once you delighted in hearing the resort staff constantly wishing you a "pleasant day," now you force yourself to smile and bite your tongue to keep from shouting, "What, are you kidding? Not at these rates!"

Because too much of a good thing is not such a good thing after all.

~

I CAN'T LEAVE BOARKE QUICKLY ENOUGH TO FIND JACK. WHERE the hell is he?

After meandering through the Hunt Club lobby where a gaggle of arm charms sport 'ho couture that would rock the Adult Entertainment Expo's fashion runway, I get the bright idea to sneak a peek in the casino.

There he is, up in the casino's mezzanine, bent over the balcony as he watches the action below, in the main gallery. His eyes follow me as I climb the curved staircase toward him, but he doesn't move when I reach his side.

Okay, time to eat crow. "It seems I owe you an apology."

He turns his head toward me. "How do you figure that?"

I lean in next to him. "You left me with the impression that you'd do whatever it took to get Julie to do our bidding."

"And by that you thought I meant falling for her bullshit come-ons, and hitting the sack with her."

"Yes...of course I did."

"Because fucking to gather intel is part of our job." He frowns. "And if the shoe were on the other foot, you too would screw whomever it takes, if the mission calls for it."

Shame weighs so heavy on me that I drop my head.

Below me is the poker table. The distraction is not great enough for me to ignore what is happening here, right now, with Jack:

Our moment of truth.

"I avoid it, whenever possible. You know that." I think back upon my missions since I met Jack. "In fact, since our 'marriage', except for a little heavy petting on the suspect's part I've been as pure as driven snow. Granted, it's helped that I've slipped a mickey or two. Or three."

"The bottom line is that you've done your job without having to put out, as quaint as that sounds."

"Yes exactly, Jack. And I'll keep doing so, as long as… well, as long as the situation allows."

His eyes lock onto mine. "Why would you presume I'd do any less?"

"Because—well, because you're…a man. Sex isn't the same to guys."

"Maybe. Personally, I've never subscribed to the theory that we humans with outies will plug into just any available outlet for a quick charge." He shrugs. "One thing I do know, under no uncertain terms: my love for you is the same as your love for me. But unfortunately, our jobs put us in compromising positions, usually with people we can't stomach. Nothing attractive there."

I have to laugh. "That's putting it mildly."

My hand rests on the balcony's rail. He puts his hand over mine. "Until I met you, I thought killing was the most gut-wrenching part of my job. It's not. It's having to get it up for women whom I honestly despise. But to do my job and complete my missions, I have to smile at them. And woo them. And do whatever it takes to get them to let down their defenses and divulge whatever it is I need from them. If needed, to kill these lovers." He pauses. "And so do you."

Yes, of course. Guns, knives, poison and missiles aren't our only weapons. Our bodies are far more dangerous—to our opponents, first and foremost. And to ourselves.

Our minds and hearts and relationships become our collateral damage.

The pain being inflicted—to us, to our loved ones—lasts a lifetime.

"Donna, before I met you, fucking the enemy was easy. It was retaliation."

Don't I know it. For Valentina's infidelity. For Carl's duplicity.

For me, fucking the enemy was revenge for Carl's supposed death. But since Jack entered my life, it's become the longest walk of shame.

With a single finger, he lifts my chin so that I can see his eyes. "As long as we're in the game, Donna, we do the role assigned to us, no questions asked, no shame felt, no jealousy to break us apart."

He has the sweetest lips. His lingering kiss takes away any doubts I have that anyone will ever come between us.

I pull back when a disgusting thought hits me. "If we were an ordinary couple—like Penelope and Peter, for example—we'd call this arrangement an 'open marriage.'"

He finds that funny. "It locks up, tight as a gnat's ass, the day we both retire. Is that a deal?"

"Deal." This mission is yet one more nail in the coffin of the Quorum. And one more step toward that glorious day when we can live normal lives. "Speaking of 'out of the ordinary,' I've got an early birthday gift for you, my love."

"Tell me that you found Mandrake's plague bacteria so we can all go home!"

"No, but hopefully it's the next best thing. I've gotten us a free pass into the VIP reserve, so at least we can look for the samples without being shot at."

His eyes grow wide. "How did you do that?"

"Boarke is gifting us a safari—and five per cent equity in any new property development—in exchange for your bank's loan. But there's a catch."

He shrugs. "Let me guess. We're about to test the promise we just made to each other."

I stick my finger in my mouth and feign a gag. Then it's time to get serious. "The VIP reserve has a truly unique prey: humans, many of whom are political prisoners, sent here on state-sanctioned death sentences."

"You're joking."

"Banging Boarke would be a joke. This is deadly serious. From what I can tell, they're holding at least a hundred people down in the basement, each in separate Plexiglass cages. The hunters get to pick out their prey, sort of like a turkey shoot. I chose Sasquatch."

"He's now in captivity?" Jack shakes his head in awe. "Good girl. It's payback time. I owe him big time. When he saw us running, he must have thought we were destined for the stockyard, too. I guess that's what he meant when he said, 'take the first plane you can, off the island'—"

"Oh my God!" I grab his arm. "Did you say 'plane'?"

"Yeah, albeit not with anywhere near Battoo's enthusiasm. Then again, he gets paid to give a shit."

"No, I mean…I've seen Sasquatch before—on the Fantasy Island plane!"

"He was on it—with us?"

"No, but he is—*was*—part of the Fantasy Air flight crew —a pilot, in fact." I take my cell phone and scroll to one of the photos Arnie passed my way. The name that aligns with his place in the photo identifies him as George Taylor. "He must have been piloting Mandrake's flight. Otherwise, how would he have known so much about him?"

Jack frowns. "Maybe Mandrake was in the stockyard with him. Or maybe Mandrake has already taken his turn, running for his life—and his head is now hanging in some sicko's trophy room."

"If that were the case, Sasquatch—I mean Taylor—wouldn't have acted as if he were still alive, or be so worried about the plague bacteria."

"That's another reason to keep him alive, Donna. Maybe he knows where it is, and can lead us to Mandrake."

"I hope so. We'll know for sure, tomorrow evening. Until then, we have a lot of work to do." Suddenly, I'm bone tired. "Thank goodness Aunt Phyllis is here, to look after the children."

"Aunt Phyllis is here, alright. Look below you."

I glance down. Yes, that's her—and from the looks of things, she's winning big at Texas Hold'em.

"But…it's after nine o'clock! Why isn't she back at Kamp KidStuff with Jeff and Mary?" I grab Jack's hand and pull him down the staircase with me.

I reach Aunt Phyllis just as another hand has been dealt. Not so gently, I tap her shoulder. "Why aren't you with the children?"

She seems surprised to see me. "Mary said you wouldn't mind if she looked after Jeff and the other boys while I go play a hand or two." She shrugs. "Okay, more like ten. But hey look, I'm ahead by a landslide!" She points across the table. "This gentleman is my lucky charm. Since he sat down, I haven't lost a hand."

She is pointing to Lee Chiffray.

My Aunt Phyllis is beating the man who won the casino's baccarat tournament? Something is terribly wrong with this picture.

"You're being much too modest, Phyllis." Chiffray's voice is deep and friendly. He may be talking to her, but he's looking at me. His smile is broad, and his handshake firm. "You say your children are on their own? With all this resort has to offer, I guess I'd be worried about that, too."

I don't appreciate his knowing chuckle. I nudge Aunt Phyllis. "Time to cash in your chips." *Or I'll cash them in for you.*

Aunt Phyllis knows better than to argue with me. "Well, I guess it's a good thing I do it now, while I'm still ahead."

"No need to call for a resort tram. I'd be happy to give you a ride back to Kamp KidStuff." Chiffray's eyes take their time as they roll up my legs. "I'd hate for you to break one of those beautiful heels."

"We'd appreciate that." Jack's tone implies the opposite.

Lee doesn't seem to catch on that he's treading on thin ice. "Great, then it's all settled." He signals a waiter, who nods at him.

He tosses the croupier a chip as a tip. With a wave, he invites Jack and me to take the lead.

Phyllis giggles as she takes his hand. "So much for 'age before beauty.' But you're right Lee. The view is much better back here. While you're staring at my niece's back-side, I can admire her husband's, and neither of them is the wiser."

Jack is clenching his fist as if he's going to belt someone. At this point, I'm hoping his target is Aunt Phyllis.

As I hold on tight to Jack's arm, I pray we make it back to Kamp KidStuff without killing someone.

THE CHILDREN AREN'T IN THE BUNGALOW.

Jack sees the frantic look in my eye. Holding me by the shoulder he murmurs, "Don't worry. We'll find them." He turns to Phyllis. "Stay here. If they come home, threaten their lives if they don't go directly to bed."

She purses her lips, but nods. She's been duly chastised.

"Donna, do you have any idea where Mary might have gone?"

"Yes, I think I do. When we walked back from the plane this morning, we noticed a group of teens hanging by the pool, both girls and boys. But they were—well, they were a few years older. I guess she ignored me when I suggested she'd be better off hanging with kids her own age."

"Yeah, like that was going to happen," Phyllis mutters under her breath.

I shoot her a dirty look. It does the trick of shutting her up.

"I might be able to help you. Do you mind if I use your concierge phone?" Chiffray asks.

"No, go ahead." I point to it, on the desk behind the el-shaped couch. "You're here with children, too. Am I right Mr. Chiffray?"

"Yes, my fiancée's. But they're closer to tots than teens." He hits a few buttons on the phone. He holds on for only a moment. "Hello, Louis, this is Mr. Chiffray. Can you do me a favor and pull up the names of Kamp KidStuff guests who have teen children?...Wonderful...Yes, now go ahead and read off their bungalow addresses." He reaches for the pad and a pen, and scribbles the information we need.

After hanging up, he tears the sheet from the pad and hands it to me.

I look over at Jack. "What are the chances that Jeff is with her, too?"

He rolls his eyes. "My guess? Slim and none. Look, why don't you hit up these bungalows while I go down to the beach, to see if Jeff is there."

He's out the door in a flash.

"I feel guilty that I kept Phyllis so long at the Hunt Club." Worry has brightened Lee's stark blue eyes. "I'd like to make it up to you. Maybe we can split up the list, if that's okay with you."

"Well…you see, Mary would never accompany you back here, because you're a stranger." He only means well. I can see that. "Do you know the locations of these other bungalows?"

"Yes. I'm an investor in the resort, so I know the property quite well."

Do you know about the human stockyard, too?

But of course he does. I clearly remember the look on Boarke's face when I faked him out by mentioning Chiffray.

I wonder why he's so concerned about Mary.

Does it really matter? His behavior isn't the priority. Finding my children is all I care about right now.

I shrug. "Sure, tag along if you want."

He smiles. "Consider me your body guard."

Ha. If only he knew that is the last thing I need.

"The kids are fine! You're worrying for nothing." Jonathan McAdams' eyes are bleary from too much good scotch.

He's not the only one. None of the guests at this dinner party hosted by him and his wife, Ginny—the parents of the friends who hang with their teen queen, Regina—are feeling any pain.

"Mr. McAdams, you say your daughter is sixteen? Well, mine is only twelve."

He smirks as he raises an eyebrow. "Jesus, no wonder you're worried! Ginny would have had a fit if Regina had been a wild child at that age. Sixteen is bad enough."

Don't judge me or my daughter, you son of a bitch.

Lee must feel my pain because he puts his hand on my arm before I can use it to beat this jerk to a pulp. "Like most girls, I'm sure Mary just wanted to be accepted. So tell us, guy. Do you know where they are?"

Of course he doesn't. He yells inside the house, "Hey, whose place are the kids destroying tonight?"

His guests' muted murmurs and nervous giggles do little to hide their embarrassment at being absentee parents.

Welcome to the club.

One woman lets loose with a loud sigh. "I think they're at our place, Jon." She sizes me up, then shrugs her delicate tanned shoulders. "Hey listen, when you get there, tell my girl, Karen, that we're right behind you. That way they have time to hide the pot and the condoms before we get home."

One of the dads slurs out, "Can you steal me a joint or two? I promise to share."

The guilty snickers of the others burn in my ears as I leap down the veranda steps. They may have given up on the fact that their children are out of control, but not me.

I'm halfway down the block before Lee catches up to me. "Donna, you're headed in the wrong direction." He points down a lane that leads to yet another row of bungalows that hug the beach.

I can barely see it through the tears veiling my eyes. I have to hold Lee's hand so that I don't trip.

I guess this isn't the best way to introduce him to parenthood. I hope his girlfriend forgives me.

Hell, I hope she's a better mother than me.

EVEN THROUGH THE SNICKERS AND LAUGHTER, I HEAR MY

daughter sobbing and shouting to let her up and out of there.

Lee doesn't knock, but enters the house and heads straight for the master bedroom.

I am close on his heels.

The teens draped over the couch in the living room quit giggling to stare at us. They are too stoned to react, and certainly too jaded to care about what's happening to someone who is younger and more innocent.

Booze is old news to them. So is pot and sex. Mary is tonight's entertainment.

The boy straddling my daughter can't be more than sixteen. He's got to be at least one hundred and ninety pounds to her one-hundred and six—in other words, a bruiser. He wears a canary yellow football jersey with royal blue letters that shout his last name, MONTROSE, in bold letters across his broad shoulders. His muscular arms have her pinned to the bed, and his thick thighs block her effort to close her legs, despite fighting him with all her might.

My punch to his nuts allows her to shove him off. She flies into my arms, babbling incoherently. I shush her and hug her close.

When I look up, I see that Lee's wide hands are now wrapped around the boy's neck and cutting off his windpipe from any oxygen. By the time I realize what is happening, the boy's eyes are already fluttering, and he is gasping.

"Lee, please! No!" It takes all my might to pull him away.

With Mary, we run out the bedroom door, and through the living room. The other four boys have sobered up in a hurry. They rub their knuckles as they weigh their allegiance to their buddy against the thought of possibly joining him in jail for attempted rape on jailbait. The cold hate lingering in

Lee's eyes must mirror my own, because the boys flinch and freeze when they look into our faces.

Smart move.

As we stumble back to my bungalow, Mary hiccups her thanks and whispers embarrassed regrets. Suddenly she looks down at her dress, and notices that the strap is broken. "Mom, I...I'm so sorry! I think that stupid creep tore your dress."

It's only then that I notice that Mary is wearing the short white frock I'd left on my bed.

Now that my daughter and I are almost exactly the same size, I hate my honeypot wardrobe. I'm quite a role model.

Mary can't read my mind. She presumes I'm disappointed in her, not in myself. "You were right. They were too old for me to hang around. I thought that wearing this"—she looks down at the white dress—"would fool them into thinking I was older, but I know they could tell. Their jokes...embarrassed me. I did...things." She ducks her head in shame.

"Mary, did you smoke pot with them?"

She cries as she nods. "And we drank, too. I didn't realize what it would do to me. I was acting so—*so crazy*! They all laughed at me. It was so stupid." Suddenly her face turns white. "Oh my God, I'm going to be sick!"

She stumbles off the path. A second later she's bending over and heaving into a bush.

I rush to hold her head, but Lee beats me to it.

It takes her a few moments to get her bearings. When she finally rights herself, she takes a good look at him. "Oh!...Thank you."

She looks over at me, with tears in her eyes. "Mom, I'd understand if you never trusted me again."

Without thinking, I glance away. I'm so taken aback with

her statement that the words fail me in describing my feelings: the relief that we got to her before the boy could hurt her; anger because she disobeyed me in the first place; and the knowledge that there are still too many lessons to be learned the hard way.

When I look back at her, her head is lowered from the weight of her shame.

I tilt her chin up so that she can look into my eyes. I hope that she sees the love I have for her. When I can finally speak, I choke on my own words. "I have no doubt you'll earn it back. Sadly, some choices we make have consequences we can't anticipate, and we can't take them back. But Mary, you'll always have my love, and that of your father's."

Her relief comes out in a long, sad sigh. She hugs me tightly, like she did when she was a little girl. Finally, she stumbles up the stairs into our bungalow.

Lee doesn't follow me up the veranda steps. Instead, he holds out his hand.

I take it, and hold on for a while. He doesn't seem to mind.

Finally, he pulls away. When I try to speak, he waves away my thanks. "She's beautiful. And I think she's learned her lesson."

I nod. "Your girlfriend is one lucky lady."

"Fiancée." He grimaces as he says it. His deep voice is hollow, empty.

I hope the sadness melts from his eyes before he gets home to her and her little ones, because he strikes me as a keeper.

Thank goodness they've got a few years yet, before they have to deal with this kind of stuff.

I ENTER THE BUNGALOW IN A TRANCE, TO WHICH I AM RUDELY awakened by the sound and fury of Cheever as he yells, "Those jerks scarred me for life!"

His face is painted white, and covered with red stripes. He is naked, except for his underwear.

What. The. Hell?

Morton and Jeff also have war paint smeared on their cheeks. Headdresses, made of feathers and lanyards and covered with intricate beading, are on their heads.

At least they're still wearing jeans.

"Whoa, whoa whoa!" I look from Cheever to Jack, who is doing his best not to laugh. "What exactly is happening?"

Jack nods over at Jeff and Morton, who are smart enough to sit still with their mouths shut. "Show her, Bing."

For the first time since I've walked in, Cheever's mouth actually snaps shut. He shakes his head adamantly.

Jack walks over to him and jerks Cheever's head down into a couch cushion. The poor kid's underpants ride up high enough that I can see what looks like a woman's breasts tattooed on his butt cheek. The words "KNOCKERS AND NOOKIE" encircle the very generous chesticles.

Yes, I am speechless.

Noting this, Jack says, "I found the boys in the jungle just beyond the Kamp KidStuff gate. Seems they've done exactly as we've asked and kept busy. Unfortunately, their projects leave a lot to be desired—extortion, racketeering, bribery."

"Wait…you sound like a Department of Justice agent."

"You're lucky I stumbled across them because I'm sure if they had shorted any of the counselors they were bribing to stay away, the Feds would have swooped down on their gang: Cheever's Beavers."

I bury my head in my hands for a moment. When I'm finally able to raise my head, it's to address Jeff. "Seriously? Is that the best name you could come up with?"

Jeff shrugs. "He won at Rock Paper Scissors."

Jack shakes his head. "Jeff, dude, he probably cheated at that, too."

Both Jeff and Morton glare at Cheever, who shrugs. "You know what they say, 'a sucker is born every minute.' You two must have been separated at birth."

"Just who was being extorted?" I ask.

Jack shrugs. "A better question is, 'who wasn't?' Any kid who wanted to take a swim had to pay Morton before entering the pool. If a boy wanted to rent a surfboard or boogie board, he had to pay Jeff."

Hearing that, I turn to my son. "That's terrible! All of those things are free amenities at the resort. What do you have to say for yourself, Jeffrey Harrison Stone?"

Jeff looks down at his feet. "I plead the fifth."

"No, sorry, young sir. This isn't a court of law. I am your judge, jury *and* executioner." I shake my head. "Go on, Jack."

"Any kid who fought the system was taken to a tribunal, in one of the jungle caves." Jack's tone is serious.

I get it. They crossed over into croc territory.

"If a kid didn't pay up, he was staked to the ground. They'd play 'pin the sword on the pinkie toe' with him."

"A sword?" I grab Morton by the scruff of his neck. "Where did you get a sword?"

Try as he might, he can't get out of my headlock. "It's fake!" he gasps. "We bought it off the King Arthur counselor, for a fiver!"

"They're lucky no one got hurt. Shows you what lousy aim they have."

"We missed on purpose," Jeff insists. "We were just trying to scare them."

Jack raises his hand to shut him up. "As it turns out, a few of the boys figured out that Cheever is a great big pussy and started a mutiny."

Jeff and Morton nod vigorously. "They stole all the money we'd saved," Morton mutters indignantly.

"Serves you right," I snap back.

"Hey, you're lucky I came upon you when I did," Jack interjects. "If I remember correctly, you two were next in line for a couple of homemade ass tats."

"We'll get back at them," Cheever declares. "We know where they live."

I shove him back down on the couch. "You're not going anywhere, you little sadist. The whole lot of you is grounded. In fact, in the morning I'm calling your mother. She's not going to like what she hears."

All the bravado seeps out of Cheever, like a water balloon pricked with a pin.

When Jeff raises his hand, my nod tells him that it's okay to speak. "Mom, this was supposed to be our vacation, too, remember? If you tell Cheever's mother, he'll be grounded for life! Instead of that, what if we make nice with the other tribe? We can sign a peace pact with them."

I think for a moment. "Sure, I can live with that."

Cheever is all smiles again. "Hey, maybe we can smoke a peace pipe to seal the deal! I know where my dad keeps his pot."

"No! And no blood pacts, either. Just sign something and live up to your word. You know, like leaders do in the real world."

For once, I'm glad that none of these kids know their American History, or World History, or PoliSci, for that matter. If they pull off peace and tranquility for the days we have left here, then this truly is a fantasy island.

Jack points in the direction of their bedroom. "Get to bed, all of you."

I wait until their door closes before I burst into tears. "I'm an awful mother."

Jack takes me in his arms. "Don't be so hard on yourself. From what I could see in this place, you've got a lot of competition. They weren't the only kids crawling out of their windows after bedtime."

"But I checked on the boys last night! They were sound asleep in their beds!"

"Apparently not. Jeff confessed that they slipped out every night. They've been sneaking over to Eden Key and looking in the windows."

"What little pervs! I hope Cheever never saw his mother with…Oh, never mind." I fall onto the couch. "And with that crocodile wandering all over the place, too."

"Trust me, one bite of Cheever, and the crocodile would swear off humans forever." Jack falls down beside me.

I lay my head on his shoulder. "Mary also had a rotten night. I shudder to think what would have happened if we hadn't gotten there in time."

Jack's face darkens when he hears this. "'We'? But Aunt Phyllis was here when we came home."

"Lee Chiffray offered to go with me. Certainly I could have handled the creep crawling all over Mary without him. If you're asking me if he went along out of anything other than concern for Mary's safety, I can tell you no."

"I believe you." The edge in his voice tells me differently. "But ask yourself, Donna: Why would he? Why wasn't he back at the Hunt Club with his girlfriend?"

"Because…"—I'm at a loss for words—"because he was concerned. He's a decent guy, Jack."

"Decent guys don't sanction human safaris."

He's got a good point.

Does Lee Chiffray know anything about the Hunt Club's dirty secret? From what I saw tonight, I'm willing to bet no.

Then again, I can't tell you where my kids are at any point in time, so I guess I'm not as smart as I think I am.

When this vacation is over, I need to take a vacation.

16

Trip Insurance

There are certain vacations in which trip insurance is not only necessary, it is mandatory. Here are two such circumstances:

Circumstance #1: If for any reason, you or your traveling companion is going to be ill, or say, meet with an unfortunate fatal accident, then by all means, take out trip insurance —on him;

Circumstance #2: If your testimony put some creep in the gray bar hotel, but he happens to be (a) well connected, (b) well-funded, or (c) soon to be released on parole, I would strongly suggest opting for both trip insurance as well as a life insurance policy that takes into account your loved one's fondness for expensive baubles.

Those of us whose line of work requires covert skullduggery and extensive use of weaponry know that there is no rest for the weary, even on holidays. That said, remember to pack some personal trip insurance, if you catch my drift: say, a nail gun and plastic bullets.

Will it get you through the TSA line? Go ahead and try it! What have you got to lose but your freedom?

Then be sure to write me from your prison cell, so that I know where to send the cake with the file.

~

"ABSOLUTELY NOT," IS RYAN'S ANSWER TO JACK AND MY request to smuggle George Taylor off the island with us. "We don't know who he is, and why he's there, and we couldn't care less. *He is not your mission.* Mandrake and the plague bacteria is your prime directive."

From the glances exchanged by Emma, Arnie, and Abu, I can tell they can't believe what they're hearing, either. Dominic's bet—that Ryan would veto the idea—is a hollow victory for him. Whatever is in the tiny flask he pulls from his tuxedo pocket is downed in one gulp.

"But Ryan, he may be able to help us find Mandrake! He was piloting the flight that took the scientist to Fantasy Island, and they must have talked at some point." I can tell by Jack's tone that he's not taking "No," for an answer.

The same goes for me. "And let's not forget, Ryan, you would have lost a valuable asset—*Jack*—if it weren't for Taylor."

"I'm very aware of that, Donna. I certainly appreciate his role in keeping Jack alive. But I don't think our client would appreciate your interference with the rendition tactics of other friendly nations. It might lead to an international incident."

"How do we know if what Boarke told Donna is true?" Emma asks. "What if those people were abducted specifically for his little shooting gallery?"

"Why don't we get a plane in here and break them out of that dungeon?" Arnie chimes in.

"The reason Boarke mentioned it to Donna in the first

place was to point out that the program had legitimate clients, and so that he could make his case for more financing." The growing irritation in Ryan's voice echoes through the phone.

I start to speak again, but Jack warns me off my soapbox with a pat on my hand. "As far as those 'friendly nations' are concerned, the people in Boarke's basement are already dead and buried. Why not release them?"

Ryan is silent for an eternity. When he finally speaks, his tone is slow but firm. "This is not a debate; the subject is closed. You have your orders."

He doesn't wait for our acknowledgment. His mood is reflected in the loud silence from the now dead phone connection.

"Well, that went well," Jack declares. His gaze moves slowly, catching the eyes of everyone in the room, one by one. Finally he comes to me. He holds out his hand. "I'm in. How about you?"

I nod. "Where thou goest, I shall go."

Even if it's on the lam.

Because once word of this jailbreak gets out, we won't be welcomed in our own country, let alone by any "friendly nation."

I take his hand in mine.

One by one, the others nod. Their hands fall over ours.

When Dominic slaps his down, he exclaims, "Bob's your uncle!"

If and when we ever get out of jail, our dog sitter bill is going to be sky high.

～

"WHERE IS HE?"

A belligerent stranger stands on our front stoop, interrupting my family's lively game of Monopoly, in which my little Scotty dog has just landed in jail.

I take this as a very bad omen.

As for the jerk in front of me, I don't know who the hell he's talking about, let alone who he is—and I certainly don't like his scowl.

"I'm sorry, do I know you?"

"Don't act coy. You were with the dude who almost killed my son last night."

Now I remember this guy. He made the remark about asking the kids to save a joint for him. "I take it, then, your last name is Montrose. Did your son happen to mention that he almost raped my twelve-year-old daughter?"

He shrugs. "Boys will be boys. So he got a little rambunctious."

And mothers will be mothers. If my children weren't on the other side of the door right now, I would have gutted this guy by now.

"I'm happy to tell you, Mr. Montrose, that I haven't seen your son since we yanked him off my daughter. Perhaps he's out molesting another underage girl."

"I saw your daughter. She doesn't look 'twelve' to me."

"Oh? Maybe she looked fourteen, then? Or fifteen? Would you say she looks eighteen?" Now we're standing nose to nose. "At what age is statutory rape okay? She was screaming her head off. If your son hadn't been holding her down against her will, he wouldn't have been roughed up." I'm jabbing his chest so hard that he almost trips as he backs off my porch. "You're lucky that I'm not reporting him to hotel security."

Really, he's lucky I didn't cut off the kid's balls.

"Okay, lady, I get it. He did a stupid thing. Believe me,

both his mother and I gave him an earful about it." There's a catch in his throat. "But that's no reason for something bad to happen to him."

I get it, too. This man is a parent, and he is worried about his child.

Welcome to the club.

"What makes you think something has happened to him?"

"He never came home last night. And his cell phone was found this morning, by the pool. None of his friends have seen him since they left Karen's last night."

I have to admit, I'd be worried too, if I were him. "Mr. Montrose, if I see your son, I'll tell him you're looking for him."

He nods as he shuffles out of the yard.

Jack sticks his head out the window. "Who was that?"

"The father of the boy who was with Mary. His son is AWOL and he's finally acting like a parent."

"Sadly, it's almost time for us to act as spies. We're to meet the others in an hour. Think we can wrap up the game by then?"

The truth is that I don't want to wrap it up. I want to hear my daughter and my son and his friends laugh and squeal and tease each other as they purchase imaginary property, or as they pass *Go* and collect two hundred dollars.

This isn't a game, it's a memory.

They think this is a vacation. I know better.

But for a little more time I can act like I have all the time in the world to spend with them.

That we are just like everyone else.

Then I remember all the people in Boarke's cages and I realize there are more important things in life than board games. Tonight I'm playing a far more important game in which real lives hang in the balance.

Wow, I just pulled a "Get Out of Jail" card. Wish I had one of those in real life.

~

BY THE TIME JACK AND I GET TO HIS SUITE AT THE HUNT CLUB, the rest of the team has assembled—

Except for Dominic. So, what else is new?

"You're tracking him through his videocam contact lenses, right? Where is he, in the lounge?" I ask Arnie.

"Nope, he's certainly not there, unless they've installed beds and naked blondes behind the bar."

I didn't save his ass from a crocodile to put up with more of his shenanigans. "I'll be right back," I say as I head out the door.

He's one floor up. When I knock, I have to wait a few minutes, so I knock again.

He opens the door wearing a robe, and nothing else. He's disappointed to see me. "I was expecting tea and crumpets."

"And I was expecting you to join us for recon, so get rid of the strumpet—*now*."

"Dominic, is that the champagne and cookies? Darling, think of where those crumbs will end up—"

I know that voice...

Babette?

I push past him, into the bedroom.

It's Babette, alright. Her arms are handcuffed to the bedposts, and her naughty bits are dotted with whipped cream.

In unison we shout, "What are you doing here?"

"You're supposed to be back in Hilldale!" Her retort is an

accusation—of what, I don't know. Does she think I'm spying on her? Hardly.

"And you're supposed to be at some beach house," I shoot back.

"We are! We're staying in my boyfriend's private villa," she says smugly.

"Is that so?" I glance into the bathroom. "Is he here, too?"

"No, of course not! He's at another one of his interminable business meetings. Or he's gambling." She shrugs. "At least he wins. Of course, they have to let him, since Lee practically owns this place."

"Wait—did you say 'Lee'? As in Chiffray?"

Her eyes narrow suspiciously. "How do you know Lee?"

I'd forgotten how jealous Babette can be. Nonchalantly I shake my head. "Through…my husband. He's here on business, with Mr. Boarke."

She smirks. "Let me guess. Boarke wants him to buy out Lee before the balloon loan comes due. Ha! Fat chance that'll happen! This place—well, not the kiddie camp, but certainly the Hunt Club—is a cash cow. Lee is willing to extend the note—for a few small concessions. He's made this perfectly clear to Boarke's little tart, Julie."

"How do you know that, my love?" Dominic asks as he dots the tip of her nose with whipped cream before putting two cream covered fingers in her mouth, which she sucks on with relish. Babette is a size zero, so she can afford the extra calories.

She grimaces. "Because Lee's got the audacity to take business calls while we make love."

"Wow," I murmur. "That's just…*sad.*"

"Who are you to judge me?" Babette kicks a pillow in my direction. "Look, I admit it, I'm high maintenance and I come with a large overhead. So yes, I'll get lost—if the price is right." She bats her eyes at Dominic. "But I never pout. I prefer to get even."

These two deserve each other—and any STDs that come with their idea of fun and games. "While you're 'getting even,' who is minding Janie and Trisha?"

Babette shrugs. "That odious Julie person—supposedly. Janie claims she spends most of her time following Lee around, like an eager little puppy. And once she caught the odious hussy in my bedroom. No surprise *there*." Jonah Breck's widow is quite familiar with the sexual peccadilloes of power rangers. "So do you mind? We're getting ready for high tea."

I pull Dominic off the bed and nudge him back into the living room with me. "Keep her busy for the next hour or two. And by the way, you're disgusting."

He chuckles as if I just charmed him with a clever *bon mot*. "*My dear*, I'm only following your orders—to get as close to Chiffray as I can." He nods toward the bedroom. "I can't get any closer, now can I? Unless the old boy is into three-ways."

He has a point.

"By the way," he continues, "Babette babbled on about something that has to do with Chiffray approving a new ventilation system for the resorts. They are testing it in one of the smaller auditoriums connected to the Hunt Club—tomorrow, in fact."

"Oh, damn! Boarke must have gotten his hands on Mandrake's plague bacteria. My guess is that it will be tested on the human livestock."

I grab my cell phone and text Arnie and Abu, so that they can monitor the air flowing throughout the Hunt Club over the next twenty-four hours.

"What are you two doing in there?" Babette shouts from

the bedroom. "Dominic, I've forgotten my safety word. What is it again?"

"Darling, I've told you a million times—it's '*slapper*.'" He turns to me and mutters, "English must be a second language to you Americans."

"In her defense, her math skills are excellent. Next time just hand her a fifty-pound note and she'll remember anything you tell her with no problem."

"Yes, I've no doubt." He pauses, and then leans into me, his eyes filled with soulful lust. "Donna, please know that these little trifles are conducted strictly in the line of duty."

"Of course, Dominic. Not to worry. There is no way in which I could think any worse of you than I already do."

He sighs with relief.

What a dumbass.

My next stop is Lee Chiffray's villa. I need to hug my baby.

In fact, I want Trisha to come home with me. The last person I'd trust to look after her is Julie.

Babette is a very close second.

One way or another, this mission ends tonight.

17

Couples Retreat

If you long for a getaway with your main squeeze—alone, just the two of you—by all means you should take what the hospitality industry euphemistically calls a "couples retreat." The best of these live up to the name if:

1: Its accommodations are both romantic and secluded. No one should be within sight, or for that matter, yelling distance. If so, don't shout out your safety word, just mime it.

2: A tub large enough for two is a must! Jacuzzi bubbles may make it harder to see your lover's naughty bits, but a generous capacity allows for lots of Kama Sutra moves. (Suggestion: Avoid positions in which someone's head has to hang below the water line, unless the other partner is certified in mouth-to-mouth resuscitation); and

3: Aromatherapy accoutrements are bountiful. This is especially important if the resort is next to a slaughterhouse, or a toxic waste dump. And of course the more fragrant the candles, the better, so make sure these are plentiful as well. (Suggestion: request a fire extinguisher, just in case your bedroom gymnastics include floor exercises worthy of an Olympic gold medal.)

DESPITE ITS SIZE, LEE CHIFFRAY'S VILLA IS NOT EASY TO FIND. IT doesn't appear on any of the resorts maps. Finally, Arnie spots it on satellite image of the island, sitting all on its lonesome on a secluded crescent of beach dotted with tall dunes, just beyond the Hunt Club. It is accessible only by a narrow road that zigzags over a cliff.

The manservant who answers the villa's stately front door barely nods at my request to see Trisha, declaring, "Little missy is on the beach."

Behind him, I hear Lee and Julie arguing.

Interesting.

I saunter in before the manservant can close the door on me. I follow the sound of their angry voices into a large living room decorated in nautical hues. Smiling sweetly, I declare, "*Yoo-hoo!*"

Lee and Julie freeze to stare at me. I can just imagine what they're thinking: *Did she hear our conversation?*

Okay, yes, but only the part where Julie said, "We've had a better offer from a French bank," and Lee retorted, "It's bogus! And besides, my deal with Boarke allows me to match any offers. I'm doing so now, whether he likes it or not."

"I'm not interrupting anything, I hope." I'm sure I sound sincere.

"No, not at all," they say together.

I'm glad I'm not standing between them, because the angry looks they exchange would incinerate a snow man, let alone little old me.

"Lee, talk about a small world! I ran into your fiancée, Babette Breck, in the Hunt Club boutique. She happens to be my neighbor, back in Hilldale. And my daughter is your guest, here in the villa. She's Janie's friend, Trisha."

His eyes narrow at this newfound knowledge. "Yes, I see the resemblance now. Trisha is adorable, too."

"Why, thank you." I take a trick out of Julie's book and bat my eyelashes as if I've awakened from a coma.

"Really?" Julie's frown only deepens. "Trisha doesn't look anything like Mr. Stone."

I notice that Lee also winces when she says this. Seems as if we're on the same page about this woman.

Taking his cue, I ignore her and address him alone. "I'll be taking Trisha now, for the rest of our stay. Where is she?"

"Playing on the beach," Julie interjects.

I stare at her. "You mean, the girls aren't here with you? But Babette told me you were babysitting them."

"Well…we…I…" For once Julie's stutter is genuine. "I was summoned by Mr. Chiffray to talk business while Janie is taking a horseback lesson. Trisha insisted that she go to the beach."

"What? No adult supervision?" I'm sure they hear the frustration in my voice. Lee knows I've been through this drill all too recently.

In a place where a pilot, a flight attendant and a scientist can disappear without a trace—not to mention all the single women Connor Reems was basting before chomping—it would be nice to have *some* accountability when it comes to a child who is not yet six.

"In fact, we can see Trisha from here." Julie waves her arm toward the wide French windows.

My heart swells to see my daughter bobbing in and out of the tall sand dunes and reeds.

Still, I shake my head in awe at Julie's audacity. I mean, come on! If anyone knows about the dangers lurking around this place, it should be her. "And what about this pirate? Trisha mentioned some counselor dressed up as one, who sometimes plays with her. You know—eye patch, peg leg, that sort of thing?"

Julie stares at me as if I'm daft. "I...I don't know what you're talking about!" She turns to Lee. "Mr. Chiffray, I promise you there hasn't been anyone else—certainly no unsanctioned employees—anywhere near your villa!"

Lee's face is as blank as it was when he was riding high at the baccarat table. Finally he smiles. "Julie, of course you wouldn't allow anyone to impede on my privacy, or that of my guests. Donna, it sounds as if Trisha has quite an active imagination."

Yes, I've seen it firsthand. At the same time, the pirate sounded so real in her texts.

The perplexed look on my face prompts Lee to add, "Perhaps she's a bit bored, here with Babette and Janie. I'm sure she'll welcome you with open arms. Oh, and don't worry about Trisha's things. The servants will have them waiting for you at the door. I'm sure we'll catch up again, back in Hilldale. Babette and I have such great chemistry."

Here's hoping he never finds out about her physical combustions with Dominic.

I have no more excuses for small talk, so I bow out through the French doors.

Now that he's taken away my opportunity to get back into the villa, I only wish I'd thought about having Arnie bug Lee's digs when we first realized the importance of his relationship with Boarke. The intel gathered would have shed a movie-premiere-sized spotlight on what we came here to find. More importantly, we might have wrapped up this mission, and I would have been reunited with Trisha even sooner.

Stupid me! Maybe I'm not cut out to be a mission leader after all. So much for wanting it all.

∼

My little girl turns cartwheels on the beach, right at the water's edge. The sun has bleached her hair almost white, and has burnished her skin to the color of golden raisins. When the surf sneaks up so close that it tickles her feet, she giggles and skips over sand that is as soft and powdery as flour sprinkled with white sugar.

I wish I could watch her play like this all day long.

But I can't—not if we're to save a hundred people from a cruel death.

She sees me before I have a chance to call out to her. "Mommy! Mommy is here," she cries as she flies across the high dunes and into my arms.

I hold her tight for as long as I can. Sheer joy has me dancing around in circles with her in my arms. The centrifugal force from my speed pulls her away, as if she's floating through the air. Her giggles are infectious. Finally, I collapse on the warm, dry sand with her on top of me.

We lay there together until the pulse of her heart mirrors mine.

This is life as it should be.

Gently I sit up, cuddling her in my arms. "Come on, sweetie. Jeff and Mary and Daddy and Aunt Phyllis are here, too. We have a bungalow at Kamp KidStuff. There are lots of fun things to do there."

But when I stand up, Trisha plops into the sand and her smile fades. "But—we can't go yet, Mommy! I'm on my way to see the pirate *now*. He's going to give me another treasure!"

I try not to laugh. "Maybe he'll bring it to you at Kamp KidStuff."

Trisha shakes her head adamantly. "He can't go anywhere. He has to stay in his cave. He's afraid they'll find him again, and put him back in the brig. Mommy, did you know 'brig' is another word for jail?"

Jail—

The livestock room.

"Trisha, did he tell you where they keep this jail?"

She squints and nods. "He says it's in a big building where there are hunters and guns."

"Where is his cave?" I try to keep my voice from sounding anxious.

"Down there, beneath the keyhole." She points down the beach. About a half-mile away, a large rock formation juts out into the surf. The wind has beaten away enough of the cliff to create a perfect hole below the ledge.

"What if I take you there now, before we go?"

"Thank you, Mommy! I'd like that." She picks up her things—tiny flip-flops, and a rope necklace lined with shells of all sizes—and hands them to me. I put them in my beach bag. Then she grabs my hand and pulls me with her along the beach.

The water rolls in and around our feet, as if it wants to pull us back to where we came from.

There is no going back now.

EVEN BEFORE WE REACH THE KEYHOLE ROCK, WE SEE HIM SITTING in front of one of the dunes, as if he doesn't have a care in the world.

He doesn't move when he sees us coming, but his smile disappears.

When we are a few yards away, he stands, shielding his eyes from the bright sun.

He truly has a peg leg. Strips of white linen cover a stump ending at his ankle. A cane gives him the ballast needed to stand up.

"Ah, my little buccaneer has come to visit me! And she's brought a friend."

Before I can stop her, Trisha runs over to him. "This is my mother. She likes pirates, too." She holds out her hand, which has three unbroken sand dollars. "I have this to swap for a treasure."

He pulls a small speckled conch shell from beneath his tattered white vest. There is a hole where he has ripped off the numbered badge, exposing his nipple and chest hair, which is already graying.

"Hold it up to your ear, and you'll hear the sea," he says to Trisha.

She does as she's told. But she must not get the analogy, because she shakes it hard and exclaims, "I hear whistling."

When he laughs at her, she joins in.

His smile disappears when he bends down over his cane so that they are face to face. "Hold tight to this shell. It's very special. Someday it will whisper to you where I've hidden the treasure."

"I cross my heart," she says solemnly.

Her hug catches him off guard. To keep his balance, he has to hold on tight. Not that he minds this. He closes his eyes. His smile expresses his bliss.

But when he opens his eyes again, sadness is reflected in them.

"I hope we find the treasure before we go home. If we don't, Mommy says you can visit whenever you want and bring the treasure with you. Can I go into your cave and play?"

He sweeps his hand toward the rock. *"Mi casa, su casa."*

Trisha runs around the rock formation to the other side, conch shell in hand.

The pirate and I are left staring at each other.

Between his size, his age, and the missing leg below his knee, assuaging my curiosity is worth a stab in the dark. I hold out my hand. "Doctor Mandrake, I presume?"

He pauses before giving me a resigned nod. "Yes, guilty as charged. And who are you?"

"It doesn't matter." I shrug. "What does matter is that your country wants you back, no questions asked—that is, if you still have the plague bacteria samples with you."

"Ah, I see." His eyes open wide at the thought. "Rest assured they are in a very safe place. As for any forgiveness on the part of my employer, to what do I owe this generosity of spirit?"

"Your timing, I suppose. When it comes to covert affairs, no news is good news. With all the so-called whistle-blowing and leaking of state secrets in the news, the Department of Defense would rather let bygones be bygones, as it were."

His mouth opens in surprise. "Uncle Sam is willing to pretend this never happened?"

"Yes—if you return the samples, and are willing to come back to work. Think of it as history repeating itself. After World War II, Germany's scientists were forgiven even worse indiscretions, as I recall." I let that sink in for a moment. "Pardon me, but I have to ask, why did you take the research with you in the first place?"

"Out of pride, I guess." He raises his lips into a mirthless smile. "Just when I'd successfully completed my research on a vaccine for a pneumonic plague bacteria, our government's latest round of budget cuts were announced. It was obvious that my project was to be put on hold, despite the Department of Defense's knowledge of the advances coming out of Russia and China in this particularly horrendous form of warfare."

He stares out at the ocean, as if looking for his next words in its still blue waters. Then he sighs. "A private entity offered me the world—money, power and most importantly, solace. All I had to do was give them the vaccine. The organization is well funded, and its representative talks a good game, going so far as to promise free worldwide distribution of the vaccine. Publicity regarding the vaccine would render the plague bacteria obsolete in warfare, and it would certainly have put me in contention for the Nobel Prize. Needless to say, I was tempted—but not by the money, or the professional prestige." He turns back to face me. "I'm tired of pork barrel politics. Defense doesn't come with the annihilation of our enemies. Such attacks only breed contempt and revenge. True defense is about the protection of our citizens. But for the right price, our so-called leaders would readily trade research that may save lives for yet another battalion of obsolete weaponry."

No arguments there. I lean back into a sand dune. "Who is the interested party?"

"A group that goes by the name of 'the Quorum.'"

Why am I not surprised?

"My lab was to be here, on Fantasy Island," Mandrake continues. "But I refused to use the 'lab rats' they provided me."

I nod. "That's certainly to your credit. I've seen the stockyard." I point down to his bandaged ankle. "What happened to your foot?"

"My change of heart got me downgraded from a suite in the Hunt Club to the stockyard. Luckily, a day later I was put out in the wild. I may have eluded my hunter, but I ran into a very hungry crocodile." He shrugs. "I owe my life to another escapee. He knew enough first aid to wrap what was left of his prison garb around the wound, along with some healing herbs."

"Was he the pilot from your flight down here?"

"Yes! How did you guess?"

"He was a good Samaritan on my behalf, too."

He shakes his head in wonder. "How did you find me?"

"Unbeknownst to you, your colonoscopy gave Uncle Sam a chance to tag you." It's my turn to laugh. "We've been following around the croc, thinking it was you."

"So, my little friend didn't lead you to me?"

"No, not at all. She kept her word to you." What good would it do to divulge Trisha's indiscreet texts? I'd prefer her pirate remember her as fondly as she will remember him.

"That's good to know. Her pilfering on my behalf relieved me of a monotonous diet of fish and tropical fruit. Of course, I knew eventually she'd be leaving the island."

"Now you'll be leaving, too."

His grin fades. "I think I owe it to my fellow prisoners to ask: can you interfere on behalf of the Hunt Club's human targets?"

"That is my goal—but in all honesty, I'm not sure if we can pull it off."

"Ah, I see that you are a kindred soul regarding the conundrum of protocol versus conscience. You do your daughter justice."

"Dr. Mandrake, is Boarke your Quorum contact?"

"Boarke? No! He's a fool—just a yes man and a property

overseer—and not even that, unless he can buy out the note on the island. He let it be known that he's talking to a money man or two." Mandrake chuckles at the thought. "From what I can tell, the power behind the throne is—"

His sudden gasp and the appearance of a tiny bullet hole at the middle of his neck occurs just a moment before Mandrake collapses face down into the sand.

Instinctively, I duck and roll between two sand dunes.

Oh my God! Where is Trisha?

In the pirate's cave.

I scramble on all fours around the rock formation, looking for some opening in the craggy cliff. Finally I find one. It's low to the ground, just a sliver wedged between fallen boulders.

The cave is dark, and larger than I would have imagined. I hear Trisha singing softly to herself.

"Trisha? Where are you?" I'm trying my best not to sound frightened.

She runs over to me. "Mommy, I think I found the pirate's treasure chest!"

Oh, no, oh God. Has she touched the plague samples?

My heart beats like a jackhammer. *Stay calm.* "Really? Let me see, too."

"Won't he mind?" She looks toward the mouth of the cave.

If she runs out there, how will I keep her from seeing Mandrake's body?

For that matter, how will I get out of this cave without getting us both killed? By now the shooter will be coming this way.

"Wait! Trisha, the pirate is gone. He had to…to go home."

"For good?" Her tiny brow furrows.

"Yes, honey. He is already far away."

"Oh." She looks around warily. "Does that mean the game is over, and I get to keep the treasure?"

"Yes. In fact, he asked that I tell you how lucky you are."

Her eyes light up. She walks over to a stone beside the far wall. With both hands, she shoves it to one side, revealing a sealed aluminum cylinder, about six inches in radius but only two inches deep.

I wonder how many Petri dishes it holds--two, maybe three at the most.

"I'll carry it," I say matter-of-factly. She hands it over, and I slip it into my beach bag. "Now Trisha, we have to go back to Janie's villa, to get your things. We have to remember to keep our promise regarding his secret treasure, okay?"

She frowns. "Mommy, you're so silly. I'm great at secrets! Not even Janie knows about the pirate."

I kiss her forehead. Clutching her hand, I murmur, "Okay sweetheart, here we go."

As I start out for the cave opening, she squeezes my hand and says, "Not that way, Mommy."

The next thing I know, Trisha is pulling me to the back of the cave—really, through another small opening. We walk through several rooms. Some are a tight fit, others are at least tall enough for me to stand upright. The glimmer of light emanating over our heads indicates that we're walking in a beeline through the narrowest part of the cliff—

And onto a different part of the beach.

I'm tempted to run, to carry her all the way to our bungalow.

But no. Whoever took out Mandrake was a crack shot—a description fitting both Julie and Lee.

If one of them is involved and we don't come back, it will be too suspicious.

We have to go back to the villa, to get Trisha's things.

THE MANSERVANT DOESN'T SMILE AS HE OPENS THE DOOR. THIS alone would give me the creeps, except for the fact that I've been here before, so I know it's just part of his charm.

As promised, her little suitcase and the matching little round hat bag containing her favorite stuffed animals are all in the front hall, waiting for us.

The place is silent. Both Julie and Lee are nowhere to be found. A part of me hopes Babette is right and that they're upstairs in the master suite, exchanging bodily fluids even as they negotiate loan terms, but I doubt that. From what I could tell, Lee could barely stomach her.

I'm almost afraid to ask, but since it may shed light on Mandrake's killer, I know I have to. "Excuse me, we're leaving now. I'd like to say goodbye to Mr. Chiffray."

"The master and Miss Julie aren't here at the moment."

I'm both relieved and concerned. Was one of them Mandrake's killer?

The sooner we get out of here, the better.

I grab everything and am just about to hustle Trisha out the door when we hear Janie's petulant plea, "No, Mrs. Stone! You can't take Trisha away!"

Janie flies down the stairs. But when Trisha wraps her arms around her little friend's waist, she's rewarded with a pout. "Why do you want to leave?"

Caught between the desire to come with me and her loyalty to her bestie, Trisha turns to me and asks, "Can Janie come, too?"

"Sorry, honey, no. I don't think her mother would want to part with her."

"Donna? Is that you?" Babette's voice floats down from the balcony.

I look up to see her standing there, in a robe. Her hair is slicked back—not with whipped cream, I hope.

I stifle the urge to wave with only my middle finger. "Ah, Babette! No longer tied up, I see."

She rewards my pun with a frown before swatting it away with the wave of her hand. "Did I hear Trisha ask if it were alright if Janie joined you on your flight home?"

"Yes…Well, no…"

"By all means, of course it's okay! In fact, her suitcase is already packed." Babette motions for the manservant to point it out to me.

Four tiny Louis Vuitton bags are stacked at the foot of the stairwell.

I can see it now: Janie, the Terrible Two, Aunt Phyllis, my Acme Team, and the Family Stone—

Oh, and let's not forget a hundred or so political prisoners, if we can get them out of this Godforsaken place.

I smile up at Babette. "Sure! What's one more?"

"Exactly! You know what they say, 'one good turn deserves another.' As much as we love hosting Trisha, it's time for a little quid pro quo, don't you think? Lee and I could certainly use some time, just the two of us."

I'm tempted to tell her how disappointed I'm sure Dominic would be, but I think better of it. Time's a-wastin'.

"By the way, Janie has a tendency toward air sickness, so do have one of those little bags handy!" Babette throws kisses down the stairs, even as she heads back down the hall toward the master suite.

"You're welcome," I mutter under my breath.

"My mommy's kisses taste sweet, like whipped cream," Janie says wistfully.

Good God, I hope she never finds out why.

As I take her bags, everything else slips out of my hand. I

sigh as I stack everything as best as I can, then I nudge the girls out the door with me.

On the way back to the bungalow, all I can think about is how to break the news to Ryan about Mandrake's death.

~

I AM AWAKENED BY THE SOFT BUZZ OF MY CELL PHONE. THE call is from "00 BRILLIANT," which is Dominic's contact ID.

Jack turns over. His subconscious refuses to acknowledge his frenemy.

Unfortunately, as mission leader I don't have the luxury of ignoring him. "This better be good," I mutter.

"*Comme ci, comme ça*, milady." He sighs mightily. "The good news: mission accomplished on accessing Julie's key."

I sit up straight in bed. "Bravo, Dominic! How did you do it?"

"She took it off when she joined me in the shower, which allowed Emma to play chambermaid. She snuck into the room and did a 3D scan of the key—although neither of them was thrilled with my suggestion that Emma join us for a wet and wild *ménage á trios*."

"I can only imagine."

"However, Emma—sly little minx, that one!—also read through the text messages on Julie's iPhone. Alas, one that stood out to her read, 'Mandrake samples found. Test set for 2230.'"

In other words, ten-thirty tonight—while Jack and I are on safari.

"But…but that can't be! I retrieved the samples myself!" I jump out of bed and scurry around the room for my beach bag. When I don't see it, I run into the living room.

No, it's not there, either.

Nor is it in Trisha and Janie's sleeping alcove.

Oh, hell. I left it in Lee and Babette's villa.

Stupid stupid me.

"Dominic, did Emma notice if the message was sent or received by Julie?"

"I asked the same thing. Unfortunately Julie and my shower shenanigans so unnerved our poor innocent Emma that she forgot to take notice of the sender and the recipient."

In other words, it could have been either Julie or Lee who found the samples in my beach bag.

The duplicate key gets us into the livestock room. Here's hoping we can get out before Boarke has a chance to run his test.

18

Last Minute Packing

Nothing is more nerve-wracking in the travel experience than the rush of last minute packing. To avoid the inevitable craziness that happens when you find yourself in a time crunch, follow these three simple steps:

First, The "Oh my God, I have nothing to wear" moment should never come within twelve hours of departure. It invites wardrobe meltdowns, and that heart-shattering moment when you realize that in your haste you made all the wrong choices. Granny panties are not in keeping with your plans for a naughty weekend rendezvous, and that too tight, too short bandage dress is not what you want to wear the first time you're meeting his beloved grandparents. The experienced traveler starts trolling her closet at least 72-hours before takeoff.

Second, shopping for clothes at a resort is like food shopping at a movie theater: you're what retailers call "a desperate customer." You'll pay double for items you'd pass up at your local mall without a second thought—including that tee-shirt that proclaims "If the Voices in My Head Don't Shut Up, I'm Going to Have to Poke Them with a Q-Tip."

Third, on a mission where you might encounter a variety of unexpected nastiness, don't just pack heat. Instead, open yourself up to an array of sophisticated weaponry! If you think a snub nose .38 will keep you safe on an island filled with dangerous creatures (both human and otherwise), think again.

Granted, packing an arsenal can be complicated, so consider false bottom suitcases with x-ray proof lining. And yes, cough up the extra money for those stupid baggage fees. There's no hope of getting a Beretta Tomcat past a TSA officer, so check your bags and suck it up.

~

"YOU KNOW I RARELY STICK MY NOSE WHERE IT'S NOT wanted—"

Aunt Phyllis' preface is outrageous, and we both know it. But because the safari takes place in less than an hour, now is not the time to run down every instance that contradicts her claim. Instead, I'll pretend I haven't spent my whole life dodging her cockamamie advice. "And you know I've always appreciated you for that."

My aunt starts again. "Hon, I'm worried about you."

Frankly, I don't think we would be having this conversation right now if she hadn't walked in on me strapping a Beretta Tomcat to the small of my back.

Thank goodness she didn't see me hiding that switchblade in my boot.

Or the grenade in my bra.

"Thanks for your concern, Aunt Phyllis. But I'll be just fine. In fact, we all will, if you follow our directions to a tee."

"Yes, yes I know. Get the kids to the airstrip no later than nine forty-five. We're not to order a tram, but carry our luggage ourselves. No one is to see or hear us depart from the resort. We're to leave all the lights on in this joint, as well as the TV, but we're to close the drapes. When we get on the tarmac, we're to look for the plane, but we don't go near it until we see some flashes, two series of two. Then Mary is to answer it by clicking her iPhone flashlight app on and off three times before we proceed to board."

She pauses for my approval. She gets my thumbs-up.

A Fantasy Island plane arrived an hour ago. It is already fueled and ready for the morning's departure.

Unfortunately, passengers booked to leave on it will have a very long delay, because it's our ticket out of here tonight.

Aunt Phyllis hesitates then adds, "Donna dear, a lot of families are having difficulties these days, making ends meet. Granted, having a loved one with a gambling problem makes it just that much harder—"

Oh no. Is this Aunt Phyllis's way of telling me that she's in over her head at the Hunt Club poker table?

"Say no more, Aunt Phyllis." I sigh. "You can imagine how upset I am."

She nods solemnly.

"Not to mention, disappointed."

"I don't blame you in the least. You have every right to be."

"So, how much?"

She stares at me, then stutters, "I wouldn't dare to guess!"

I wince. "Ten thousand?"

She plops down on the bed, shaking her head. "Honey, you know me better than that. I'm not good at guessing games."

"Twenty…thirty thousand?" I close my eyes at the thought.

"Jesus, Mary and Joseph! It's worse than I thought!"

She's telling me.

I sit down beside her. "Tonight, I'll…I'll do what I can to scrape together the cash, but…well, I may have to borrow some of it."

"I guess I can dip into my savings," she whispers.

I shake my head adamantly. "No, never. You've always been there for me. Now it's my time to be here, for you."

I pull out my very last Acme check. Ryan will hit the roof, but I'll work something out. He can dock my pay for the next few hits, or something. I'll even throw in a pie or two, to seal the deal. How can he say no to my apple rhubarb?

I write out the check with a flourish, to CASH. "Here, take it. But Aunt Phyllis, I hope you realize I can't be bailing you out all the time—"

"What do you mean, 'bailing *me* out'? I was talking about your husband! Isn't this"—she points to the check—"for his debts?"

"His debts? Why do you think he owes anyone anything?"

"Well…" she's at a loss for words. "Because he's never here! He's always at the Hunt Club with that woman who manages the finances at the casino, that 'Miss Julie.'" She curls her fingers into quote marks as she spits out Julie's name. "And isn't it the reason we're sneaking out of here like thieves, in the middle of the night?"

"No! He doesn't even gamble! He's meeting with Julie because his bank may be financing the resorts, not because he owes her anything."

My aunt smiles. "Well now, that's a relief! I thought he was paying off his debt with…well, you know, services rendered."

"Rest assured he's not rendering anything to anyone other than me."

"Then tell me again, why the heck are we sneaking out in the middle of the night?"

Oh boy, how should I answer this? "We…we got a very special rate on a chartered red-eye flight. But it's first come, first served. Since there's so many of us—well, you know how it is."

Aunt Phyllis waves me away. "Say no more! But quite frankly I'd be surprised anyone would ever want to leave this paradise."

If only she knew.

She glances at my back. "One more question. Why are you packing heat?"

"We're going on a safari, remember? I don't want to run out of bullets."

She's about to stuff the check in her bra, but I snatch it out of her hand and tear it up. "See you in a few hours. Just be on time."

"I DON'T GET IT. WHY AREN'T WE SEEING THE STOCKYARD ROOM via the Hunt Club's security videos?" I lean over Arnie's shoulder in the hope that seeing the screen on his computer will help clear up my concern.

He shakes his head. "It must have its own feed. I'll scan all the satellite downlinks into the island. Unfortunately, that may take a while."

"We don't have 'a while.' They release the plague bacteria at ten-thirty, in order to test the antidote. If you're going to open those cages, it's got to happen between nine forty-five and ten fifteen."

In just a few minutes, Jack and I must leave to meet Battoo in the Safari staging area. If all goes well, Arnie will have tapped into the livestock room's security system, so that on our command he can (a) put all guard station security monitors on a loop; (b) lock the air vents; (c) open all the cages; (d) and via the intercom, command the prisoners to run out to the plane via the secret tunnel between the Hunt Club and the Fantasy Island airstrip.

Abu, Emma, and Dominic will be there in the tunnel to lead the way.

Between Jack and George of the Jungle, we'll be onboard and have wheels up by 22:20.

Well, a girl can dream, can't she?

Jack takes my hand. "We'd better get going. Don't worry, boss lady. Emma and Arnie can start cross-referencing every ComSat signal hitting the island. They'll have it done long before you give them the order to get this show on the road."

Emma's fingers are now flying across her computer keyboard. Arnie's are also moving at warp speed. Still, I have to temper Jack's bravado with Arnie's double-take. It doesn't help when he gives Jack a sidelong glance and mouths, *Are you crazy?*

Here's hoping he's not.

One hundred and thirteen lives depend on it.

As instructed, we get to the safari staging room at ten minutes to eight.

Battoo is nowhere to be found.

"Ah, there you are, Mrs. Stone!" Julie's cheery hello, coming from behind me, sends a shiver up my spine.

What the hell is she doing here?

I cover my concern with an air kiss. "We were under the impression that Battoo was to be our guide."

She opens her arms in mock exasperation. "He's tied up at the moment."

In this place, that is never a good thing.

She motions toward the gun room. "Shall we get started? Feel free to pick out any gun you like."

When we enter, there is no one else there—not even Abu, who is supposed to be working tonight.

Strange.

Jack and I scan the gun racks until we find rifles to our liking. For him, it's a 45.70 Marlin, while I choose a Ruger 1B and hope that I don't have to use it.

She takes our guns. "Here, let me load them for you."

She walks down the counter until she finds the right bullet drawers. In no time at all she's loaded both guns. She hands them to us, along with two hunting vests. "Safety first," she purrs.

Her next task is to choose a gun for herself—a Marlin 338MX. "Ah, here's my baby!" She kisses each bullet before loading them into her gun.

Jack and I exchange glances. "Then you'll be joining us, I take it?"

She nods. "I wouldn't be much of a guide if I didn't have your backs, now would I?"

I won't let her get anywhere near my back. Or Jack's for that matter.

She better watch her own.

"AH, THERE'S YOUR PREY!" JULIE POINTS THROUGH THE thicket.

She's right. George kneels, gasping. He's put on a good show. We've finally cornered him in a marsh just a few hundred yards from the beach.

He's been running for the past half hour, but we're never more than one hundred yards behind him. This may have something to do with the fact that the medallion on his shirt is really a tracker, plus his tunic and pants are dyed with something that glows so that it can be seen, with or without our night goggles.

Not to mention that if the pygmies find him first, their darts, tainted with a sedative, will slow him down, Julie explained so matter-of-factly. To top it off, George hasn't been fed all day. "We find that a hungry prey is less challenging to track." She patted Jack's arm. "We aim to please."

In other words, this isn't a safari. It's a shooting gallery.

Like me, Jack has had enough of this. Neither of us is planning on shooting George.

Not that Julie knows this.

In truth, she should worry about herself.

Jack lifts his hand, indicating that he'll go in first, and that we're to stay back here, behind the brush.

I nod, but Julie starts after him. I grab her arm. "The kill is supposed to be his, remember?"

"The hunter has to be in view of his guide at all times. It's Hunt Club protocol."

The shot from Jack's gun is loud. Birds screech and scatter in the skies.

Julie looks at George's GPS signal on her cell phone screen. It isn't moving. "Well, well, well! Your husband should be congratulated. He's had his first kill."

I look down at the screen, too. Suddenly I hear Arnie's voice in my earbud. "We're in...sort of!"

"What does that mean?" I say under my breath.

Julie looks up and smirks. "What do you think it means? The prey is dead."

Suddenly I realize she thought I was talking to her. "Oh!...Well, of course, it would be. He loves to hunt—deer, bison, elk, big game—"

The dot on her cell screen is moving again.

She sees it, too.

Her reaction is faster than mine. She breaks the grip on my rifle by slamming the butt of her gun into my gut.

As I double over, she prods me upright with her rifle.

"But he won't shoot an innocent man." She laughs. "It's all the proof we needed that neither of you are who you pretend to be. Congratulations on finding Dr. Mandrake, Mrs. Stone. We certainly appreciate you leading us to your daughter's imaginary pirate. But what stupidity, leaving the bacteria samples in Mr. Chiffray's foyer!"

Her jibe hits its mark. When I wince, she laughs. "Let's see, how can I earn back your husband's sympathy after I kill you?" She fakes a look of innocent shock. "Oops, I tripped and fell, and my gun went off! Too bad it shot poor old Donna in the back."

How dare she call me old! I've got four years on her, at the most.

Okay, maybe six.

She takes a step back, raises her gun, and puts me in her sights.

The bang is even more deafening than Jack's shot.

I wait for the bullet—

But I don't go down.

When I turn around, she's staring at me. She may be stunned, but she's knows an angry woman when she sees one. She shoots again—

Again, the bang is loud.

I flinch again—

And yet, I'm still standing.

Abu's voice comes in over my earbud. "Hey, I don't know if I mentioned this, but this afternoon I changed out all the bullets in the gun room with ones that are blanks. Got to love FedEx when it absolutely, positively has to be there on time. Even here on Fantasy Island, they got those blanks here in a twenty-four hour turnaround."

Now he tells me.

With a flick of my wrist, my knife is out of my boot.

It finds its mark in her thigh.

But only because I want to take her alive. We've got a few questions about the Quorum that need answered.

Julie screams and clutches the knife. She tugs gingerly, but it is buried too deeply in muscle.

She stumbles backward, into a murky pond. With only one leg to stand on, she falls backward.

The marsh seems to suck her down. She tries to raise her arms over her head, but she can't. It's as if they are stuck in the muck.

She must be in quicksand.

And she's sinking fast. The more she struggles, the quicker she sinks. In no time at all it is over her chest, then up to her neck. "I…I can't get out! I can't move! I—"

She gulps and gasps as the guck fills her mouth.

By the time Jack and George reach me, she's in over her head.

"Where did she go?" George wonders.

I point to the quicksand pit.

When Jack sees me, he grabs me in a hug, as if he'll never let me go.

But he has to, and we both know it. We still have a lot of work to do.

We've got to get to the prisoners before it's too late.

"I never gave you a proper thank you," I say to George as I give him a hug.

Then I strip him out of his tunic. His broad shoulders glimmer with the sweat that comes from running for your life.

Jack looks from me to George and back again. "Um… what the hell are you doing?"

"The emblem on his tunic has a built in tracking device," I explain. "Abu and Dominic, are you listening? Just in case all the prisoners are being tracked, please make sure to cut the emblems off their tunics. Have the prisoners leave them in their cages."

"We're already aware of this, milady," Dominic's voice can be heard on our earbuds. "Battoo warned us. In fact, he's one of those being released. Julie caught him neutralizing the sedative used in the pygmy darts."

I'm glad to hear he's getting off this cursed rock as well.

I turn to George. "You were one of the Fantasy Air pilots, weren't you?"

He nods. "Jack told me you deduced I'd flown Mandrake to the island, on one of Fantasy Air's smaller jets. The Quorum didn't realize I had the guest compartment's surveillance system engaged, and was listening in on their pitch to Mandrake. Laura, the attendant on the flight, heard it, too. When Mandrake never made any of the flights off the island, I got suspicious. My mistake was asking too many questions. I was summoned to Julie's office. She must have drugged me, because I woke up in a cage. My hunt took place two days later. I grew up hiking and fishing. I learned a few tricks about survival along the way." He pounds one hand with the other's fist. "Laura never had a chance. She must have asked Julie about it, too."

I nod. "We found Laura's body in a mass grave."

He tears up. "Thank God you've decided to do the right thing about the other prisoners."

"Oh yeah, about that," Arnie begins. "As I started to say, we've hit a little glitch in our game plan."

"It's almost ten o'clock. Don't leave us in suspense, Arnie." I nudge Jack and George back on the path toward our jeep. I pray that Julie left the keys in it. Otherwise, we're going to have to hotwire it.

"The great news is that Emma tracked down the satellite feed for the livestock room's security cameras. We were able to put it on a loop. The guards in the control booth aren't any wiser to what's happening right under their noses. Neither are the guards in the hallway."

"Sounds great so far." I know that Arnie is stalling on the bad news, a frequent habit for him.

"Also, Abu and Dominic immobilized the men guarding the tunnel to the tarmac. Already your family is on the plane, as are most of the prisoners."

We're in luck. The keys are in the jeep. When we jump in, I take the wheel.

The Hunt Club is ten minutes down the road and the airstrip another five beyond it. The road is bumpy, so my voice shakes as I say, "I like what I'm hearing. Can you cut to the chase?"

"Unfortunately, Dominic broke the key in one of the locks. If we can't find the master switch that opens all the cages simultaneously, we'll be leaving twelve of the prisoners behind."

"Unacceptable," Jack, George and I say at the same time.

"Is there any way around it?" I ask.

"Electronically, I'm trying as many combinations as possible. But as you know, we've only got another twenty-six—make that *twenty-five*—minutes before the gas is released."

"We'll be there in ten," Jack says firmly.

We're now doing over sixty miles an hour. I'm hugging every curve.

I know what the guys are thinking, even if they don't say it: *woman driver*.

At this point, just getting there alive will be a miracle.

Make that two. Even if we get there in time, the odds of saving them are still slim to none.

WHEN WE REACH THE TUNNEL, IT'S ALREADY TEN-FOURTEEN.

Here comes the hard part. "Okay, both of you—get on the plane and secure it for take-off."

Jack does a double-take. "What? Are you crazy? If you don't get on that plane, then I don't either!"

"You'll get on it, and that's an order from your faux wife *and* your mission leader." If one doesn't convince him, the other should.

"I don't care." He crosses his arms. He's just as stubborn as ever.

"I do, Jack. About my children. About you. About my team members."

I kiss him. It's long, and deep and hard, and makes all kinds of promises—

That I'll be back in time, because I don't plan on dying.

That when the plane is wheels up, I'll be on it.

That we'll enjoy a long and happy life together.

He must have gotten the message, because he doesn't stop me.

I don't look back. Otherwise I can't look forward to all I've just promised him.

~

"So much for fun and games," Dominic mutters as he bangs on the recessed lock holding the key.

It secures the cell holding the little Middle Eastern girl. She sobs uncontrollably. Having watched the others escape, she wonders out loud why Allah has forsaken her.

I want to hold her to tell her that he has not.

Without thinking, I jam my hand into my vest pocket. Inside is the key ring holding the jeep's car key.

In fact, it holds all sorts of keys—

Including the brass one we need—Julie's original key.

I whoop as I turn the locks of the cages still holding prisoners—

—Including the missing Montrose boy who almost went too far with Mary. *How did he end up here?*

He glances back at me, but only for a second. His survival instincts keep him moving forward with the others, who are running for the exit.

The only cage I can't open belongs to the little girl.

My hand is just small enough to slip into the recess, and my nails are just long enough to lift the broken tip of the key, very slowly, through the key hole—

It comes out.

I insert Julie's key in its place and the door swings open.

The girl runs out. She is so happy that she leaps onto me in delirious gratitude. Together we topple to the floor. Her hugs are tight, and her kisses are furious.

Realizing we've got only seconds to go, Dominic picks her up and runs out with her.

I'm on his heels—

But that's still not fast enough. It's exactly ten-thirty. The steel doors slide shut, just as I reach them.

It's going to be interesting to see how long I can hold my breath.

19

Repeat after me: "There's no place like home..."

Whenever one goes on vacation, inevitably there comes a time when homesickness kicks in. One of the most heartfelt scenes in The Wizard of Oz is about just that:

Dorothy wants to go home.

Ah, if only it were so easy to click your heels three times and end up in your own bed. But since you don't own a pair of ruby slippers, here's how to make the trip home, safely and soundly:

First, don't hitchhike. The guy who picks you up may be a good Samaritan. On the other hand, he may be a perv. Your odds are fifty-fifty. Those aren't good odds in any game of chance, so cough up the price of a Greyhound ticket and away you go.

Next, double your estimated time of arrival, or ETA. No one ever gets anywhere on time. Los Angeles traffic is proof of that, as is the Atlanta International Airport, or as it's known in the business world, "the seventh circle of hell."

And finally, not everyone will welcome you home with open arms—and that's okay. Remember, you went away for a reason. Now that you're rested, you've probably come back with a plan.

Stick with it. Or find a new home. And a good pair of ruby slippers.

~

I CAN BREATHE.

But I can't see.

And I can't move.

Am I dead?

No. From what I can tell, I am blindfolded. My arms are shackled over my head, while the bindings on my legs leave them spread apart.

My legs and arms ache. How long have I been hanging here?

As if reading my mind, Boarke laughs heartily. "Ah, Mrs. Stone, after almost a full day, you are finally awake!"

My shock at the lost time comes with an involuntary spasm.

"Very soon, you'll regret missing your flight." The tone of his voice is as dark as Hell. "But you'll be pleased to know that between Mandrake's chicanery and your little stunt with the prisoners, I was almost ruined. When word gets out of the prisoners' escape, no country will do business with me again."

I try not to smile at the news that the others got off the island. Then I remember that I'll never again see Jack or my children, and my heart sinks to the pit of my gut.

At least the blindfold keeps my tears from rolling down my face.

I'm almost afraid to ask, but I know I have to. "What do you mean, 'Mandrake's chicanery'?"

"Why do you think you're even alive, you little bitch?

The plague bacteria sample he brought with him was a fake!"

Well, what do you know.

I can't help myself. I laugh, even through my tears.

Boarke slaps me hard, across the face. When I flinch, he laughs.

"You pig," I mutter. "You had children in here—a little girl, even a teenage boy who was one of your guests."

"You can make an enemy at any age. You of all people must know that."

I spit blood in the direction of his voice. I guess it hit its mark because he slaps me again. "You think you're so funny?"

I steel myself for another smack.

"As it turns out, your pretty little head"—even as he says this, he presses my forehead into the wall—"has a high price on it." He chuckles. "At least, to two of my benefactors."

"What the hell are you talking about?"

"It seems you are to be my collateral for Fantasy Island. By selling you to the highest bidder, I've secured my loan." His face is so close to mine that he sprays me with his joyous declaration. "I can only imagine what the winner will do with you. I know what I would have done, had I kept you."

I'm glad I'll never find out. And he should be happy he'll never find out what I'd do in return.

"I've always relied on the kindness of strangers. Who were my bidders, if you don't mind me asking?"

"Not at all. You met one of them during your stay here—Mr. Chiffray."

Lee.

With what I've seen about him, the offer might have been made out of pity or kindness. He was helpful in locating Mary, and certainly kind to Trisha. Should he hang in with silly Babette, we may even be neighbors—that is, if he had the highest bid.

If so, they'll have free babysitting for life, not to mention all the pie they can stomach.

"The other is an old acquaintance: Carl."

Oh.

Fuck.

The look on my face sends him into a convulsion of laughter. "Ah, then it looks like I made the right choice! Mr. Chiffray was very disappointed. But from what I can see, that coquette, Babette, certainly knows how to make it up to him. What do I care at this point? I own my island free and clear! And I owe it all to you."

His hand encircles my neck. For just a moment his fingers tighten around me—

No air…I'm about to black out.

He releases me.

As I slump against the wall, I hear him shout to the guards, "Put her in the Presidential suite…No, not the one at Eden Key, you idiots! That one is reserved for President Putin. He doesn't need to buy his sluts. They crawl out of the woodwork. That Super Bowl ring is quite an aphrodisiac. Take this one upstairs, here, to the Hunt Club's penthouse suite. And tell the pygmies to prepare for a hunt tomorrow evening."

THE GUARDS HAVE TOO MUCH FUN WITH ME. THEY RIP OFF MY tunic and threaten to 'give me what I deserve' in every orifice, but they don't dare touch the merchandise. Apparently they've witnessed the wrath of Carl. I guess a tweak of my breast isn't worth losing a hand over.

Works for me.

With my blindfold on, I can't see him when he enters, but the click of the door and his footsteps tell me he is now here, in front of me.

I can hear him breathing.

I've only got my ears in which to gauge his distance from me. I know his height and build well enough that if my legs weren't cuffed together, I'd kick him in the nutsack.

Yes, as far as we're concerned, the rose is off the bloom.

I feel him walking around me. Is he admiring me, or imagining ways to make me scream out in pain until I beg him to stop whatever fresh hell he has planned for me?

It will never happen. He has no intention of stopping.

Until I am a corpse.

For Carl Stone, revenge is pleasurable, but never sweet.

I feel his hand touching my hair. The other one falls onto my shoulder. It nudges my hair to one side, exposing my neck. I brace myself for what is to come next. Will he bite me and laugh as I bleed? Will he strangle me until a death rattle rises from my throat?

No. Instead, he kisses it gently.

Then he unties my blindfold.

I stare into his eyes. There is no smirk on his face. It is blank, fathomless.

His eyes are even greener than I remembered them. However, his face seems off-kilter. It is obvious he has had plastic surgery. His forehead is relaxed, the lines of tension and anger smoothed from it.

As he lifts his arms, I brace myself for his punch, his slap—

For his touch.

But instead of taking me, he grabs his face—

And pulls it off.

He's wearing…a mask?

My captor is Jack.

I'm so stunned that I drop to the floor, shaking.

When he reaches down to take me in his arms, I don't know whether to laugh, or cry, or beat him to a bloody pulp.

"I know, I know," he whispers to me as he holds me. "Worst joke ever."

"That's putting it mildly!" My voice is shaking so hard because my teeth are still rattling. "What the hell, Jack?"

"I took a chance that Boarke knows—or knew—Carl. It was the only way I could get back on the island without being shot."

"The fact that you weren't thrown in a cage means Carl is still alive." The very thought has me slumping out of Jack's hug.

"Not necessarily. Quite frankly, he seemed shocked to see me, as if he'd seen a ghost. But he was too shaken up to question what was before his eyes, let alone to deny me any request"—Jack's smile promises the moon—"which was you, on a silver platter."

"That's what scared me—the thought of what Carl would do with me, should he still be alive." I shudder. "Jack, what happens if Boarke calls some of his Quorum buddies for verification?"

"He can't. Arnie figured a way to block all satellite, cell and cable transmissions within a fifty-mile radius of the island. But we don't have much time. The block is scheduled to be lifted just as we're wheels down in Los Angeles. Thank goodness you woke up when you did."

"I hear you paid a pretty penny for me. What did you do, take a second mortgage on our house?"

"Are you kidding? That wouldn't have bought your pinky,

let alone all of your bodacious bod. Instead, Arnie robbed a bank—sort of. The funds wired to Boarke's Swiss bank account were really transferred from another account inside the same institution. This little 'accounting mistake,' has already been discovered, and rectified. Not that Boarke is aware of it yet. He won't be, until he can get access to a phone. By then, we'll be long gone." He pulls me back up on my feet. "Come on, let's blow this joint. I've got us seats on the next flight out."

"Good because I've had enough fantasy. I want the real world."

And my real life. With the *real* love of my life.

Jack is my home. And I am his.

It's time to go home.

But I've got one more task to complete.

"Wait here for me," I murmur to him through a kiss.

He wants to ask what trouble I'm up to, but he won't.

Smart man.

In this case, don't ask, don't tell is a good thing.

No one is supposed to know that Russia's president, Vladimir Putin, is here on Fantasy Island, at Eden Key. But hey, unlike some of the bimbos lounging around the pool who think the term "foreign relations" means a night ending in a walk of shame spent with some guy who pays in Euros, I'd know that distinctive sneer anywhere—

Not to mention the bling he's sporting: the 2005 Super Bowl ring he allegedly lifted from the New England Patriots' owner, Robert Kraft.

Okay, let's give him the benefit of the doubt when he says he didn't take it. I still find it hard to believe that he found the time to play pro football in 2004 *and* be the prime minister of Russia.

Apparently I'm not the only one who isn't buying his bullshit. No other woman around the pool is falling for the middle-aged Russian blowhard who's flashing the notorious ring and boasting about the fifty-yard pass he threw, with only twenty-three seconds to go in the fourth quarter to win the game.

Now it's my turn to win one for the Gipper.

First, I take the chaise next to his. Next, I pull off my flimsy bikini cover-up with a stretch that puts my Victoria's Secret's add-two-cups bikini halter top front and center to his sight line.

By the time I deliver my innocent request for an all-over rubdown with my Hawaiian Tropic Deep Tanning lotion, he's drooling.

When he asks where I'm from, I tell him I'm a Georgia Rebel. He frowns at first, but then he realizes I mean the Deep South.

When I ask him about his accent, he claims he's from Minneapolis.

He wishes.

He's slathering oil on my legs when his cell phone rings. He feels safe enough with this little hick from the sticks to talk in his native tongue. My Russian may be rusty, but I know the term *chyort voz'mi*! Let me give you a hint. It is a universal one, expressing shock at something totally out of your control, including the bodily function just declared. In this case it is shouted angrily, along with the name "Teddy Grodin."

So I guess it's official: word has leaked that Teddy now swims with the fishes after his ill-conceived jump from that private jet ride we generously offered him.

Putin is too angry to notice me slipping away.

He's also too upset to realize his Super Bowl ring has come right off his finger, thanks to my super-slippery suntan oil and a little sleight of hand.

By the time I make it to the tarmac, Jack has already boarded the plane. I fairly run up the air stairs, not because Putin's dogs are on my tail, but because there's no place like home.

Now, repeat that three times…

———————————————————————

20

Check-Out Time

———————————————————————

It's inevitable that such a relaxing vacation must come to an end. When it's time to check out of your hotel, here are some smart tips:

First, take any free toiletries. The hotels presume you will do so, which is why they put their logo on all those cute little bottles. That said, cleaning out the maid's cart is not good form. However, leaving her a tip makes you an angel.

Next, check your bill carefully. Do you see any meals charged to your room, that you don't remember? How about porn? How about negligees from the gift shop? Hmmm. Maybe your boyfriend wasn't "out on the golf course" after all.

And finally, check around the room for all your belongings. Look under your pillow, your bed, and through your bed sheets. When doing so, if you find a thong that isn't yours, it's logical to jump to the conclusion that your boyfriend has been playing off on you—

But don't.

At least, not until you've tortured him sufficiently. By taking the hotel iron and applying it to his backside, you'll give him something to remember you by, always—a brand that painfully shows every other girl that his ass is yours for life.

Just another fun day in the neighborhood.

With no clouds in the azure sky, a faint whisper of a breeze nudges a few of the hot pink petals from the bougainvillea vine clamoring up the lattice fence surrounding the Hilldale Country Club pool. They drift skyward, only to waft down into the tot pool, where Trisha and the other little ones try to catch them before they fall.

Penelope and her besties—Tiffy Swift and the unfortunately named Hayley Coxhead—are sitting catty-corner from me, only six lounge chairs away. And yet they chose to ignore my welcoming wave. I guess Penelope is still angry that Cheever came home without his flip-flops, and sporting a boob tattoo on his butt.

I won't dare tell her he almost came home without a toe, or that the tattoo is a whole lot better than a croc bite.

The pool is so jam-packed that at first I don't see what I'm looking for: the heads of Jeff, Cheever and Morton, who for the last hour have been lurking just beneath the water's surface, watching for the bikini bottoms of Hilldale's *teen fatales.*

In unison, Hayley, Tiffy and Penelope's heads tilt up, as if drawn by some imaginary tractor beam. The tips of their pink tongues peek out of plumped lips, in anticipation—

Of what?

The sun is so bright that even with sunglasses I must shield my eyes in order to see the object of their interest.

Ah, I'm not surprised—Jack.

His biceps pump like pistons and the muscles roll under

his wide, tan shoulders as he climbs the ladder of the tallest diving board. Once at the top, he centers himself on it. I envision him tuning out the shouts and murmurs of the throngs of bathers in the recreational pool next door.

His eyes are focused straight ahead. His toes arch and his calves flex in tandem, making the board bounce ever so slightly. Then he heads to the back of the board. Turning around again, he runs four steps down the board before taking a leap—

Of faith? No. Jack is too self-assured of his abilities for that.

While high in the air, he raises his arms and circles them backward. By the time they are back over his head, he has folded himself into a perfect jack knife—

—Before straightening up and cutting the water cleanly, like a hot blade piercing butter.

Hilldale's mean mommies melt back into their chaises with awed sighs.

"Beautiful," Abu murmurs.

I look up at him. A portable ice cream freezer is strapped over his Good Humor uniform. He raises his voice to say: "Here's the Strawberry Shortcake bar you ordered."

I nod, but I frown because I know the treat comes with a cost beyond its three-dollar price tag. We're being called up for another mission, which is written on the inside of the wrapper.

As I read it, my eyes grow big. It's a doozy, alright.

By the time I look up again, Jack is pulling himself out of the pool. Water droplets glisten all over his well-oiled body. The ones clinging to the hairs on his chest sparkle, like tiny silver bells. The way the eyes of all the poolside moms follow as he moves past them, you'd think he emits a silent high-pitched sound, like a dog whistle.

Trisha jumps out of the pool and runs to him. He picks her up as he saunters my way.

Janie runs after them. She'd much rather hang with us than with her latest nanny, who has turned the Breck Mansion into party central.

When the puma is away, the kittens will play.

Jack stands over me, watching me lick the melting ice cream. If I think that putting the whole thing in my mouth looks seductive, he sets me straight when he bends down to wipe away a splotch of strawberry on my cheek. "You're a mess, but I love you anyway."

"You'll be a mess, too when you hear what Ryan needs us to do next week—on the first day of school, no less! Cover a possible assassination attempt on one of the presidential primary candidates."

He plops down on the chair beside me. "No rest for the weary, is there?"

Trisha has brought her bag of treasures to the pool with her. She holds Mandrake's conch shell to her ear and shakes it hard, then stares down at it.

"Mommy, look! The shell has a message, just like a fortune cookie." She hands it to me.

Strange. A sliver of folded paper is now visible, coiled in the upper ear of the shell.

I pull it out and unfold it. The note is handwritten, not with pencil or ink but with dye from a plant. It reads:

NSA – BIN 4265

I hand it over to Jack. "What do you think this means?"

He stares down at it. "I think we may have found the missing plague samples."

He grabs his cell phone from my new beach bag and

hops up out of the chair. Each purposeful stride is scrutinized by our neighbors, who presume he's in the middle of a red hot business negotiation.

If only his job were so pat, so safe.

Ten minutes later, he's back. He's all smiles. "Ryan is calling the client, to see if it means anything to him. One thing is certain—Mandrake was determined that the plague vaccine wouldn't fall into the wrong hands."

We both look up as a stanza of *Easy Street* blares from Janie's cell phone. "Oh! Mummy is calling," the little girl squeals. She hits the TALK button.

Even with the phone at Janie's ear, I can hear Babette's imperious voice. But it's Janie's face that makes the greatest impact on me. At first, her eyes open wide in shock. A moment later her little pillowy lips turn down sadly. Finally, she nods listlessly and whispers, "I'm so happy for you, Mummy. Congratulations."

After clicking off, she drops the cell into her tiny purse.

Her head stays down until she can smile again. Still, she can't hide the tears in her eyes.

Gently with her thumb, Trisha wipes away her friend's tear. "What's wrong, Janie?"

"My mother got married today." The nonchalance in Janie's voice sounds forced. "She never thought she would. She's afraid men would be after her money."

I can imagine her saying that—albeit not to a six-year-old.

I bend down so that I'm face to face with the little girl. "I'm sure your mother has found it lonely this past year. And since her new husband, Mr. Chiffray, has money, too, she must feel he loves her for all the right reasons."

"But what if he *doesn't* love her?"

"Only time will tell if that's the case," I reason.

She nods uncertainly, as if accepting a death sentence. Finally she sighs. "Can we go home now?"

She'll get no argument from me.

It's been a long day.

And tomorrow is another day—hopefully, again not with the Quorum.

~

BABETTE AND LEE CHIFFRAY'S WEDDING RECEPTION HAS ALL OF our Hilldale neighbors in a tizzy. In widowhood, she kept to herself. Bereavement calls and visits were ignored. Condolence cards weren't opened. Casseroles, left on the front entrance of her palatial mansion to give her solace, were pawned off on the help.

The latter had more to do with her strict Size Zero dieting regimen than with her grieving process.

I don't blame her. It's hard to mourn a rapist.

At least, now she's found someone to share her billions.

Everyone in town wants to meet the lucky guy. Unfortunately, he's been in the study on a business call since the event started.

The invitation said garden party, but this is no mere weenie roast. Butlers in white tie and tuxes pass platters laden with creative canapés topped with slivers of roasted vegetables and savory meats.

On a stadium-sized backlit screen, pictures from the elopement rotate on a loop. Truly, it was a grand tour: The wedding took place in Venice. Afterward they visited Paris, London, and Lake Como.

Janie stayed home and cried her eyes out.

I hope Lee's sensitive side picks up on her trepidation. If not, then he isn't the man I thought he was.

Babette's guests wear chic sundresses—Escada in linen, Kate Spade in eyelet, and Cavalli silks. Their hats are worthy of Ascot.

And alas, it seems that envy never goes out of fashion.

Still, no one outdoes the new bride. Her dress—short and virginal white—is a mist of tulle over a slim, skimming bodice. Her matching hat sports a tiny veil that could pass as a white spider's web.

I wonder: who was predator, and who was prey?

Janie's ensemble is a tiny replica of her mother's. While most of her little friends turn cartwheels on a lawn as plush as velveteen, their little hostess slumps morosely in a chair. Trisha, a true friend, stands stoically at her friend's side, but her mouth is turned down at the ends.

Suddenly her eyes light up. I look to see what has caught her attention.

Dominic Fleming.

Talk about audacity.

She runs up to him and grabs his hand, pulling him toward me.

We haven't seen each other since the night of the prison break. I think Jack will forgive me for gracing Dominic with a kiss on the cheek.

He pats the spot gently. "Truly stingy of you, my dear. Then again, beggars can't be choosers, now can they?"

"You seem to have your fair share of admirers here, Dominic—my daughter included." I nod toward Trisha, who stands at his feet, fixated in adoration.

She's not the only one. Already Penelope, Hayley and Tiffy are eyeing him as if he's a braised lamb chop.

Dominic may be speaking to me, but he's grinning at them. "Ah yes, the bountiful Mrs. Bing! Met her in Fantasy Island's dungeon, in fact."

"Don't tell me Penelope was one of the prisoners we released!"

His laughter is boisterous, to say the least. Then again, the king of the pride must have the loudest roar. "I meant the BSDM playroom, in Eden Key." He smiles. "She wields quite a whip! Should she ever be in want of a profession, I know of several private clubs that would welcome her expertise. I'm surprised Peter can sit upright at all."

The thought of their bedroom antics leaves me wincing.

"Speaking of Peter," Dominic continues, "I was quite taken with his knowledge of your local real estate. Thanks to his guidance, I'll soon be closing on the most charming little bungalow, right here in Hilldale."

I drop a chopped liver canapé on the grass. With the speed of a Wimbledon ball-boy, a butler swoops down and runs off with it.

As shocking as that is, Dominic's news takes the cake. "You're moving here? But I thought you loved London!"

"The charm of one doesn't preclude the other. Besides, I consider it my duty."

"Oh? Why is that?"

"Ryan wants to put this Quorum bother to rest, once and for all. This isn't to say you and Jack haven't done a brilliant job at nudging the sleeping beast."

"Is that what Ryan said, that we've only 'nudged' it? Seems to me that it's been all quiet on the Quorum front, thanks to our efforts!"

"No need to get your knickers in a twist, old girl. Acme's coverage of the presidential candidate next week is a perfect example. The Quorum will do anything to control the Oval Office. Taking out a frontrunner is very much its cuppa, believe you me. Ryan merely suggested that more manpower will be needed, if we're to deliver an all-around thumping."

I'll say someone needs an all-around thumping. Unfortunately I left my baseball bat at home.

"I dare say, a second home allows for a welcomed change of pace." His eyes sweep over me. "A much needed respite from the role of international man of mystery."

His slow wink could spark a flame on a matchstick.

Now *I* feel like the lamb chop.

Trisha tugs at the sash of my sundress. "Mommy, on the plane Mr. Fleming told me I should never worry about you. He thinks you're one of the smartest ladies he's ever met."

"How very sweet." I stare at Dominic. Is he blushing?

"In fact, Mr. Fleming said if anything should happen to him, I should give this to you, because you know how he feels about you."

Trisha pulls a baby blue Tiffany box from her pocket.

Oh. My. God.

I open it and find a ring so big that it might have once belonged to the Queen of England. Oh hell, I hope Dominic didn't lift this from the royal collection.

Looking back, as much as I tried to deny it, certainly the signs were all there. His flirtatiousness. His soulful looks. His aggressive pursuit of me. And when we were trapped by the crocodile he tried to confess…something—

Was it his love for me?

Wait…*there's a Tiffany store on Fantasy Island?* Boy, that place really *does* have everything!

I'm just about to tell Dominic how flattered I am when I notice that Babette has sidled over to us. Apparently she's heard the whole conversation. She can't take her eyes off the ring. "But—but Donna Stone is already married! Why in the hell would you want a frumpy, flatchested mouse like her, when you could have had these"—she juts her inflated breasts in his direction—"and all my money to boot?"

Dominic grabs my fist before it ruins Babette's perfect nose job. "Stop me if I'm wrong, Babette, but didn't you just tie the knot with Lee?" I ask.

"What?...Okay, true, but"—She looks up at him, pleadingly—"if Dominic had asked me first, I would have said yes. It's not as if I need Lee's money or anything. And he works all the damn time." Her glare moves from Dominic to me. "Ha! I wonder what your husband will think when he finds out!"

"Find out what?" At the sound of Jack's voice, we all turn at the same time.

"Donna is considering leaving you for this pompous stud," Babette declares as she slaps Dominic's arm. Her sympathetic gaze at Jack comes off like a cat eyeing a mouse.

"That's not true! In the first place, I'm already married. In the second, I'd never consider anything so ludicrous." I cross my arms under my chest. I guess Jack is smiling because he knows I'm doing my best not to slap her silly.

"No doubt I'd be heartbroken. I guess I'd have to find some way to console myself," Jack says as he waves broadly at his fan club—Penelope, Tiffy and Hayley—who are staring our way.

His attention is too much for Penelope. She passes out.

Oddly, her pals do nothing to break her fall to the ground. So much for friendship.

Being scorned twice at her own reception is more than Babette can bear. She storms off angrily.

Dominic pats Jack on the back. "You don't have to worry, old chap. Donna is all yours—and always was."

"I never doubted if for a moment," says Jack.

Dominic and I burst out laughing at the same time.

We've been in sync on so much that I wouldn't be surprised if we're both thinking the same thing:

As if.

"I needed to make it clear to Babette, once and for all, that our fun and games are over," Dominic explains. "Your little Trisha is quite an actress. The way she delivered her lines, I've no doubt you've got another Cate Blanchett in the making."

I look down at the Tiffany box. "Do I get to keep the ring?"

"Feel free, my dear. The box is real, but the ring is a diamond simulant. The best Amora Moissanite that money can buy."

I snicker. "With all of Babette's baubles, you'd think she'd know a real one from a fake by now."

"Speaking of the real thing, Ryan wanted you to know that your lead on the missing plague bacteria and antidote samples was spot on. Someone placed it in a warehouse dead file by mistake. Turns out it was under the NSA's nose the whole time."

Jack and I exchange glances. Mandrake made sure it never left the building. Had he lived, his position and his reputation would have stayed intact.

If a true philanthropic organization had offered him a chance to distribute the antidote for free, would he have taken it? I guess we'll never know, but I'd like to think this would have been the case.

"Donna old girl, word on the street is that your cooking is excellent, but otherwise you're all corners, as they say on my side of the pond. I can only imagine that your monopoly on the most eligible man at this soirée has only put you deeper in Dutch with your neighbors." Dominic nods toward Hilldale's horniest momtourage.

"You're right, Dominic. Thank you for so thoughtfully pointing this out. You have my blessing to mingle to your heart's content. I'll make sure to put a map to the Free Clinic in your Welcome Wagon basket."

Dominic doesn't waste any time. Five strides puts him in their midst.

His choice has me shaking my head. "If Dominic is serious about bed-hopping through Hilldale, I wonder how long it will take him to realize he's not the predator but the prey?"

"Everyone needs a hobby, right?" Jack's smile fades when he sees Lee on the terrace. Lee waves at us, but his attempt at a smile is tepid at best.

"I'd like to figure out his angle," Jack mutters.

"What do you mean by that?"

"Something just isn't quite right. Don't you find it odd that Babette's boyfriend ends up taking her to Fantasy Island, of all places?"

"His firm held the note on the place—or still does, I guess, now that it's gone into default. Considering that he's such a workaholic, I'm not at all surprised he chose a getaway that would allow him to combine business with pleasure."

"You give him too much credit. He knew the Hunt Club's dirty little secret. The fact that he bid against 'Carl' for you is proof of that."

"I'm just happy that the best man won." I tuck a tuft of his hair behind his ear. Can he feel the love in my touch? His smile shows me so.

"I'm also happy he chose not to outbid me. Although something tells me he could have done so, easily." Jack gazes down at me. "I have to admit I'm a bit curious what he would have done with you."

I've seen how Lee looks at me. And I saw his uncontrollable rage toward the boy who almost raped Mary.

I suddenly remember Boarke's boast—that one of my bidders arranged for the boy to be put in the stockyard. Since it wasn't Jack, it had to be Lee.

I don't want to go there.

I want to stay here—at Jack's side. For as long as we both shall live.

"By the way, I heard they found Boarke's body deep in the jungle." Jack shrugs. "The parts not eaten by a crocodile were riddled with pygmy darts."

"A sad but appropriate ending." I shudder. "Maybe they'll use his 'resignation' as an excuse to go in a different direction with the resorts. You know, less swinger slashers and human safaris—more sun, sand and surf."

Jack laughs. "Mrs. Stone, where is your sense of adventure?"

"I left it in the croc nest on Fantasy Island. Admit it, Jack Craig—there is something to be said for sitting on a beach and staring off at the ocean, without a care in the world."

His arms feel warm and strong as they circle my waist. "I'm glad you think so. I've booked a room, just for the two of us, at Post Ranch Inn, outside of Big Sur. We can do some staring of our own."

My squeal has him cupping his ears, but he doesn't fight off my barrage of kisses.

When I stop suddenly and frown, he holds up a hand. "I know what you're thinking. I've had all the kids and Aunt Phyllis sign oaths to be on their best behavior while we're gone."

"Not in blood, I hope."

"Jeff suggested that, but I vetoed the idea. However, I

caught Aunt Phyllis talking Pig Latin to the kids. I think she said, 'what happens in Hilldale stays in Hilldale.'"

Seeing my face fall to the ground, he adds, "Just kidding!"

He'd better be.

If I'm going to keep my family in line, I'll need a croc of my own. Next stop: the pet store.

Trisha runs over and grabs our hands. "They're going to cut the cake!"

We let her swing between us. Each step between us and the buffet table is her chance to chant out one of the new words she learned while texting on Janie's iPhone.

"Q...U...O...R—"

Jack and I stop cold. We exchange looks.

By the time he's kneeling in front of Trisha, he has a smile on his face. "That's a big new word for you, isn't it Trisha?"

Her eyes light up, proudly. "Yes! Really, it's spelled Q-U-O-R-U-M. Mrs. Breck—I mean Mrs. Chiffray taught it to me."

Jack and I scan the crowd for Babette.

She has just cut a piece of the cake. Lee already has a chunk of it in his hand. Their fingers find each other's mouths, and the bites are generous.

They should be smiling and staring into each other's eyes, but they aren't.

They are looking at us.

The applause and laughter is boisterous.

Jack and I aren't clapping.

All work and no play can make Donna one mean lady.

The Chiffrays are about to find that out, the hard way.

—THE END—

270

Next Up for Donna!

The Housewife Assassin's Recipes for Disaster

(Book 6)

Donna must stop the assassinations of both US political parties' presidential candidates. But when she discovers she has a long-term vendetta with one of the targets, can she put aside her animosity long enough to save the candidate's life?

Other Books by Josie Brown

The True Hollywood Lies Series

Hollywood Hunk

Hollywood Whore

The Totlandia Series

The Onesies - Book 1 (Fall)

The Onesies - Book 2 (Winter)

The Onesies - Book 3 (Spring)

The Onesies - Book 4 (Summer)

The Twosies - Book 5 (Fall)

The Twosies – Book 6 (Winter)

The Twosies - Book 7 (Spring)

The Twosies - Book 8 (Summer)

More Josie Brown Novels

The Candidate

Secret Lives of Husbands and Wives

The Baby Planner

How to Reach Josie

To write Josie, go to:
mailfromjosie@gmail.com

To find out more about Josie, or to get on her eLetter list for book launch announcements, go to her website:
www.JosieBrown.com

You can also find her at:

www.AuthorProvocateur.com

twitter.com / JosieBrownCA

facebook.com / josiebrownauthor

pinterest.com / josiebrownca

instagram.com / josiebrownnovels